HAVE
SPACE SUIT—
WILL
TRAVEL

Robert A. Heinlein

A Del Rey® Book
BALLANTINE BOOKS • NEW YORK

FOR HARRY AND BARBARA STINE

RLI: VL: 7 & up
     IL: 7 & up

A Del Rey® Book
Published by Ballantine Books

Cover art by Darrell K. Sweet

http://www.randomhouse.com

ISBN 0-345-32441-2

This edition published by arrangement with Charles Scribner's Sons

Printed in Canada

First Ballantine Books Edition: December 1977

25 24 23 22

Chapter 1

You see, I had this space suit.

How it happened was this way:

"Dad," I said, "I want to go to the Moon."

"Certainly," he answered and looked back at his book. It was Jerome K. Jerome's *Three Men in a Boat*, which he must know by heart.

I said, "Dad, please! I'm serious."

This time he closed the book on a finger and said gently, "I said it was all right. Go ahead."

"Yes . . . but *how?*"

"Eh?" He looked mildly surprised. "Why, that's your problem, Clifford."

Dad was like that. The time I told him I wanted to buy a bicycle he said, "Go right ahead," without even glancing up—so I had gone to the money basket in the dining room, intending to take enough for a bicycle. But there had been only eleven dollars and forty-three cents in it, so about a thousand miles of mowed lawns later I bought a bicycle. I hadn't said any more to Dad because if money wasn't in the basket, it wasn't anywhere; Dad didn't bother with banks—just the money basket and one next to it marked "UNCLE SAM," the contents of which he bundled up and mailed to the government once a year. This caused the Internal Revenue Service considerable headache and once they sent a man to remonstrate with him.

First the man demanded, then he pleaded. "But, Dr. Russell, we know your background. You've no excuse for not keeping proper records."

"But I do," Dad told him. "Up here." He tapped his forehead.

"The law requires written records."

"Look again," Dad advised him. "The law can't even require a man to read and write. More coffee?"

The man tried to get Dad to pay by check or money order. Dad read him the fine print on a dollar bill, the part about "legal tender for all debts, public and private."

In a despairing effort to get *something* out of the trip he asked Dad *please* not to fill in the space marked "occupation" with "Spy."

"Why not?"

"What? Why, because you *aren't*—and it upsets people."

"Have you checked with the F.B.I.?"

"Eh? No."

"They probably wouldn't answer. But you've been very polite. I'll mark it 'Unemployed Spy.' Okay?"

The tax man almost forgot his brief case. Nothing fazed Dad, he meant what he said, he wouldn't argue and he never gave in. So when he told me I could go to the Moon but the means were up to me, he meant just that. I could go tomorrow—provided I could wangle a billet in a space ship.

But he added meditatively, "There must be a number of ways to get to the Moon, son. Better check 'em all. Reminds me of this passage I'm reading. They're trying to open a tin of pineapple and Harris has left the can opener back in London. They try several ways." He started to read aloud and I sneaked out—I had heard that passage five hundred times. Well, three hundred.

I went to my workshop in the barn and thought about ways. One way was to go to the Air Academy at Colorado Springs—if I got an appointment, if I graduated, *if* I managed to get picked for the Federation Space Corps, there was a chance that someday I would be ordered to Lunar Base, or at least one of the satellite stations.

Another way was to study engineering, get a job in jet propulsion, and buck for a spot that would get me sent to the Moon. Dozens, maybe hundreds, of engineers had been to the Moon, or were still there—for all sorts of work: electronics, cryogenics, metallurgy, ceramics, air conditioning, as well as rocket engineering.

Oh, yes! Out of a million engineers a handful got picked for the Moon. Shucks, I rarely got picked even playing post office.

Or a man could be an M.D., or a lawyer, or geologist, or toolmaker, and wind up on the Moon at a fat salary—provided they wanted him and nobody else. I didn't care about salary—but how do you arrange to be number one in your specialty?

And there was the straightforward way: trundle in a wheelbarrow of money and buy a ticket.

This I would never manage—I had eighty-seven cents at that moment—but it had caused me to think about it steadily. Of the boys in our school half admitted that they wanted to space, half pretended not to care, knowing how feeble the chances were—plus a handful of creeps who wouldn't leave Earth for any reason. But we talked about it and some of us were determined to go. I didn't break into a rash until American Express and Thos. Cook & Son announced tourist excursions.

I saw their ads in *National Geographic* while waiting to have my teeth cleaned. After that I never was the same.

The idea that any rich man could simply lay cash on the line and *go* was more than I could stand. I just *had* to go. I would never be able to pay for it—or, at least, that was so far in the future there was no use thinking about it. So what could I do to be *sent?*

You see stories about boys, poor-but-honest, who go to the top because they're smarter than anyone in the county, maybe the state. But they're not talking about me. I was in the top quarter of my graduating class but they do not give scholarships to M.I.T. for that—not from Centerville High. I am stating a fact; our high school isn't very good. It's great to go to—we're league champions in basketball and our square-dance team is state runner-up and we have a swell sock hop every Wednesday. Lots of school spirit.

But not much studying.

The emphasis is on what our principal, Mr. Hanley, calls "preparation for life" rather than on trigonometry. Maybe it does prepare you for life; it certainly doesn't prepare you for CalTech.

I didn't find this out myself. Sophomore year I brought home a questionnaire cooked up by our group project in "Family Living" in social studies. One question read: "How is your family council organized?"

At dinner I said, "Dad, how is our family council organized?"

Mother said, "Don't disturb your father, dear."

Dad said, "Eh? Let me see that."

He read it, then told me to fetch my textbooks. I had not brought them home, so he sent me to school to get them. Fortunately the building was open—rehearsals for the Fall Blow-Out. Dad rarely gave orders but when he did he expected results.

I had a swell course that semester—social study, commercial arithmetic, applied English (the class had picked "slogan writing" which was fun), handicrafts (we were building sets for the Blow-Out), and gym—which was basketball practice for me; I wasn't tall enough for first team but a reliable substitute gets his varsity letter his senior year. All in all, I was doing well in school and knew it.

Dad read all my textbooks that night; he is a fast reader. In social study I reported that our family was an informal democracy; it got by—the class was arguing whether the chairmanship of a council should rotate or be elective, and whether a grandparent living in the home was eligible. We decided that a grandparent was a member but should not be chairman, then we formed committees to draw up a constitution for an ideal family organization, which we would present to our families as the project's findings.

Dad was around school a good bit the next few days, which worried me—when parents get overactive they are always up to something.

The following Saturday evening Dad called me into his study. He had a stack of textbooks on his desk and a chart of Centerville High School's curriculum, from American Folk Dancing to Life Sciences. Marked on it was my course, not only for that semester but for junior and senior years the way my faculty advisor and I had planned it.

Dad stared at me like a gentle grasshopper and said mildly, "Kip, do you intend to go to college?"

"Huh? Why, certainly, Dad!"

"With what?"

I hesitated. I knew it cost money. While there had been times when dollar bills spilled out of the basket onto the floor, usually it wouldn't take long to count what was in it. "Uh, maybe I'll get a scholarship. Or I could work my way."

He nodded. "No doubt . . . if you want to. Money problems can always be solved by a man not frightened by them. But when I said, 'With what?' I was talking about up *here*." He tapped his skull.

I simply stared. "Why, I'll graduate from high school, Dad. That'll get me into college."

"So it will. Into our State University, or the State Aggie, or State Normal. But, Kip, do you know that they are flunking out 40 per cent of each freshman class?"

"I wouldn't flunk!"

"Perhaps not. But you will if you tackle any serious subject—engineering, or science, or pre-med. You would,

9

that is to say, if your preparation were based on *this*." He waved a hand at the curriculum.

I felt shocked. "Why, Dad, Center is a swell school." I remembered things they had told us in P.T.A. Auxiliary. "It's run along the latest, most scientific lines, approved by psychologists, and—"

"—and paying excellent salaries," he interrupted, "for a staff highly trained in modern pedagogy. Study projects emphasize practical human problems to orient the child in democratic social living, to fit him for the vital, meaningful tests of adult life in our complex modern culture. Excuse me, son; I've talked with Mr. Hanley. Mr. Hanley is sincere—and to achieve these noble purpposes we are spending more per student than is any other state save California and New York."

"Well . . . what's wrong with that?"

"What's a dangling participle?"

I didn't answer. He went on, "Why did Van Buren fail of re-election? How do you extract the cube root of eighty-seven?"

Van Buren had been a president; that was all I remembered. But I could answer the other one. "If you want a cube root, you look in a table in the back of the book."

Dad sighed. "Kip, do you think that table was brought down from on high by an archangel?" He shook his head sadly. "It's my fault, not yours. I should have looked into this years ago—but I had assumed, simply because you liked to read and were quick at figures and clever with your hands, that you were getting an education."

"You think I'm not?"

"I know you are not. Son, Centerville High is a delightful place, well equipped, smoothly administered, beautifully kept. Not a 'blackboard jungle,' oh, no!—I think you kids love the place. You should. But *this*—"

Dad slapped the curriculum chart angrily. "Twaddle! Beetle tracking! Occupational therapy for morons!"

I didn't know what to say. Dad sat and brooded. At last he said, "The law declares that you must attend school until you are eighteen or have graduated from high school."

"Yes, sir."

"The school you are in is a waste of time. The toughest course we can pick won't stretch your mind. But it's either this school, or send you away."

I said, "Doesn't that cost a lot of money?"

He ignored my question. "I don't favor boarding schools, a teen-ager belongs with his family. Oh, a tough prep school back east can drill you so that you can enter Stanford, or Yale, or any of the best—but you can pick up false standards, too—nutty ideas about money and social position and the right tailor. It took me years to get rid of ones I acquired that way. Your mother and I did not pick a small town for your boyhood unpurposefully. So you'll stay in Centerville High."

I looked relieved.

"Nevertheless you intend to go to college. Do you intend to become a professional man? Or will you look for snap courses in more elaborate ways to make bayberry candles? Son, your life is yours, to do with as you wish. But if you have any thought of going to a good university and studying anything of importance, then we must consider how to make best use of your next three years."

"Why, gosh, Dad, of course I want to go to a good—"

"See me when you've thought it over. Good night."

I did for a week. And, you know, I began to see that Dad was right. Our project in "Family Living" was twaddle. What did those kids know about running a family? Or Miss Finchley?—unmarried and no kids. The class decided unanimously that every child should have a room of his own, and be given an allowance

11

"to teach him to handle money." Great stuff . . . but how about the Quinlan family, nine kids in a five-room house? Let's not be foolish.

Commercial arithmetic wasn't silly but it was a waste of time. I read the book through the first week; after that I was bored.

Dad switched me to algebra, Spanish, general science, English grammar and composition; the only thing unchanged was gym. I didn't have it too tough catching up; even those courses were watered down. Nevertheless, I started to learn, for Dad threw a lot of books at me and said, "Clifford, you would be studying these if you were not in overgrown kindergarten. If you soak up what is in them, you should be able to pass College Entrance Board Examinations. Possibly."

After that he left me alone; he meant it when he said that it was my choice. I almost bogged down—those books were *hard,* not the predigested pap I got in school. Anybody who thinks that studying Latin by himself is a snap should try it.

I got discouraged and nearly quit—then I got mad and leaned into it. After a while I found that Latin was making Spanish easier and vice versa. When Miss Hernandez, my Spanish teacher, found out I was studying Latin, she began tutoring me. I not only worked my way through Virgil, I learned to speak Spanish like a Mexicano.

Algebra and plane geometry were all the math our school offered; I went ahead on my own with advanced algebra and solid geometry and trigonometry and might have stopped so far as College Boards were concerned—but math is worse than peanuts. Analytical geometry seems pure Greek until you see what they're driving at—then, if you know algebra, it bursts on you and you race through the rest of the book. Glorious!

I had to sample calculus and when I got interested in electronics I needed vector analysis. General science was the only science course the school had and pretty general it was, too—about Sunday supplement level. But when you read about chemistry and physics you want to do it, too. The barn was mine and I had a chem lab and a darkroom and an electronics bench and, for a while, a ham station. Mother was perturbed when I blew out the windows and set fire to the barn—just a small fire—but Dad was not. He simply suggested that I not manufacture explosives in a frame building.

When I took the College Boards my senior year I passed them.

It was early March my senior year that I told Dad I wanted to go to the Moon. The idea had been made acute by the announcement of commercial flights but I had been "space happy" ever since the day they announced that the Federation Space Corps had established a lunar base. Or earlier. I told Dad about my decision because I felt that he would know the answer. You see, Dad always found ways to do anything he decided to do.

When I was little we lived lots of places—Washington, New York, Los Angeles, I don't know where—usually in hotel apartments. Dad was always flying somewhere and when he was home there were visitors; I never saw him much. Then we moved to Centerville and he was always home, his nose in a book or working at his desk. When people wanted to see him they had to come to him. I remember once, when the money basket was empty, Dad told Mother that "a royalty was due." I hung around that day because I had never seen a king (I was eight) and when a visitor showed up I was disappointed because he didn't wear a crown. There was money in the basket the next day so I decided that he had been incognito (I was reading *The Little Lame Prince*) and had tossed Dad a purse of gold—it was at least a year before I found out that a "royalty" could be money from a patent or a book or business stock, and some of the glamour went out of life. But this visitor, though not king, thought he could make Dad do what he wanted rather than what Dad wanted:

"Dr. Russell, I concede that Washington has an atrocious climate. But you will have air-conditioned offices."

"With clocks, no doubt. And secretaries. And soundproofing."

"Anything you want, Doctor."

"The point is, Mr. Secretary, I don't want them. This household has no clocks. Nor calendars. Once I had a large income and a larger ulcer; I now have a small income and no ulcer. I stay here."

"But the job needs *you*."

"The need is not mutual. Do have some more meat loaf."

Since Dad did not want to go to the Moon, the problem was mine. I got down college catalogs I had collected and started listing engineering schools. I had no idea how I could pay tuition or even eat—but the first thing was to get myself accepted by a tough school with a reputation.

If not, I could enlist in the Air Force and try for an appointment. If I missed, I could become an enlisted specialist in electronics; Lunar Base used radar and astrar techs. One way or another, I was going.

Next morning at breakfast Dad was hidden behind the *New York Times* while Mother read the *Herald-Trib.* I had the *Centerville Clarion* but it's fit only for wrapping salami. Dad looked over his paper at me. "Clifford, here's something in your line."

"Huh?"

"Don't grunt; that is an uncouth privilege of seniors. This." He handed it to me.

It was a soap ad.

It announced that tired old gimmick, a gigantic super-colossal prize contest. This one promised a thousand prizes down to a last hundred, each of which was a year's supply of Skyway Soap.

Then I spilled cornflakes in my lap. The first prize was—

"—AN ALL-EXPENSE TRIP TO THE MOON!!!"

That's the way it read, with three exclamation points —only to me there were a dozen, with bursting bombs and a heavenly choir.

Just complete this sentence in twenty-five words or less: "I use Skyway Soap because . . . . . ."

(And send in the usual soap wrapper or reasonable facsimile.)

There was more about "—joint management of American Express and Thos. Cook—" and "—with the cooperation of the United States Air Force—" and a list of lesser prizes. But all I saw, while milk and soggy cereal soaked my pants, was:

"—TRIP TO THE MOON!!!"

Chapter 2

First I went sky-high with excitement . . . then as far down with depression. I didn't win contests—why, if I bought a box of Cracker Jack, I'd get one they forgot to put a prize in. I had been cured of matching pennies. If I ever—

"Stop it," said Dad.

I shut up.

"There is no such thing as luck; there is only adequate or inadequate preparation to cope with a statistical universe. Do you intend to enter this?"

"Do I!"

"I assume that to be affirmative. Very well, make a systematic effort."

I did and Dad was helpful—he didn't just offer me more meat loaf. But he saw to it I didn't go to pieces; I finished school and sent off applications for college and kept my job—I was working after school that semester at Charton's Pharmacy—soda jerk, but also learning about pharmacy. Mr. Charton was too conscientious to let me touch anything but packaged items, but I learned—materia medica and nomenclature and what various antibiotics were for and why you had to be careful. That led into organic chemistry and biochemistry and he lent me *Walker, Boyd and Asimov*—biochemistry makes atomic physics look simple, but presently it begins to make sense.

Mr. Charton was an old widower and pharmacology was his life. He hinted that someone would have to carry on the pharmacy someday—some young fellow with a degree in pharmacy and devotion to the profession. He said that he might be able to help such a person get through school. If he had suggested that I could someday run the dispensary at Lunar Base, I might have taken the bait. I explained that I was dead set on spacing, and engineering looked like my one chance.

He didn't laugh. He said I was probably right—but that I shouldn't forget that wherever Man went, to the Moon, on Mars, or the farthest stars, pharmacists and dispensaries would go along. Then he dug out books for me on space medicine—Strughold and Haber and Stapp and others. "I once had ideas along that line, Kip," he said quietly, "but now it's too late."

Even though Mr. Charton was not really interested in anything but drugs, we sold everything that drugstores sell, from bicycle tires to home permanent kits.

Including soap, of course.

We were selling darned little Skyway Soap; Centerville is conservative about new brands—I'll bet some of them made their own soap. But when I showed up for work that day I had to tell Mr. Charton about it. He dug out two dust-covered boxes and put them on the counter. Then he phoned his jobber in Springfield.

He really did right by me. He marked Skyway Soap down almost to cost and pushed it—and he almost always got the wrappers before he let the customer go. Me, I stacked a pyramid of Skyway Soap on each end of the fountain and every coke was accompanied by a spiel for good old Skyway, the soap that washes cleaner, is packed with vitamins, and improves your chances of Heaven, not to mention its rich creamy lather, finer ingredients, and refusal to take the Fifth Amendment. Oh, I was shameless! Anybody who got away without buying was deaf or fast on his feet.

If he bought soap without leaving the wrappers with me he was a magician. Adults I talked out of it; kids, if I had to, I paid a penny for each wrapper. If they brought in wrappers from around town, I paid a dime a dozen and threw in a cone. The rules permitted a contestant to submit any number of entries as long as each was written on a Skyway Soap wrapper or reasonable facsimile.

I considered photographing one and turning out facsimiles by the gross, but Dad advised me not to. "It is within the rules, Kip, but I've never yet known a skunk to be welcome at a picnic."

So I used soap. And I sent in wrappers with slogans: "I use Skyway Soap because—
—it makes me feel so *clean.*"
—highway or byway, there's no soap like Skyway!"
—its quality is sky-high."
—it is pure as the Milky Way."
—it is pure as Interstellar Space."
—it leave me fresh as a rain-swept sky."

And so on endlessly, until I tasted soap in my dreams. Not just my own slogans either; Dad thought them up, and so did Mother and Mr. Charton. I kept a notebook and wrote them down in school or at work or in the middle of the night. I came home one evening and found that Dad had set up a card file for me and after that I kept them alphabetically to avoid repeating. A good thing, too, for toward the last I sent in as many as a hundred a day. Postage mounted, not to mention having to buy some wrappers.

Other kids in town were in the contest and probably some adults, but they didn't have the production line I had. I'd leave work at ten o'clock, hurry home with the day's slogans and wrappers, pick up more slogans from Dad and Mother, then use a rubber stamp on the inside of each wrapper: "I use Skyway Soap because—" with my name and address. As I typed, Dad filled out file cards. Each morning I mailed the bunch on my way to school.

I got laughed at but the adults most inclined to kid me were quickest to let me have their wrappers.

All but one, an oaf called "Ace" Quiggle. I shouldn't

class Ace as an adult; he was an over-age juvenile delinquent. I guess every town has at least one Ace. He hadn't finished Centerville High, a distinction since Mr. Hanley believed in promoting everybody "to keep age groups together." As far back as I remember Ace hung around Main Street, sometimes working, mostly not.

He specialized in "wit." He was at our fountain one day, using up two dollars' worth of space and time for one thirty-five-cent malt. I had just persuaded old Mrs. Jenkins to buy a dozen cakes and had relieved her of the wrappers. As she left, Ace picked one off my counter display and said, "You're selling these, Space Cadet?"

"That's right, Ace. You'll never find such a bargain again."

"You expect to go to the Moon, just selling soap, Captain? Or should I say 'Commodore'? Yuk yuk yukkity yuk!" That's how Ace laughed, like a comic strip.

"I'm trying," I said politely. "How about some?"

"You're sure it's good soap?"

"Positive."

"Well, I'll tell you. Just to help you out—I'll buy one bar."

A plunger. But this might be the winning wrapper. "Sure thing, Ace. Thanks a lot." I took his money, he slipped the cake into his pocket and started to leave. "Just a second, Ace. The wrapper. Please?"

He stopped. "Oh, yes." He took out the bar, peeled it, held up the wrapper. "You want this?"

"Yes, Ace. Thanks."

"Well, I'll show you how to get the best use of it." He reached across to the cigar lighter on the tobacco counter and set fire to it, lit a cigarette with it, let the wrapper burn almost to his fingers, dropped it and stepped on it.

Mr. Charton watched from the window of the dispensary.

Ace grinned. "Okay, Space Cadet?"

I was gripping the ice-cream scoop. But I answered, "Perfectly okay, Ace. It's your soap."

Mr. Charton came out and said, "I'll take the fountain, Kip. There's a package to deliver."

That was almost the only wrapper I missed. The contest ended May 1 and both Dad and Mr. Charton decided to stock up and cleaned out the last case in the store. It was almost eleven before I had them written up, then Mr. Charton drove me to Springfield to get them postmarked before midnight.

I had sent in five thousand seven hundred and eighty-two slogans. I doubt if Centerville was ever so scrubbed.

The results were announced on the Fourth of July. I chewed my nails to the elbows in those nine weeks. Oh, other things happened. I graduated and Dad and Mother gave me a watch and we paraded past Mr. Hanley and got our diplomas. It felt good, even though what Dad had persuaded me to learn beat what I learned at dear old Center six ways from zero. Before that was Sneak Day and Class Honeymoon and Senior Prom and the Class Play and the Junior-Senior Picnic and all the things they do to keep the animals quiet. Mr. Charton let me off early if I asked, but I didn't ask often as my mind wasn't on it and I wasn't going steady anyhow. I had been earlier in the year, but she—Elaine McMurty—wanted to talk boys and clothes and I wanted to talk space and engineering so she put me back into circulation.

After graduation I worked for Mr. Charton full time. I still didn't know how I was going to college. I didn't think about it; I just dished sundaes and held my breath until the Fourth of July.

It was to be on television at 8 P.M. We had a TV—a black and white flat-image job—but it hadn't been turned on in months; after I built it I lost interest. I dug it out, set it up in the living room and tested the picture. I killed a couple of hours adjusting it, then spent the rest of the day chewing nails. I couldn't eat dinner. By seven-thirty I was in front of the set, not-watching a comedy team and fiddling with my file cards. Dad came in, looked sharply at me, and said, "Take a grip on yourself, Kip. Let me remind you again that the chances are against you."

I gulped. "I know, Dad."

"Furthermore, in the long run it won't matter. A man almost always gets what he wants badly enough. I am sure you will get to the Moon someday, one way or another."

"Yes, sir. I just wish they would get it over with."

"They will. Coming, Emma?"

"Right away, dearest," Mother called back. She came in, patted my hand and sat down.

Dad settled back. "Reminds me of election nights."

Mother said, "I'm glad you're no longer up to your ears in *that*."

"Oh, come now, sweetheart, you enjoyed every campaign."

Mother sniffed.

The comics went back where comics go, cigarettes did a cancan, then dived into their packs while a soothing voice assured us that carcinogenous factors were unknown in Coronets, the safe, Safe, SAFE smoke with the true tobacco flavor. The program cut to the local station; we were treated to a thrilling view of Center Lumber & Hardware and I started pulling hairs out of the back of my hand.

The screen filled with soap bubbles; a quartet sang that this was the Skyway Hour, as if we didn't know. Then the screen went blank and sound cut off and I swallowed my stomach.

The screen lighted up with: "Network Difficulty—Do Not Adust Your Sets."

I yelped, "Oh, they can't do that! They can't!"

Dad said, "Stop it, Clifford."

I shut up. Mother said, "Now, dearest, he's just a boy."

Dad said, "He is not a boy; he is a man. Kip, how do you expect to face a firing squad calmly if this upsets you?"

I mumbled; he said, "Speak up." I said I hadn't really planned on facing one.

"You may need to, someday. This is good practice. Try the Springfield channel; you may get a skip image."

I tried, but all I got was snow and the sound was like two cats in a sack. I jumped back to our local station.

"—jor General Bryce Gilmore, United States Air Force, our guest tonight, who will explain to us, later in this program, some hitherto unreleased pictures of Federation Lunar Base and the infant Luna City, the fastest growing little city on the Moon. Immediately after announcing the winners we will attempt a television linkage with Lunar Base, through the cooperation of the Space Corps of the—"

I took a deep breath and tried to slow my heartbeat, the way you steady down for a free-throw in a tie game. The gabble dragged on while celebrities were introduced, the contest rules were explained, an improbably sweet young couple explained to each other why they always used Skyway Soap. My own sales talks were better.

At last they got to it. Eight girls paraded out; each held a big card over her head. The M.C. said in an awe-struck voice: "And now . . . and *now*—the winning Skyway slogan for the . . . FREE TRIP TO THE MOON!"

I couldn't breathe.

The girls sang, "I like Skyway Soap because—" and went on, each turning her card as a word reached her:

"—it . . . is . . . as . . . pure . . . as . . . the . . . sky . . . itself!"

I was fumbling cards. I thought I recognized it but couldn't be sure—not after more than five thousand slogans. Then I found it—and checked the cards the girls were holding.

"Dad! Mother! I've won, I've *won!*"

Chapter 3

"Hold it, Kip!" Dad snapped. "Stop it."

Mother said, "Oh, *dear!*"

I heard the M.C. saying, "—present the lucky winner, Mrs. Xenia Donahue, of Great Falls, Montana. . . . Mrs. *Donahue!*"

To a fanfare a little dumpy woman teetered out. I read the cards again. They still matched the one in my hand. I said, "Dad, what happened? That's *my* slogan."

"You didn't listen."

"They've cheated me!"

"Be quiet and listen."

"—as we explained earlier, in the event of duplicate entries, priority goes to the one postmarked first. Any remaining tie is settled by time of arrival at the contest office. Our winning slogan was submitted by eleven contestants. To them go the first eleven prizes. Tonight we have with us the six top winners—for the trip to the Moon, the weekend in a satellite space station, the jet flight around the world, the flight to Antarctica, the—"

"Beaten by a postmark. A *postmark!*"

"—sorry we can't have every one of the winners with us tonight. To the rest this comes as a surprise." The M.C. looked at his watch. "Right this minute, in a thousand homes across the land . . . right this *second*—there is a lucky knock on a lucky door of some loyal friend of Skyway—"

There was a knock on *our* door.

I fell over my feet. Dad answered. There were three men, an enormous crate, and a Western Union messenger singing about Skyway Soap. Somebody said, "Is this where Clifford Russell lives?"

Dad said, "Yes."

"Will you sign for this?"

"What is it?"

"It just says 'This Side Up.' Where do you want it?"

Dad passed the receipt to me and I signed, somehow. Dad said, "Will you put it in the living room, please?"

They did and left and I got a hammer and sidecutters. It looked like a coffin and I could have used one.

I got the top off. A lot of packing got all over Mother's rugs. At last we were down to it.

It was a space suit.

Not much, as space suits go these days. It was an obsolete model that Skyway Soap had bought as surplus material—the tenth-to-hundredth prizes were all space suits. But it was a real one, made by Goodyear, with air conditioning by York and auxiliary equipment by General Electric. Its instruction manual and maintenance-and-service log were with it and it had racked up more than eight hundred hours in rigging the second satellite station.

I felt better. This was no phony, this was no toy. It had been out in space, even if I had not. But I would!— someday. I'd learn to use it and someday I'd wear it on the naked face of the Moon.

Dad said, "Maybe we'd better carry this to your workshop. Eh, Kip?"

Mother said, "There's no rush, dearest. Don't you want to try it on, Clifford?"

I certainly did. Dad and I compromised by toting the crate and packing out to the barn. When we came back, a reporter from the *Clarion* was there with a photographer—the paper had known I was a winner before I did, which didn't seem right.

They wanted pictures and I didn't mind.

I had an awful time getting into it—dressing in an upper berth is a cinch by comparison. The photographer said, "Just a minute, kid. I've seen 'em do it at Wright Field. Mind some advice?"

"Uh? No. I mean, yes, tell me."

"You slide in like an Eskimo climbing into a kayak. Then wiggle your right arm in—"

It was fairly easy that way, opening front gaskets wide and sitting down in it, though I almost dislocated a shoulder. There were straps to adjust for size but we didn't bother; he stuffed me into it, zippered the gaskets, helped me to my feet and shut the helmet.

It didn't have air bottles and I had to live on the air inside while he got three shots. By then I knew that the suit had seen service; it smelled like dirty socks. I was glad to get the helmet off.

Just the same, it made me feel good to wear it. Like a spacer.

They left and presently we went to bed, leaving the suit in the living room.

About midnight I catfooted down and tried it on again.

The next morning I moved it out to my shop before I went to work. Mr. Charton was diplomatic; he just said he'd like to see my space suit when I had time. Everybody knew about it—my picture was on the front page of the *Clarion* along with the Pikes Peak Hill Climb and the holiday fatalities. The story had been played for laughs, but I didn't mind. I had never really *believed* I would win—and I had an honest-to-goodness space suit, which was more than my classmates had.

That afternoon Dad brought me a special delivery letter from Skyway Soap. It enclosed a property title to one suit, pressure, serial number so-and-so, ex-US-AF. The letter started with congratulations and thanks but the last paragraphs meant something:

Skyway Soap realizes that your prize may not be of immediate use to you. Therefore, as mentioned in para-

graph 4 (a) of the rules, Skyway offers to redeem it for a cash premium of five hundred dollars ($500.00). To avail yourself of this privilege you should return the pressure suit via express collect to Goodyear Corporation (Special Appliances Division, attn: Salvage), Akron, Ohio, on or before the 15th of September.

Skyway Soap hopes that you have enjoyed our Grand Contest as much as we have enjoyed having you and hopes that you will retain your prize long enough to appear with it on your local television station in a special Skyway Jubilee program. A fee of fifty dollars ($50.00) will be paid for this appearance. Your station manager will be in touch with you. We hope that you will be our guest.

All good wishes from Skyway, the Soap as Pure as the Sky Itself.

I handed it to Dad. He read it and handed it back.

I said, "I suppose I should."

He said, "I see no harm. Television leaves no external scars."

"Oh, that. Sure, it's easy money. But I meant I really ought to sell the suit back to them." I should have felt happy since I needed money, while I needed a space suit the way a pig needs a pipe organ. But I didn't, even though I had never had five hundred dollars in my life.

"Son, any statement that starts 'I really ought to—' is suspect. It means you haven't analyzed your motives."

"But five hundred dollars is tuition for a semester, almost."

"Which has nothing to do with the case. Find out what you want to do, then do it. Never talk yourself into doing something you don't want. Think it over." He said good-bye and left.

I decided it was foolish to burn my bridges before I crossed them. The space suit was mine until the middle of September even if I did the sensible thing—by then I might be tired of it.

But I didn't get tired of it; a space suit is a marvelous piece of machinery—a little space station with everything miniaturized. Mine was a chrome-plated helmet and shoulder yoke which merged into a body of silicone, asbestos, and glass-fibre cloth. This hide was stiff except at the joints. They were the same rugged material but were "constant volume"—when you bent a knee a bellows arrangement increased the volume over the knee cap as much as the space back of the knee was squeezed. Without this a man wouldn't be able to move; the pressure inside, which can add up to several tons, would hold him rigid as a statue. These volume compensators were covered with dural armor; even the finger joints had little dural plates over the knuckles.

It had a heavy glass-fibre belt with clips for tools, and there were the straps to adjust for height and weight. There was a back pack, now empty, for air bottles, and zippered pockets inside and out, for batteries and such.

The helmet swung back, taking a bib out of the yoke with it, and the front opened with two gasketed zippers; this left a door you could wiggle into. With helmet clamped and zippers closed it was impossible to open the suit with pressure inside.

Switches were mounted on the shoulder yoke and on the helmet; the helmet was monstrous. It contained a drinking tank, pill dispensers six on each side, a chin plate on the right to switch radio from "receive" to "send," another on the left to increase or decrease flow of air, an automatic polarizer for the face lens, microphone and earphones, space for radio circuits in a bulge back of the head, and an instrument board arched over the head. The instrument dials read backwards because they were reflected in an inside mirror in front of the wearer's forehead at an effective fourteen inches from the eyes.

Above the lens or window there were twin headlights. On top were two antennas, a spike for broadcast and a horn that squirted microwaves like a gun—you aimed it by facing the receiving station. The horn antenna was armored except for its open end.

This sounds as crowded as a lady's purse but everything was beautifully compact; your head didn't touch anything when you looked out the lens. But you could tip your head back and see reflected instruments, or tilt it down and turn it to work chin controls, or simply turn your neck for water nipple or pills. In all remaining space sponge-rubber padding kept you from banging your head no matter what.

My suit was like a fine car, its helmet like a Swiss watch.

But its air bottles were missing; so was radio gear except for built-in antennas; radar beacon and emergency radar target were gone, pockets inside and out were empty, and there were no tools on the belt. The manual told what it ought to have—it was like a stripped car.

I decided I just had to make it work right.

First I swabbed it out with Clorox to kill the lockerroom odor. Then I got to work on the air system.

It's a good thing they included that manual; most of what I thought I knew about space suits was wrong.

A man uses around three pounds of oxygen a day—pounds mass, not pounds per square inch. You'd think a man could carry oxygen for a month, expecially out in space where mass has no weight, or on the Moon where three pounds weigh only half a pound. Well, that's okay for space stations or ships or frogmen; they run air through soda lime to take out carbon dioxide, and breathe it again. But not space suits.

Even today people talk about "the bitter cold of outer space"—but space is vacuum and if vacuum were cold, how could a Thermos jug keep hot coffee hot? Vacuum is *nothing*—it has no temperature, it just insulates.

Three-fourths of your food turns into heat—a lot of heat, enough each day to melt fifty pounds of ice and more. Sounds preposterous, doesn't it? But when you have a roaring fire in the furnace, you are *cooling* your body; even in the winter you keep a room about thirty degrees cooler than your body. When you turn up a furnace's thermostat, you are picking a more comfortable rate for cooling. Your body makes so much heat you have to get rid of it, exactly as you have to cool a car's engine.

Of course, if you do it too fast, say in a sub-zero wind, you can freeze—but the usual problem in a space suit is to keep from being boiled like a lobster. You've got vacuum all around you and it's *hard* to get rid of heat.

Some radiates away but not enough, and if you are in sunlight, you pick up still more—this is why space ships are polished like mirrors.

So what can you do?

Well, you can't carry fifty-pound blocks of ice. You get rid of heat the way you do on Earth, by convection and evaporation—you keep air moving over you to evaporate sweat and cool you off. Oh, they'll learn to build space suits that recycle like a space ship but today the practical way is to let used air escape from the suit, flushing away sweat and carbon dioxide and excess heat—while wasting most of the oxygen.

There are other problems. The fifteen pounds per square inch around you includes three pounds of oxygen pressure. Your lungs can get along on less than half that, but only an Indian from the high Andes is likely to be comfortable on less than two pounds oxygen pressure. Nine-tenths of a pound is the limit. Any less than nine-tenths of a pound won't force oxygen into blood—this is about the pressure at the top of Mount Everest.

Most people suffer from hypoxia (oxygen shortage)

long before this, so better use two p.s.i. of oxygen. Mix an inert gas with it, because pure oxygen can cause a sore throat or make you drunk or even cause terrible cramps. Don't use nitrogen (which you've breathed all your life) because it will bubble in your blood if pressure drops and cripple you with "bends." Use helium which doesn't. It gives you a squeaky voice, but who cares?

You can die from oxygen shortage, be poisoned by too much oxygen, be crippled by nitrogen, drown in or be acid-poisoned by carbon dioxide, or dehydrate and run a killing fever. When I finished reading that manual I didn't see how anybody could stay alive anywhere, much less in a space suit.

But a space suit was in front of me that had protected a man for hundreds of hours in empty space.

Here is how you beat those dangers. Carry steel bottles on your back; they hold "air" (oxygen and helium) at a hundred and fifty atmospheres, over 2000 pounds per square inch; you draw from them through a reduction valve down to 150 p.s.i. and through still another reduction valve, a "demand" type which keeps pressure in your helmet at three to five pounds per square inch—two pounds of it oxygen. Put a silicone-rubber collar around your neck and put tiny holes in it, so that the pressure in the body of your suit is less, the air movement still faster; then evaporation and cooling will be increased while the effort of bending is decreased. Add exhaust valves, one at each wrist and ankle—these have to pass water as well as gas because you may be ankle deep in sweat.

The bottles are big and clumsy, weighing around sixty pounds apiece, and each holds only about five mass pounds of air even at that enormous pressure; instead of a month's supply you will have only a few hours—my suit was rated at eight hours for the bottles it used to have. But you will be okay for those hours—if everything works right. You can stretch time, for you don't die from overheating very fast and can stand too much carbon dioxide even longer—but let your oxygen run out and you die in about seven minutes. Which gets us back where we started—it takes oxygen to stay alive.

To make darn sure that you're getting enough(your nose can't tell) you clip a little photoelectric cell to your ear and let it see the color of your blood; the redness of the blood measures the oxygen it carries. Hook this to a galvanometer. If its needle gets into the danger zone, start saying your prayers.

I went to Springfield on my day off, taking the suit's hose fittings, and shopped. I picked up, second hand, two thirty-inch steel bottles from a welding shop—and got myself disliked by insisting on a pressure test. I took them home on the bus, stopped at Pring's Garage and arranged to buy air at fifty atmospheres. Higher pressures, or oxygen or helium, I could get from the Springfield airport, but I didn't need them yet.

When I got home I closed the suit, empty, and pumped it with a bicycle pump to two atmospheres absolute, or one relative, which gave me a test load of almost four to one compared with space conditions. Then I tackled the bottles. They needed to be mirror bright, since you can't afford to let them pick up heat from the Sun. I stripped and scraped and wire-brushed, and buffed and polished, preparatory to nickel-plating.

Next morning, Oscar the Mechanical Man was limp as a pair of long johns.

Getting that old suit not just airtight but helium-tight was the worst headache. Air isn't bad but the helium molecule is so small and agile that it migrates right through ordinary rubber—and I wanted this job to be *right,* not just good enough to perform at home but okay for space. The gaskets were shot and there were slow leaks almost impossible to find.

I had to get new silicone-rubber gaskets and patch-ing compound and tissue from Goodyear; small-town hardware stores don't handle such things. I wrote a letter explaining what I wanted and why—and they didn't even charge me. They sent me some mimeographed sheets elaborating on the manual.

It still wasn't easy. But there came a day when I pumped Oscar full of pure helium at two atmospheres absolute.

A week later he was still tight as a six-ply tire.

That day I wore Oscar as a self-contained environment. I had already worn him many hours without the helmet, working around the shop, handling tools while hampered by his gauntlets, getting height and size adjustments right. It was like breaking in new ice skates and after a while I was hardly aware I had it on —once I came to supper in it. Dad said nothing and Mother has the social restraint of an ambassador; I discovered my mistake when I picked up my napkin.

Now I wasted helium to the air, mounted bottles charged with air, and suited them. Then I clamped the helmet and dogged the safety catches.

Air sighed softly into the helmet, its flow through the demand valve regulated by the rise and fall of my chest—I could reset it to speed up or slow down by the chin control. I did so, watching the gauge in the mirror and letting it mount until I had twenty pounds absolute inside. That gave me five pounds more than the pressure around me, which was as near as I could come to space conditions without being in space.

I could feel the suit swell and the joints no longer felt loose and easy. I balanced the cycle at five pounds differential and tried to move—

And almost fell over. I had to grab the workbench.

Suited up, with bottles on my back, I weighed more than twice what I do stripped. Besides that, although the joints were constant-volume, the suit didn't work as freely under pressure. Dress yourself in heavy fishing waders, put on an overcoat and boxing gloves and a bucket over your head, then have somebody strap two sacks of cement across your shoulders and you will know what a space suit feels like under one gravity.

But ten minutes later I was handling myself fairly well and in half an hour I felt as if I had worn one all my life. The distributed weight wasn't too great (and I knew it wouldn't amount to much on the Moon). The joints were just a case of getting used to more effort. I had had more trouble learning to swim.

It was a blistering day: I went outside and looked at the Sun. The polarizer cut the glare and I was able to look at it. I looked away; polarizing eased off and I could see around me.

I stayed cool. The air, cooled by semi-adiabatic expansion (it said in the manual), cooled my head and flowed on through the suit, washing away body heat and used air through the exhaust valves. The manual said that heating elements rarely cut in, since the usual problem was to get rid of heat; I decided to get dry ice and force a test of thermostat and heater.

I tried everything I could think of. A creek runs back of our place and beyond is a pasture. I sloshed through the stream, lost my footing and fell—the worst trouble was that I could never see where I was putting my feet. Once I was down I lay there a while, half floating but mostly covered. I didn't get wet, I didn't get hot, I didn't get cold, and my breathing was as easy as ever even though water shimmered over my helmet.

I scrambled heavily up the bank and fell again, striking my helmet against a rock. No damage, Oscar was built to take it. I pulled my knees under me, got up, and crossed the pasture, stumbling on rough ground but not falling. There was a haystack there and I dug into it until I was buried.

Cool fresh air . . . no trouble, no sweat.

After three hours I took it off. The suit had relief arrangements like any pilot's outfit but I hadn't rigged it yet, so I had come out before my air was gone. When I hung it in the rack I had built, I patted the shoulder yoke. "Oscar, you're all right," I told it. "You and I are partners. We're going places."

I would have sneered at five thousand dollars for Oscar.

While Oscar was taking his pressure tests I worked on his electrical and electronic gear. I didn't bother with a radar target or beacon; the first is childishly simple, the second is fiendishly expensive. But I did want radio for the space-operations band of the spectrum—the antennas suited only those wavelengths. I could have built an ordinary walkie-talkie and hung it outside—but I would have been kidding myself with a wrong frequency and gear that might not stand vacuum. Changes in pressure and temperature and humidity do funny things to electronic circuits; that is why the radio was housed inside the helmet.

The manual gave circuit diagrams, so I got busy. The audio and modulating circuits were no problem, just battery-operated transistor circuitry which I could make plenty small enough. But the microwave part—

It was a two-headed calf, each with transmitter and receiver—one centimeter wavelength for the horn and three octaves lower at eight centimeters for the spike in a harmonic relationship, one crystal controlling both. This gave more signal on broadcast and better aiming when squirting out the horn and also meant that only part of the rig had to be switched in changing antennas. The output of a variable-frequency oscillator was added to the crystal frequency in tuning the receiver. The circuitry was simple—on paper.

But microwave circuitry is never easy; it takes precision machining and a slip of a tool can foul up the impedance and ruin a mathematically calculated resonance.

Well, I tried. Synthetic precision crystals are cheap from surplus houses and some transistors and other components I could vandalize from my own gear. And I made it work, after the fussiest pray-and-try-again I have ever done. But the consarned thing simply would *not* fit into the helmet.

Call it a moral victory—I've never done better work.

I finally bought one, precision made and embedded in plastic, from the same firm that sold me the crystal. Like the suit it was made for, it was obsolete and I paid a price so low that I merely screamed. By then I would have mortgaged my soul—I wanted that suit to *work*.

The only thing that complicated the rest of the electrical gear was that everything had to be either "failsafe" or "no-fail"; a man in a space suit can't pull into the next garage if something goes wrong—the stuff *has* to keep on working or he becomes a vital statistic. That was why the helmet had twin headlights; the second cut in if the first failed—even the peanut lights for the dials over my head were twins. I didn't take short cuts; every duplicate circuit I kept duplicate and tested to make sure that automatic changeover always worked.

Mr. Charton insisted on filling the manual's list on those items a drugstore stocks—maltose and dextrose and amino tablets, vitamins, dexedrine, dramamine, aspirin, antibiotics, antihistamines, codeine, almost any pill a man can take to help him past a hump that might kill him. He got Doc Kennedy to write prescriptions so that I could stock Oscar without breaking laws.

When I got through Oscar was in as good shape as he had ever been in Satellite Two. It had been more fun than the time I helped Jake Bixby turn his heap into a hotrod.

But summer was ending and it was time I pulled out of my daydream. I still did not know where I was going to school, or how—or if. I had saved money but it wasn't nearly enough. I had spent a little on postage and soap wrappers but I got that back and more by one fifteen-minute appearance on television and I hadn't spent a dime on girls since March—too busy. Oscar cost surprisingly little; repairing Oscar had been mostly sweat and screwdriver. Seven dollars out of every ten I had earned was sitting in the money basket.

But it wasn't enough.

I realized glumly that I was going to have to sell Oscar to get through the first semester. But how would I get through the rest of the year? Joe Valiant the all-American boy always shows up on the campus with fifty cents and a heart of gold, then in the last chapter is tapped for Skull-and-Bones and has money in the bank. But I wasn't Joe Valiant, not by eight decimal places. Did it make sense to start if I was going to have to drop out about Christmas? Wouldn't it be smarter to stay out a year and get acquainted with a pick and shovel?

Did I have a choice? The only school I was sure of was State U.—and there was a row about professors being fired and talk that State U. might lose its accredited standing. Wouldn't it be comical to spend years slaving for a degree and then have it be worthless because your school wasn't recognized?

State U. wasn't better than a "B" school in engineering even before this fracas.

Rensselaer and CalTech turned me down the same day—one with a printed form, the other with a polite letter saying it was impossible to accept all qualified applicants.

Little things were getting my goat, too. The only virtue of that television show was the fifty bucks. A person looks foolish wearing a space suit in a television studio and our announcer milked it for laughs, rapping the helmet and asking me if I was still in there. Very funny. He asked me what I wanted with a space suit and when I tried to answer he switched off the mike in my suit and patched in a tape with nonsense about space pirates and flying saucers. Half the people in town thought it was my voice.

It wouldn't have been hard to live down if Ace Quiggle hadn't turned up. He had been missing all summer, in jail maybe, but the day after the show he took a seat at the fountain, stared at me and said in a loud whisper, "Say, ain't you the famous space pirate and television star?"

I said, "What'll you have, Ace?"

"Gosh! Could I have your autograph? I ain't never seen a real live space pirate before!"

"Give me your order, Ace. Or let someone else use that stool."

"A choc malt, Commodore—and leave out the soap."

Ace's "wit" went on every time he showed up. It was a dreadfully hot summer and easy to get tempery. The Friday before Labor Day weekend the store's cooling system went sour, we couldn't get a repairman and I spent three bad hours fixing it, ruining my second-best pants and getting myself reeking. I was back at the fountain and wishing I could go home for a bath when Ace swaggered in, greeting me loudly with "Why, if it isn't Commander Comet, the Scourge of the Spaceways! Where's your blaster gun, Commander? Ain't you afraid the Galactic Emperor will make you stay in after school for running around bare-nekkid? Yuk yuk yukkity yuk!"

A couple of girls at the fountain giggled.

"Lay off, Ace," I said wearily. "It's a hot day."

"That's why you're not wearing your rubber underwear?" The girls giggled again.

Ace smirked. He went on: "Junior, seein' you got that

clown suit, why don't you put it to work? Run an ad in the *Clarion*: 'Have Space Suit—Will Travel.' Yukkity yuk! Or you could hire out as a scarecrow."

The girls snickered. I counted ten, then again in Spanish, and in Latin, and said tensely, "Ace, just tell me what you'll have."

"My usual. And snap it up—I've got a date on Mars."

Mr. Charton came out from behind his counter, sat down and asked me to mix him a lime cooler, so I served him first. It stopped the flow of wit and probably saved Ace's life.

The boss and I were alone shortly after. He said quietly, "Kip, a reverence for life does not require a man to respect Nature's obvious mistakes."

"Sir?"

"You need not serve Quiggle again. I don't want his trade."

"Oh, I don't mind. He's harmless."

"I wonder how harmless such people are? To what extent civilization is retarded by the laughing jackasses, the empty-minded belittlers? Go home; you'll want to make an early start tomorrow."

I had been invited to the Lake of the Forest for the long Labor Day weekend by Jake Bixby's parents. I wanted to go, not only to get away from the heat but also to chew things over with Jake. But I answered, "Shucks, Mr. Charton, I ought not to leave you stuck."

"The town will be deserted over the holiday; I may not open the fountain. Enjoy yourself. This summer has worn you a bit fine, Kip."

I let myself be persuaded but I stayed until closing and swept up. Then I walked home, doing some hard thinking.

The party was over and it was time to put away my toys. Even the village half-wit knew that I had no sensible excuse to have a space suit. Not that I cared what Ace thought . . . but I did have no use for it—and I needed money. Even if Stanford and M.I.T. and Carnegie and the rest turned me down, I was going to start this semester. State U. wasn't the best—but neither was I and I had learned that more depended on the student than on the school.

Mother had gone to bed and Dad was reading. I said hello and went to the barn, intending to strip my gear off Oscar, pack him into his case, address it, and in the morning phone the express office to pick it up. He'd be gone before I was back from the Lake of the Forest. Quick and clean.

He was hanging on his rack and it seemed to me that he grinned hello. Nonsense, of course. I went over and patted his shoulder. "Well, old fellow, you've been a real chum and it's been nice knowing you. See you on the Moon—I hope."

But Oscar wasn't going to the Moon. Oscar was going to Akron, Ohio, to "Salvage." They were going to unscrew parts they could use and throw the rest of him on the junk pile.

My mouth felt dry.

("It's okay, pal," Oscar answered.)

See that? Out of my silly head! Oscar didn't really speak; I had let my imagination run wild too long. So I quit patting him, hauled the crate out and took a wrench from his belt to remove the gas bottles.

I stopped.

Both bottles were charged, one with oxygen, one with oxy-helium. I had wasted money to do so because I wanted, just once, to try a spaceman's mix.

The batteries were fresh and power packs were charged.

"Oscar," I said softly, "we're going to take a last walk together. Okay?"

("Swell!")

I made it a dress rehearsal—water in the drinking tank, pill dispensers loaded, first-aid kit inside, vacuum-proof duplicate (I hoped it was vacuum-proof) in an outside pocket. All tools on belt, all lanyards tied so that tools wouldn't float away in free fall. Everything.

Then I heated up a circuit that the F.C.C. would have squelched had they noticed, a radio link I had salvaged out of my effort to build a radio for Oscar, and had modified as a test rig for Oscar's ears and to let me check the aiming of the directional antenna. It was hooked in with an echo circuit that would answer back if I called it—a thing I had bread-boarded out of an old Webcor wire recorder, vintage 1950.

Then I climbed into Oscar and buttoned up. "Tight?" ("Tight!")

I glanced at the reflected dials, noticed the blood-color reading, reduced pressure until Oscar almost collapsed. At nearly sea-level pressure I was in no danger from hypoxia; the trick was to avoid too much oxygen.

We started to leave when I remembered something. "Just a second, Oscar." I wrote a note to my folks, telling them that I was going to get up early and catch the first bus to the lake. I could write while suited up now, I could even thread a needle. I stuck the note under the kitchen door.

Then we crossed the creek into the pasture. I didn't stumble in wading; I was used to Oscar now, sure-footed as a goat.

Out in the field I keyed my talkie and said, "June-bug, calling Peewee. Come in, Peewee."

Seconds later my recorded voice came back: " 'June-bug, calling Peewee. Come in, Peewee.' "

I shifted to the horn antenna and tried again. It wasn't easy to aim in the dark but it was okay. Then I shifted back to spike antenna and went on calling Peewee while moving across the pasture and pretending that I was on Venus and had to stay in touch with base because it was unknown terrain and unbreathable atmosphere. Everything worked perfectly and if it had been Venus, I would have been all right.

Two lights moved across the southern sky, planes I thought, or maybe helis. Just the sort of thing yokels like to report as "flying saucers." I watched them, then moved behind a little rise that would tend to spoil reception and called Peewee. Peewee answered and I shut up; it gets dull talking to an idiot circuit which can only echo what you say to it.

Then I heard: "Peewee to Junebug! Answer!"

I thought I had been monitored and was in trouble—then decided that some ham had picked me up. "Junebug here. I read you. Who are you?"

The test rig echoed my words.

Then the new voice shrilled, "Peewee here! Home me in!"

This was silly. But I found myself saying, "Junebug to Peewee, shift to directional frequency at one centimeter—and keep talking, keep talking!" I shifted to the horn antenna.

"Junebug, I read you. Fix me. One, two, three, four, five, six, seven—"

"You're due south of me, about forty degrees. Who are you?"

It must be one of those lights. It had to be.

But I didn't have time to figure it out. A space ship almost landed on me.

Chapter 4

I said "space ship," not "rocket ship." It made no noise but a whoosh and there weren't any flaming jets—it seemed to move by clean living and righteous thoughts.

I was too busy keeping from being squashed to worry about details. A space suit in one gravity is no track suit; it's a good thing I had practiced. The ship sat down where I had just been, occupying more than its share of pasture, a big black shape.

The other one whooshed down, too, just as a door opened in the first. Light poured through the door; two figures spilled out and started to run. One moved like a cat; the other moved clumsily and slowly—handicapped by a space suit. S'help me, a person in a space suit does look silly. This one was less than five feet tall and looked like the Gingerbread Man.

A big trouble with a suit is your limited angle of vision. I was trying to watch both of them and did not see the second ship open. The first figure stopped, waiting for the one in the space suit to catch up, then suddenly collapsed—just a gasping sound, "Eee*ah!*"— and clunk.

You can tell the sound of pain. I ran to the spot at a lumbering dogtrot, leaned over and tried to see what was wrong, tilting my helmet to bring the beam of my headlight onto the ground.

A bug-eyed monster—

That's not fair but it was my first thought. I couldn't believe it and would have pinched myself except that it isn't practical when suited up.

An unprejudiced mind (which mine wasn't) would have said that this monster was rather pretty. It was small, not more than half my size, and its curves were

43

graceful, not as a girl is but more like a leopard, although it wasn't shaped like either one. I couldn't grasp its shape—I didn't have any pattern to fit it to; it wouldn't add up.

But I could see that it was hurt. Its body was quivering like a frightened rabbit. It had enormous eyes, open but milky and featureless, as if nictitating membranes were across them. What appeared to be its mouth—

That's as far as I got. Something hit me in the spine, right between the gas bottles.

I woke up on a bare floor, staring at a ceiling. It took several moments to recall what had happened and then I shied away because it was so darn silly. I had been out for a walk in Oscar . . . and then a space ship had landed . . . and a bug-eyed—

I sat up suddenly as I realized that Oscar was gone. A light cheerful voice said, "Hi, there!"

I snapped my head around. A kid about ten years old was seated on the floor, leaning against a wall. He —I corrected myself. Boys don't usually clutch rag dolls. This kid was the age when the difference doesn't show much and was dressed in shirt, shorts and dirty tennis shoes, and had short hair, so I didn't have much to go on but the rag dolly.

"Hi, yourself," I answered. "What are we doing here?"

"I'm surviving. I don't know about you."

"Huh?"

"Surviving. Pushing my breath in and out. Conserving my strength. There's nothing else to do at the moment; they've got us locked in."

I looked around. The room was about ten feet across, four-sided but wedge-shaped, and nothing in it but us. I couldn't see a door; if we weren't locked, we might as well be. "Who locked us in?"

"Them. Space pirates. And *him*."

"Space pirates? Don't be silly!"

The kid shrugged. "Just my name for them. But better not think they're silly if you want to keep on surviving. Are you 'Junebug'?"

"Huh? You sound like a junebug yourself. Space pirates, my aunt!" I was worried and very confused and this nonsense didn't help. Where was Oscar? And where was I?

"No, no, not a junebug but 'Junebug'—a radio call. You see, I'm Peewee."

I said to myself, Kip old pal, walk slowly to the nearest hospital and give yourself up. When a radio rig you wired yourself starts looking like a skinny little girl with a rag doll, you've flipped. It's going to be wet packs and tranquilizers and no excitement for you—you've blown every fuse. "You're 'Peewee'?"

"That's what I'm called—I'm relaxed about it. You see, I heard, 'Junebug, calling Peewee,' and decided that Daddy had found out about the spot I was in and had alerted people to help me land. But if you aren't 'Junebug,' you wouldn't know about that. Who are you?"

"Wait a minute, I *am* 'Junebug.' I mean I was using that call. But I'm Clifford Russell—'Kip' they call me."

"How do you do, Kip?" she said politely.

"And howdy to you, Peewee. Uh, are you a boy or a girl?"

Peewee looked disgusted. "I'll make you regret that remark. I realize I am undersized for my age but I'm actually eleven, going on twelve. There's no need to be rude. In another five years I expect to be quite a dish—you'll probably beg me for every dance."

At the moment I would as soon have danced with a kitchen stool, but I had things on my mind and didn't want a useless argument. "Sorry, Peewee. I'm still groggy. You mean you were in that first ship?"

Again she looked miffed. "I was piloting it."

Sedation every night and a long course of psycho-analysis. At *my* age. "You were—piloting?"

"You surely don't think the Mother Thing could? She wouldn't fit their controls. She curled up beside me and coached. But if you think it's easy, when you've never piloted anything but a Cessna with your Daddy at your elbow and never made *any* kind of landing, then think again. I did very well!—and your landing instructions weren't too specific. What have they done with the Mother Thing?"

"The what?"

"You don't know? Oh, dear!"

"Wait a minute, Peewee. Let's get on the same frequency. I'm 'Junebug' all right and I homed you in—and if you think *that's* easy, to have a voice out of nowhere demand emergency landing instructions, you better think again, too. Anyhow, a ship landed and another ship landed right after it and a door opened in the first ship and a guy in a space suit jumped out—"

"That was I."

"—and something else jumped out—"

"The Mother Thing."

"Only she didn't get far. She gave a screech and flopped. I went to see what the trouble was and something hit me. The next thing I know you're saying, 'Hi, there.' " I wondered if I ought to tell her that the rest, including her, was likely a morphine dream because I was probably lying in a hospital with my spine in a cast.

Peewee nodded thoughtfully. "They must have blasted you at low power, or you wouldn't be here. Well, they caught you and they caught me, so they almost certainly caught her. Oh, dear! I do hope they didn't hurt her."

"She looked like she was dying."

"As if she *were* dying," Peewee corrected me. "Subjunctive. I rather doubt it; she's awfully hard to kill—

46

and they wouldn't kill her except to keep her from escaping; they need her alive."

"Why? And why do you call her 'the Mother Thing'?"

"One at a time, Kip. She's the Mother Thing because . . . well, because she *is*, that's all. You'll know, when you meet her. As to why they wouldn't kill her, it's because she's worth more as a hostage than as a corpse —the same reason they kept me alive. Although she's worth incredibly more than I am—they'd write me off without a blink if I became inconvenient. Or you. But since she was alive when you saw her, then it's logical that she's a prisoner again. Maybe right next door. That makes me feel *much* better."

It didn't make me feel better. "Yes, but where's *here?*"

Peewee glanced at a Mickey Mouse watch, frowned and said, "Almost halfway to the Moon, I'd say."

"*What?!*"

"Of course I don't *know*. But it makes sense that they would go back to their nearest base; that's where the Mother Thing and I scrammed from."

"You're telling me we're in that ship?"

"Either the one I swiped or the other one. Where did you think you were, Kip? Where else *could* you be?"

"A mental hospital."

She looked big-eyed and then grinned. "Why, Kip, surely your grip on reality is not that weak?"

"I'm not sure about anything. Space pirates—Mother Things."

She frowned and bit her thumb. "I suppose it must be confusing. But trust your ears and eyes. My grip on reality is quite strong, I assure you—you see, I'm a genius." She made it a statement, not a boast, and somehow I was not inclined to doubt the claim, even though it came from a skinny-shanked kid with a rag doll in her arms.

But I didn't see how it was going to help.

Peewee went on: " 'Space pirates' . . . mmm. Call them what you wish. Their actions are piratical and they operate in space—you name them. As for the Mother Thing . . . wait until you meet her."

"What's she doing in this hullabaloo?"

"Well, it's complicated. She had better explain it. She's a cop and she was after them—"

"A cop?"

"I'm afraid that is another semantic inadequacy. The Mother Thing knows what we mean by 'cop' and I think she finds the idea bewildering if not impossible. But what would you call a person who hunts down miscreants? A cop, no?"

"A cop, yes, I guess."

"So would I." She looked again at her watch. "But right now I think we had better hang on. We ought to be at halfway point in a few minutes—and a skew-flip is disconcerting even if you are strapped down."

I had read about skew-flip turn-overs, but only as a theoretical maneuver; I had never heard of a ship that could do one. If this was a ship. The floor felt as solid as concrete and as motionless. "I don't see anything to hang on to."

"Not much, I'm afraid. But if we sit down in the narrowest part and push against each other, I think we can brace enough not to slide around. But let's hurry; my watch might be slow."

We sat on the floor in the narrow part where the angled walls were about five feet apart. We faced each other and pushed our shoes against each other, each of us bracing like an Alpinist inching his way up a rock chimney—my socks against her tennis shoes, rather, for my shoes were still on my workbench, so far as I knew. I wondered if they had simply dumped Oscar in the pasture and if Dad would find him.

"Push hard, Kip, and brace your hands against the desk."

I did so. "How do you know when they'll turn over, Peewee?"

"I haven't been unconscious—they just tripped me and carried me inside—so I know when we took off. If we assume that the Moon is their destination, as it probably is, and if we assume one gravity the whole jump— which can't be far off; my weight feels normal. Doesn't yours?"

I considered it. "I think so."

"Then it probably is, even though my own sense of weight may be distorted from being on the Moon. If those assumptions are correct, then it is almost exactly a three-and-a-half-hour trip and—" Peewee looked at her watch. "—E.T.A. should be nine-thirty in the morning and turn-over at seven-forty-five. Any moment now."

"Is it that late?" I looked at my watch. "Why, I've got a quarter of two."

"You're on your zone time. I'm on Moon time—Greenwich time, that is. Oh, oh! Here we go!"

The floor tilted, swerved, and swooped like a roller coaster, and my semicircular canals did a samba. Things steadied down as I pulled out of acute dizziness.

"You all right?" asked Peewee.

I managed to focus my eyes. "Uh, I think so. It felt like a one-and-a-half gainer into a dry pool."

"This pilot does it faster than I dared to. It doesn't really hurt, after your eyes uncross. But that settles it. We're headed for the Moon. We'll be there in an hour and three quarters."

I still couldn't believe it. "Peewee? What kind of a ship can gun at one gee all the way to the Moon? They been keeping it secret? And what were *you* doing on the Moon anyhow? And why were you stealing a ship?"

She sighed and spoke to her doll. "He's a quiz kid, Madame Pompadour. Kip, how can I answer three questions at once? This is a flying saucer, and—"

"Flying saucer! Now I've heard everything."

"It's rude to interrupt. Call it anything you like; there's nothing official about the term. Actually it's shaped more like a loaf of pumpernickel, an oblate spheroid. That's a shape defined—"

"I know what an oblate spheroid is," I snapped. I was tired and upset from too many things, from a cranky air conditioner that had ruined a good pair of pants to being knocked out while on an errand of mercy. Not to mention Ace Quiggle. I was beginning to think that little girls who were geniuses ought to have the grace not to show it.

"No need to be brisk," she said reprovingly. "I am aware that people have called everything from weather balloons to street lights 'flying saucers.' But it is my considered opinion—by Occam's Razor—that—"

"Whose razor?"

"Occam's. Least hypothesis. Don't you know anything about logic?"

"Not much."

"Well . . . I suspected that about every five-hundredth 'saucer sighting' was a ship like this. It adds up. As for what I was doing on the Moon—" She stopped and grinned. "I'm a pest."

I didn't argue it.

"A long time ago when my Daddy was a boy, the Hayden Planetarium took reservations for trips to the Moon. It was just a publicity gag, like that silly soap contest recently, but Daddy got his name on the list. Now, years and years later, they are letting people go to the Moon—and sure enough, the Hayden people turned the list over to American Express—and American Express notified the applicants they could locate that they would be given preference."

"So your father took you to the Moon?"

"Oh, heavens, no! Daddy filled out that form when he was only a boy. Now he is just about the biggest man at the Institute for Advanced Study and hasn't time for such pleasures. And Mama wouldn't go if you paid her. So I said *I* would. Daddy said '*No!*' and Mama said '*Good gracious, no!*' . . . and so I went. I can be an awful nuisance when I put my mind on it," she said proudly. "I have talent for it. Daddy says I'm an amoral little wretch."

"Uh, do you suppose he might be right?"

"Oh, I'm sure he is. He understands me, whereas Mama throws up her hands and says she can't cope. I was perfectly beastly and unbearable for two whole weeks and at last Daddy said 'For Blank's sake let her go!— maybe we'll collect her insurance!' So I did."

"Mmmmm . . . that still doesn't explain why you are here."

"Oh, that. I was poking around where I shouldn't, doing things they told us not to. I always get around; it's very educational. So they grabbed me. They would rather have Daddy but they hope to swap me for him. I couldn't let that happen, so I had to escape."

I muttered, " 'The butler did it.' "

"What?"

"Your story has as many holes as the last chapter of most whodunits."

"Oh. But I assure you it is the simple—oh, oh! here we go again!"

All that happened was that the lighting changed from white to blue. There weren't any light fixtures; the whole ceiling glowed. We were still sprawled on the floor. I started to get up—and found I couldn't.

I felt as if I had just finished a cross-country race, too weak to do anything but breathe. Blue light can't do that; it's merely wavelengths 4300 to 5100 angstroms and sunlight is loaded with it. But whatever they used with the blue light made us as limp as wet string.

Peewee was struggling to tell me something. "If . . . they're coming for us . . . don't resist . . . and . . . above all—"

The blue light changed to white. The narrow wall started to slide aside.

Peewee looked scared and made a great effort. "—above all . . . don't antagonize . . . *him.*"

Two men came in, shoved Peewee aside, strapped my wrists and ankles and ran another strap around my middle, binding my arms. I started to come out of it—not like flipping a switch, as I still didn't have energy enough to lick a stamp. I wanted to bash their heads but I stood as much chance as a butterfly has of hefting a bar bell.

They carried me out. I started to protest. "Say, where are you guys taking me? What do you think you're doing? I'll have you arrested. I'll—"

"Shaddap," said one. He was a skinny runt, fifty or older, and looked as if he never smiled. The other was fat and younger, with a petulant babyish mouth and a dimple in his chin; he looked as if he could laugh if he weren't worried. He was worrying now.

"Tim, this can get us in trouble. We ought to space him—we ought to space both of 'em—and tell *him* it was an accident. We can say they got out and tried to escape through the lock. *He* won't know the dif—"

"Shaddap," answered Tim with no inflection. He added, "You want trouble with *him?* You want to chew space?"

"But—"

"Shaddap."

They carried me around a curved corridor, into an inner room and dumped me on the floor.

I was face up but it took time to realize this must be the control room. It didn't look like anything any human would design as a control room, which wasn't surprising as no human had. Then I saw *him.*

Peewee needn't have warned me; I didn't want to antagonize *him.*

The little guy was tough and dangerous, the fat guy

was mean and murderous; they were cherubs compared with *him*. If I had had my strength I would have fought those two any way they liked; I don't think I'm too afraid of any human as long as the odds aren't impossible.

But not *him*.

He wasn't human but that wasn't what hurt. Elephants aren't human but they are very nice people. *He* was built more like a human than an elephant is but that was no help—I mean he stood erect and had feet at one end and a head at the other. He was no more than five feet tall but that didn't help either; he dominated us the way a man dominates a horse. The torso part was as long as mine; his shortness came from very squat legs, with feet (I guess you would call them feet) which bulged out, almost disc-like. They made squashy, sucking sounds when he moved. When he stood still a tail, or third leg, extruded and turned him into a tripod—he didn't need to sit down and I doubt if he could.

Short legs did not make him slow. His movements were blurringly fast, like a striking snake. Does this mean a better nervous system and more efficient muscles? Or a native planet with higher gravity?

His arms looked like snakes—they had more joints than ours. He had two sets, one pair where his waist should have been and another set under his head. No shoulders. I couldn't count his fingers, or digit tendrils; they never held still. He wasn't dressed except for a belt below and above the middle arms which carried whatever such a thing carries in place of money and keys. His skin was purplish brown and looked oily.

Whatever *he* was, he was *not* the same race as the Mother Thing.

He had a faint sweetish musky odor. Any crowded room smells worse on a hot day, but if I ever whiff that odor again, my skin will crawl and I'll be tongue-tied with fright.

I didn't take in these details instantly; at first all I could see was his face. A "face" is all I can call it. I haven't described it yet because I'm afraid I'll get the shakes. But I will, so that if you ever see one, you'll shoot first, before your bones turn to jelly.

No nose. He was an oxygen breather but where the air went in and out I couldn't say—some of it through the mouth, for he could talk. The mouth was the second worst part of him; in place of jawbone and chin he had mandibles that opened sideways as well as down, gaping in three irregular sides. There were rows of tiny teeth but no tongue that I could see; instead the mouth was rimmed with cilia as long as angleworms. They never stopped squirming.

I said the mouth was "second worst"; he had eyes. They were big and bulging and protected by horny ridges, two on the front of his head, set wide apart.

They scanned. They scanned like radar, swinging up and down and back and forth. He never looked at you and yet was *always* looking at you.

When he turned around, I saw a third eye in back. I think he scanned his whole surroundings at all times, like a radar warning system.

What kind of brain can put together everything in all directions at once? I doubt if a human brain could, even if there were any way to feed in the data. He didn't seem to have room in his head to stack much of a brain, but maybe he didn't keep it there. Come to think of it, humans wear their brains in an exposed position; there may be better ways.

But he certainly had a brain. He pinned me down like a beetle and squeezed out what he wanted. He didn't have to stop to brainwash me; he questioned and I gave, for an endless time—it seemed more like days than hours. He spoke English badly but understandably. His labials were all alike—"buy" and "pie" and "vie" sounded the same. His gutturals were harsh and his dentals had a clucking quality. But I could usually understand and when I didn't, he didn't threaten or punish; he just tried again. He had no expression in his speech.

He kept at it until he had found out who I was and what I did and as much of what I knew as interested him. He asked questions about how I happened to be where I was and dressed the way I was when I was picked up. I couldn't tell whether he liked the answers or not.

He had trouble understanding what a "soda jerk" was and, while he learned about the Skyway Soap contest, he never seemed to understand why it took place. But I found that there were a lot of things I didn't know either—such as how many people there are on Earth and how many tons of protein we produce each year.

After endless time he had all he wanted and said, "Take it out." The stooges had been waiting. The fat boy gulped and said, "Space him?"

He acted as if killing me or not were like saving a piece of string. "No. It is ignorant and untrained, but I may have use for it later. Put it back in the pen."

"Yes, boss."

They dragged me out. In the corridor Fatty said, "Let's untie his feet and make him walk."

Skinny said, "Shaddap."

Peewee was just inside the entrance panel but didn't move, so I guess she had had another dose of that blue-light effect. They stepped over her and dumped me. Skinny chopped me on the side of the neck to stun me. When I came to, they were gone, I was unstrapped, and Peewee was sitting by me. She said anxiously, "Pretty bad?"

"Uh, yeah," I agreed, and shivered. "I feel ninety years old."

"It helps if you don't look *at him*—especially his eyes.

Rest a while and you'll feel better." She glanced at her watch. "It's only forty-five minutes till we land. You probably won't be disturbed before then."

"Huh?" I sat up. "I was in there only an *hour?*"

"A little less. But it seems forever. I know."

"I feel like a squeezed orange." I frowned, remembering something. "Peewee, I wasn't too scared when they came for me. I was going to demand to be turned loose and insist on explanations. But I never asked *him* a question, not one."

"You never will. I tried. But your will just drains out. Like a rabbit in front of a snake."

"Yes."

"Kip, do you see why I had to take just any chance to get away? You didn't seem to believe my story—do you believe it now?"

"Uh, yes. I believe it."

"Thanks. I always say I'm too proud to care what people think, but I'm not, really. I had to get back to Daddy and tell him . . . because he's the only one in the entire world who would simply believe me, no matter how crazy it sounded."

"I see. I guess I see. But how did you happen to wind up in Centerville?"

"Centerville?"

"Where I live. Where 'Junebug' called 'Peewee.' "

"Oh. I never meant to go there. I meant to land in New Jersey, in Princeton if possible, because I had to find Daddy."

"Well, you sure missed your aim."

"Can you do better? I would have done all right but I had my elbow joggled. Those things aren't hard to fly; you just aim and push for where you want to go, not like the complicated things they do about rocket ships. And I had the Mother Thing to coach me. But I had to slow down going into the atmosphere and compensate for Earth's spin and I didn't know quite how. I found myself too far west and they were chasing me and I didn't know *what* to do . . . and then I heard you on the space-operations band and thought everything was all right—and there I was." She spread her hands. "I'm sorry, Kip."

"Well, you landed it. They say any landing you walk away from is a good one."

"But I'm sorry I got you mixed up in it."

"Uh . . . don't worry about that. It looks like somebody has to get mixed up in it. Peewee . . . what's *he* up to?"

"*They,* you mean."

"Huh? I don't think the other two amount to anything. *He* is the one."

"I didn't mean Tim and Jock—they're just people gone bad. I mean *them—him* and others like him."

I wasn't at my sharpest—I had been knocked out three times and was shy a night's sleep and more confusing things had happened than in all my life. But until Peewee pointed it out I hadn't considered that there could be more than one like *him*—one seemed more than enough.

But if there was one, then there were thousands—maybe millions or billions. I felt my stomach twist and wanted to hide. "You've seen others?"

"No. Just *him*. But the Mother Thing told me."

"Ugh! Peewee . . . what are they up to?"

"Haven't you guessed? They're moving in on us."

My collar felt tight, even though it was open. "How?"

"I don't know."

"You mean they're going to kill us off and take over Earth?"

She hesitated. "It might not be anything that nice."

"Uh . . . make slaves of us?"

"You're getting warmer. Kip—I think they eat meat."

I swallowed. "You have the jolliest ideas, for a little girl."

"You think I like it? That's why I had to tell Daddy."

There didn't seem to be anything to say. It was an old, old fear for human beings. Dad had told me about an invasion-from-Mars radio broadcast when he was a kid—pure fiction but it had scared people silly. But people didn't believe in it now; ever since we got to the Moon and circled Mars and Venus everybody seemed to agree that we weren't going to find life anywhere.

Now here it was, in our laps. "Peewee? Are these things Martians? Or from Venus?"

She shook her head. "They're not from anywhere close. The Mother Thing tried to tell me, but we ran into a difficulty of understanding."

"Inside the Solar System?"

"That was part of the difficulty. Both yes and no."

"It can't be both."

"*You* ask her."

"I'd like to." I hesitated, then blurted, "I don't care where they're from—we can shoot them down . . . if we don't have to look at them!"

"Oh, I hope so!"

"It figures. You say these are flying saucers . . . real saucer sightings, I mean; not weather balloons. If so, they have been scouting us for years. Therefore they aren't sure of themselves, even if they do look horrible enough to curdle milk. Otherwise they would have moved in at once the way we would on a bunch of animals. But they haven't. That means we can kill them —if we go about it right."

She nodded eagerly. "I hope so. I hoped Daddy would see a way. But—" She frowned. "—we don't know much about them . . . and Daddy always warned me not to be cocksure when data was incomplete. 'Don't make so much stew from one oyster, Peewee,' he always says."

"But I'll bet we're right. Say, who is your Daddy? And what's your full name?"

"Why, Daddy is Professor Reisfeld. And my name is Patricia Wynant Reisfeld. Isn't that awful? Better call me Peewee."

"Professor Reisfeld— What does he teach?"

"Huh? You don't *know?* You don't know about Daddy's Nobel Prize? Or anything?"

"I'm just a country boy, Peewee. Sorry."

"You must be. Daddy doesn't *teach* anything. He *thinks.* He thinks better than anybody . . . except me, possibly. He's the synthesist. Everybody else specializes. Daddy knows everything and puts the pieces together."

Maybe so, but I hadn't heard of him. It sounded like a good idea . . . but it would take an awfully smart man—if I had found out anything, it was that they could print it faster than I could study it. Professor Reisfeld must have three heads. Five.

"Wait till you meet him," she added, glancing at her watch. "Kip, I think we had better get braced. We'll be landing in a few minutes . . . and *he* won't care how he shakes up passengers."

So we crowded into the narrow end and braced each other. We waited. After a bit the ship shook itself and the floor tilted. There was a slight bump and things got steady and suddenly I felt very light. Peewee pulled her feet under her and stood up. "Well, we're on the Moon."

Chapter 5

When I was a kid, we used to pretend we were making the first landing on the Moon. Then I gave up romantic notions and realized that I would have to go about it another way. But I never thought I would get there penned up, unable to see out, like a mouse in a shoe box.

The only thing that proved I was on the Moon was my weight. High gravity can be managed anywhere, with centrifuges. Low gravity is another matter; on Earth the most you can squeeze out is a few seconds going off a high board, or by parachute delay, or stunts in a plane.

If low gravity goes on and on, then wherever you are, you are *not* on Earth. Well, I wasn't on Mars; it had to be the Moon.

On the Moon I should weigh a little over twenty-five pounds. It felt about so—I felt light enough to walk on a lawn and not bend the grass.

For a few minutes I simply exulted in it, forgetting *him* and the trouble we were in, just heel-and-toe around the room, getting the wonderful feel of it, bouncing a little and bumping my head against the ceiling and feeling how slowly, slowly, slowly I settled back to the floor. Peewee sat down, shrugged her shoulders and gave a little smile, an annoyingly patronizing one. The "Old Moon-Hand"—all of two weeks more of it than I had had.

Low gravity has its disconcerting tricks. Your feet have hardly any traction and they fly out from under you. I had to learn with muscles and reflexes what I had known only intellectually: that when weight goes down, mass and inertia do not. To change direction, even in walking, you have to lean the way you would to round a turn on a board track—and even then if you don't have traction (which I didn't in socks on a smooth floor) your feet go out from under you.

A fall doesn't hurt much in one-sixth gravity but Pee-wee giggled. I sat up and said, "Go and laugh, smartie. You can afford to—you've got tennis shoes."

"I'm sorry. But you looked silly, hanging there like a slow-motion picture and grabbing air."

"No doubt. Very funny."

"I said I was sorry. Look, you can borrow my shoes."

I looked at her feet, then at mine, and snorted. "Gee, thanks!"

"Well . . . you could cut the heels out, or something. It wouldn't bother me. Nothing ever does. Where are your shoes, Kip?"

"Uh, about a quarter-million miles away—unless we got off at the wrong stop."

"Oh. Well, you won't need them much, here."

"Yeah." I chewed my lip, thinking about "here" and no longer interested in games with gravity. "Peewee? What do we do now?"

"About what?"

"About *him*."

"Nothing. What *can* we do?"

"Then what do we do?"

"Sleep."

"Huh?"

"Sleep. 'Sleep, that knits up the ravell'd sleave of care.' 'Tired Nature's sweet restorer, balmy sleep.' 'Blessings on him who invented sleep, the mantle that covers all human thoughts.' "

"Quit showing off and talk sense!"

"I *am* talking sense. At the moment we're as helpless as goldfish. We're simply trying to survive—and the first principle of survival is not to worry about the impossible and concentrate on what's possible. I'm hungry and thirsty and uncomfortable and very, very tired . . . and all I can do about it is sleep. So if you will kindly keep quiet, that's what I'll do."

"I can take a hint. No need to snap at me."

"I'm sorry. But I get cross as two sticks when I'm tired and Daddy says I'm simply frightful before breakfast." She curled up in a little ball and tucked that filthy rag doll under her chin. "G'night, Kip."

"Good night, Peewee."

I thought of something and started to speak . . . and saw that she was asleep. She was breathing softly and her face had smoothed out and no longer looked alert and smart-alecky. Her upper lip pooched out in a baby pout and she looked like a dirty-faced cherub. There were streaks where she had apparently cried and not wiped it away. But she had never let me see her crying.

Kip, I said to myself, you get yourself into the darndest things; this is much worse than bringing home a stray pup or a kitten.

But I had to take care of her . . . or die trying.

Well, maybe I would. Die trying, I mean. It didn't look as if I were any great shakes even taking care of myself.

I yawned, then yawned again. Maybe the shrimp had more sense than I had, at that. I was more tired than I had ever been, and hungry and thirsty and not comfortable other ways. I thought about banging on the door panel and trying to attract the fat one or his skinny partner. But that would wake Peewee—and it might antagonize *him*.

So I sprawled on my back the way I nap on the living-room rug at home. I found that a hard floor does not require any one sleeping position on the Moon; one-sixth gravity is a better mattress than all the foam rubber ever made—that fussy princess in Hans Christian Andersen's story would have had no complaints.

I went to sleep at once.

It was the wildest space opera I had ever seen, loaded with dragons and Arcturian maidens and knights in shining space armor and shuttling between King Arthur's Court and the Dead Sea Bottoms of Barsoom. I didn't mind that but I did mind the announcer. He had the voice of Ace Quiggle and the face of *him*. He leaned out of the screen and leered, those wormy cilia writhing. "Will Beowulf conquer the Dragon? Will Tristan return to Iseult? Will Peewee find her dolly? Tune in this channel tomorrow night and in the meantime, wake up and hurry to your neighborhood druggist for a cake of Skyway's Kwikbrite Armor Polish, the better polish used by the better knights *sans peur et sans reproche*. Wake up!" He shoved a snaky arm out of the screen and grabbed my shoulder.

I woke up.

"Wake up," Peewee was saying, shaking my shoulder. "Please wake up, Kip."

"Lea' me alone!"

"You were having a nightmare."

The Arcturian princess had been in a bad spot. "Now I'll never know how it came out. Wha' did y' want to wake me for? I thought the idea was to sleep?"

"You've slept for hours—and now perhaps there is something we can do."

"Breakfast, maybe?"

She ignored that. "I think we should try to escape."

I sat up suddenly, bounced off the floor, settled back. "Wups! How?"

"I don't know exactly. But I think they have gone away and left us. If so, we'll never have a better chance."

"They have? What makes you think so?"

"Listen. Listen hard."

I listened. I could hear my heart beat, I could hear Peewee breathing, and presently I could hear her heart beating. I've never heard deeper silence in a cave.

I took my knife, held it in my teeth for bone conduction and pushed it against a wall. Nothing. I tried the floor and the other walls. Still nothing. The ship ached with silence—no throb, no thump, not even those vibrations you can sense but not hear. "You're right, Peewee."

"I noticed it when the air circulation stopped."

I sniffed. "Are we running out of air?"

"Not right away. But the air stopped—it comes out of those tiny holes up there. You don't notice it but I missed something when it stopped."

I thought hard. "I don't see where this gets us. We're still locked up."

"I'm not sure."

I tried the blade of my knife on a wall. It wasn't metal or anything I knew as plastic, but it didn't mind a knife. Maybe the Comte de Monte Cristo could have dug a hole in it—but he had more time. "How do you figure?"

"Every time they've opened or closed that door panel, I've heard a click. So after they took you out I stuck a wad of bubble gum where the panel meets the wall, high up where they might not notice."

"You've got some gum?"

"Yes. It helps, when you can't get a drink of water. I—"

"Got any more?" I asked eagerly. I wasn't fresh in any way but thirst was the worst—I'd never been so thirsty.

Peewee looked upset. "Oh, poor Kip! I haven't any more . . . just an old wad I kept parked on my belt buckle and chewed when I felt driest." She frowned. "But you can have it. You're welcome."

"Uh, thanks, Peewee. Thanks a lot. But I guess not."

She looked insulted. "I assure you, Mr. Russell, that I do not have anything contagious. I was merely trying to—"

"Yes, yes," I said hastily. "I'm sure you were. But—"

"I assumed that these were emergency conditions.

It is surely no more unsanitary than kissing a girl—but then I don't suppose you've ever kissed a girl!"

"Not lately," I evaded. "But what I want is a drink of clear cold water—or murky warm water. Besides, you used up your gum on the door panel. What did you expect to accomplish?"

"Oh. I told you about that click. Daddy says that, in a dilemma, it is helpful to change any variable, then reexamine the problem. I tried to introduce a change with my bubble gum."

"Well?"

"When they brought you back, then closed the door, I didn't hear a click."

"*What?* Then you thought you had bamboozled their lock hours and hours ago—and you didn't tell *me?*"

"That is correct."

"Why, I ought to spank you!"

"I don't advise it," she said frostily. "I bite."

I believed her. And scratch. And other things. None of them pleasant. I changed the subject. "Why didn't you tell me, Peewee?"

"I was afraid you might try to get out."

"Huh? I certainly would have!"

"Precisely. But I *wanted* that panel closed . . . as long as *he* was out there."

Maybe she was a genius. Compared with me. "I see your point. All right, let's see if we can get it open." I examined the panel. The wad of gum was there, up high as she could reach, and from the way it was mashed it did seem possible that it had fouled the groove panel slid into, but I couldn't see any crack down the edge.

I tried the point of my big blade on it. The panel seemed to creep to the right an eighth of an inch—then the blade broke.

I closed the stub and put the knife away. "Any ideas?"

"Maybe if we put our hands flat against it and tried to drag it?"

"Okay." I wiped sweat from my hands on my shirt. "Now . . . easy does it. Just enough pressure for friction."

The panel slid to the right almost an inch—and stopped firmly.

But there was a hairline crack from floor to ceiling.

I broke off the stub of the big blade this time. The crack was no wider. Peewee said, "Oh, dear!"

"We aren't licked." I backed off and ran toward the door.

"Toward," not "to"—my feet skidded, I leveled off and did a leisurely bellywhopper. Peewee didn't laugh.

I picked myself up, got against the far wall, braced one foot against it and tried a swimming racing start.

I got as far as the door panel before losing my footing. I didn't hit it very hard, but I felt it spring. It bulged a little, then sprang back.

"Wait a sec, Kip," said Peewee. "Take your socks off. I'll get behind you and push—my tennis shoes don't slip."

She was right. On the Moon, if you can't get rubber-soled shoes, you're better off barefooted. We backed against the far wall, Peewee behind me with her hands on my hips. "One . . . two . . . three . . . Go!" We advanced with the grace of a hippopotamus.

I hurt my shoulder. But the panel sprung out of its track, leaving a space four inches wide at the bottom and tapering to the top.

I left skin on the door frame and tore my shirt and was hampered in language by the presence of a girl. But the opening widened. When it was wide enough for my head, I got down flat and peered out. There was nobody in sight—a foregone conclusion, with the noise I had made, unless they were playing cat-and-mouse. Which I wouldn't put past them. Especially *him*.

Peewee started to wiggle through; I dragged her back.

"Naughty, naughty! I go first." Two more heaves and it was wide enough for me. I opened the small blade of my knife and handed it to Peewee. "With your shield or on it, soldier."

"You take it."

"I won't need it. 'Two-Fisted Death,' they call me around dark alleys." This was propaganda, but why worry her? *Sans peur et sans reproche*—maiden-rescuing done cheaply, special rates for parties.

I eased out on elbows and knees, stood up and looked around. "Come on out," I said quietly.

She started to, then backed up suddenly. She reappeared clutching that bedraggled dolly. "I almost forgot Madame Pompadour," she said breathlessly.

I didn't even smile.

"Well," she said defensively, "I have to have her to get to sleep at night. It's my one neurotic quirk—but Daddy says I'll outgrow it."

"Sure, sure."

"Well, don't look so smug! It's not fetishism, not even primitive animism; it's merely a conditioned reflex. I'm aware that it's just a doll—I've understood the pathetic fallacy for . . . oh, years and years!"

"Look, Peewee," I said earnestly, "I don't care how you get to sleep. Personally I hit myself over the head with a hammer. But quit yakking. Do you know the layout of these ships?"

She looked around. "I think this is the ship that chased me. But it looks the same as the one I piloted."

"All right. Should we head for the control room?"

"Huh?"

"You flew the other heap. Can you fly this one?"

"Unh . . . I guess so. Yes, I can."

"Then let's go." I started in the direction they had lugged me.

"But the other time I had the Mother Thing to tell me what to do! Let's find her."

I stopped. "Can you get it off the ground?"

"Well . . . yes."

"We'll look for her after we're in the air—'in space,' I mean. If she's aboard we'll find her. If she's not, there's not a thing we can do."

"Well . . . all right. I see your logic; I don't have to like it." She tagged along. "Kip? How many gravities can you stand?"

"Huh? I haven't the slightest idea. Why?"

"Because these things can go lots faster than I dared try when I escaped before. That was my mistake."

"Your mistake was in heading for New Jersey."

"But I had to find Daddy!"

"Sure, sure, eventually. But you should have ducked over to Lunar Base and yelled for the Federation Space Corps. This is no job for a popgun; we need help. Any idea where we are?"

"Mmm . . . I think so. If *he* took us back to their base. I'll know when I look at the sky."

"All right. If you can figure out where Lunar Base is from here, that's where we'll go. If not— Well, we'll head for New Jersey at all the push it has."

The control-room door latched and I could not figure out how to open it. Peewee did what she said should work—which was to tuck her little finger into a hole mine would not enter—and told me it must be locked. So I looked around.

I found a metal bar racked in the corridor, a thing about five feet long, pointed on one end and with four handles like brass knucks on the other. I didn't know what it was—the hobgoblin equivalent of a fire ax, possibly—but it was a fine wrecking bar.

I made a shambles of that door in three minutes. We went in.

My first feeling was gooseflesh because here was where I had been grilled by *him*. I tried not to show it. If *he* turned up, I was going to let him have his wrecking bar right between his grisly eyes. I looked around, really seeing the place for the first time. There was sort of a nest in the middle surrounded by what could have been a very fancy coffee maker or a velocipede for an octopus; I was glad Peewee knew which button to push. "How do you see out?"

"Like this." Peewee squeezed past and put a finger into a hole I hadn't noticed.

The ceiling was hemispherical like a planetarium. Which was what it was, for it lighted up. I gasped.

It was suddenly not a floor we were on, but a platform, apparently out in the open and maybe thirty feet in the air. Over me were star images, thousands of them, in a black "sky"—and facing toward me, big as a dozen full moons and green and lovely and beautiful, was Earth!

Peewee touched my elbow. "Snap out of it, Kip."

I said in a choked voice, "Peewee, don't you have any poetry in your soul?"

"Surely I have. Oodles. But we haven't time. I know where we are, Kip—back where I started from. Their base. See those rocks with long jagged shadows? Some of them are ships, camouflaged. And over to the left—that high peak, with the saddle?—a little farther left, almost due west, is Tombaugh Station, forty miles away. About two hundred miles farther is Lunar Base and beyond is Luna City."

"How long will it take?"

"Two hundred, nearly two hundred and fifty miles? Uh, I've never tried a point-to-point on the Moon—but it shouldn't take more than a few minutes."

"Let's go! They might come back any minute."

"Yes, Kip." She crawled into that jackdaw's nest and bent over a sector.

Presently she looked up Her face was white and thin and very little-girlish. "Kip . . . we aren't going anywhere. I'm sorry."

I let out a yelp. "What! What's the matter? Have you forgotten how to run it?"

"No. The 'brain' is gone."

"The which?"

"The 'brain.' Little black dingus about the size of a walnut that fits in this cavity." She showed me. "We got away before because the Mother Thing managed to steal one. We were locked in an empty ship, just as you and I are now. But she had one and we got away." Peewee looked bleak and very lost. "I should have known that *he* wouldn't leave one in the control room—I guess I did and didn't want to admit it. I'm sorry."

"Uh . . . look, Peewee, we won't give up that easily. Maybe I can make something to fit that socket."

"Like jumping wires in a car?" She shook her head. "It's not that simple, Kip. If you put a wooden model in place of the generator in a car, would it run? I don't know quite what it does, but I called it the 'brain' because it's very complex."

"But—" I shut up. If a Borneo savage had a brand-new car, complete except for spark plugs, would he get it running? Echo answers mournfully. "Peewee, what's the next best thing? Any ideas? Because if you haven't, I want you to show me the air lock. I'll take this—" I shook my wrecking bar "—and bash anything that comes through."

"I'm stumped," she admitted. "I want to look for the Mother Thing. If she's shut up in this ship, she may know what to do."

"All right. But first show me the air lock. You can look for her while I stand guard." I felt the reckless anger of desperation. I didn't see how we were ever going to get out and I was beginning to believe that we weren't—but there was still a reckoning due. *He* was going to learn that it wasn't safe to push people around. I was sure—I was fairly sure—that I could sock him before my spine turned to jelly. Splash that repulsive head. If I didn't look at his eyes.

Peewee said slowly, "There's one other thing—"

"What?"

"I hate to suggest it. You might think I was running out on you."

"Don't be silly. If you've got an idea, spill it."

"Well . . . there's Tombaugh Station, over that way about forty miles. If my space suit is in the ship—"

I suddenly quit feeling like Bowie at the Alamo. Maybe the game would go an extra period— "We can walk it!"

She shook her head. "No, Kip. That's why I hesitated to mention it. *I* can walk it . . . if we find my suit. But you couldn't wear my suit even if you squatted."

"I don't need your suit," I said impatiently.

"Kip, Kip! This is the Moon, remember? No air."

"Yes, yes, sure! Think I'm an idiot? But if they locked up your suit, they probably put mine right beside it and—"

"*You've* got a space suit?" she said incredulously.

Our next remarks were too confused to repeat but finally Peewee was convinced that I really did own a space suit, that in fact the only reason I was sending on the space-operations band twelve hours and a quarter of a million miles back was that I was wearing it when they grabbed me.

"Let's tear the joint apart!" I said. "No—show me that air lock, then *you* take it apart."

"All right."

She showed me the lock, a room much like the one we had been cooped in, but smaller and with an inner door built to take a pressure load. It was not locked. We opened it cautiously. It was empty, and its outer door was closed or we would never been able to open the inner. I said, "If Wormface had been a suspenders-and-belt man, he would have left the outer door open, even though he had us locked up. Then— Wait a second! Is there a way to latch the inner door open?"

"I don't know."

"We'll see." There was, a simple hook. But to make sure that it couldn't be unlatched by button-pushing from outside I wedged it with my knife. "You're sure this is the only air lock?"

"The other ship had only one and I'm pretty certain they are alike."

"We'll keep our eyes open. Nobody can get at us through this one. Even old Wormface has to use an air lock."

"But suppose he opens the outer door anyhow?" Peewee said nervously. "We'd pop like balloons."

I looked at her and grinned. "*Who* is a genius? Sure we would . . . if he did. But he won't. Not with twenty, twenty-five tons of pressure holding it closed. As you reminded me, this is the Moon. No air outside, remember?"

"Oh." Peewee looked sheepish.

So we searched. I enjoyed wrecking doors; Wormface wasn't going to like me. One of the first things we found was a smelly little hole that Fatty and Skinny lived in. The door was not locked, which was a shame. That room told me a lot about that pair. It showed that they were pigs, with habits as unattractive as their morals. The room also told me that they were not casual prisoners; it had been refitted for humans. Their relationship with Wormface, whatever it was, had gone on for some time and was continuing. There were two empty racks for space suits, several dozen canned rations of the sort sold in military-surplus stores, and best of all, there was drinking water and a washroom of sorts—and something more precious than fine gold or frankincense if we found our suits: two charged bottles of oxy-helium.

I took a drink, opened a can of food for Peewee—it

opened with a key; we weren't in the predicament of the *Three Men in a Boat* with their tin of pineapple—told her to grab a bite, then search that room. I went on with my giant toad sticker; those charged air bottles had given me an unbearable itch to find our suits—and get out!—before Wormface returned.

I smashed a dozen doors as fast as the Walrus and the Carpenter opened oysters and found all sorts of things, including what must have been living quarters for wormfaces. But I didn't stop to look—the Space Corps could do that, if and when—I simply made sure that there was not a space suit in any of them.

And found them!—in a compartment next to the one we had been prisoners in.

I was so glad to see Oscar that I could have kissed him. I shouted, "Hi, Pal! *Mirabile visu!*" and ran to get Peewee. My feet went out from under me again but I didn't care.

Peewee looked up as I rushed in. "I was just going to look for you."

"Got it! Got it!"

"You found the Mother Thing?" she said eagerly.

"Huh? No, no! The space suits—yours and mine! Let's go!"

"Oh." She looked disappointed and I felt hurt. "That's good . . . but we have to find the Mother Thing first."

I felt tried beyond endurance. Here we had a chance, slim but real, to escape a fate-worse-than-death (I'm not using a figure of speech) and *she* wanted to hang around to search for a bug-eyed monster. For any human being, even a stranger with halitosis, I would have done it. For a dog or cat I would, although reluctantly.

But what was a bug-eyed monster to me? All this one had done was to get me into the worst jam I had ever been in.

I considered socking Peewee and stuffing her into her

suit. But I said, "Are you crazy? We're leaving—right now!"

"We can't go till we find her."

"Now I know you're crazy. We don't even know she's here . . . and if we do find her, we can't take her with us."

"Oh, but we will!"

"How? This is the Moon, remember? No air. Got a space suit for her?"

"But—" That stonkered her. But not for long. She had been sitting on the floor, holding the ration can between her knees. She stood up suddenly, bouncing a little, and said, "Do as you like; I'm going to find her. Here." She shoved the can at me.

I should have used force. But I am handicapped by training from early childhood never to strike a female, no matter how richly she deserves it. So the opportunity and Peewee both slid past while I was torn between common sense and upbringing. I simply groaned helplessly.

Then I became aware of an unbearably attractive odor. I was holding that can. It contained boiled shoe leather and gray gravy and smelled ambrosial.

Peewee had eaten half; I ate the rest while looking at what she had found. There was a coil of nylon rope which I happily put with the air bottles; Oscar had fifty feet of clothesline clipped to his belt but that had been a penny-saving expedient. There was a prospector's hammer which I salvaged, and two batteries which would do for headlamps and things.

The only other items of interest were a Government Printing Office publication titled *Preliminary Report on Selenology*, a pamphlet on uranium prospecting, and an expired Utah driver's license for "Timothy Johnson"—I recognized the older man's mean face. The pamphlets interested me but this was no time for excess baggage.

The main furniture was two beds, curved like contour chairs and deeply padded; they told me that Skinny and Fatty had ridden this ship at high acceleration.

When I had mopped the last of the gravy with a finger, I took a big drink, washed my hands—using water lavishly because I didn't care if that pair died of thirst—grabbed my plunder and headed for the room where the space suits were.

As I got there I ran into Peewee. She was carrying the crowbar and looking overjoyed. "I found her!"

"Where?"

"Come on! I can't get it open, I'm not strong enough."

I put the stuff with our suits and followed her. She stopped at a door panel farther along the corridor than my vandalism had taken me. "In there!"

I looked and I listened. "What makes you think so?"

"I know! Open it!"

I shrugged and got to work with the nutpick. The panel went *sprung!* and that was that.

Curled up in the middle of the floor was a creature. So far as I could tell, it might or might not have been the one I had seen in the pasture the night before. The light had been poor, the conditions very different, and my examination had ended abruptly. But Peewee was in no doubt. She launched herself through the air with a squeal of joy and the two rolled over and over like kittens play-fighting.

Peewee was making sounds of joy, more or less in English. So was the Mother Thing, but not in English. I would not have been surprised if she had spoken English, since Wormface did and since Peewee had mentioned things the Mother Thing had told her. But she didn't.

Did you ever listen to a mockingbird? Sometimes singing melodies, sometimes just sending up a joyous noise unto the Lord? The endlessly varied songs of a mockingbird are nearest to the speech of the Mother Thing.

At last they held still, more or less, and Peewee said, "Oh, Mother Thing, I'm so happy!"

The creature sang to her. Peewee answered, "Oh. I'm forgetting my manners. Mother Thing, this is my dear friend Kip."

The Mother Thing sang to me:

—and I understood.

What she said was: "I am very happy to know you, Kip."

It didn't come out in words. But it might as well have been English. Nor was this half-kidding self-deception, such as my conversations with Oscar or Peewee's with Madame Pompadour—when I talk with Oscar I am both sides of the conversation; it's just my conscious talking to my subconscious, or some such. This was not that.

The Mother Thing sang to me and I understood.

I was startled but not unbelieving. When you see a rainbow you don't stop to argue the laws of optics. There it is, in the sky.

I would have been an idiot not to know that the Mother Thing was speaking to me because I *did* understand and understood her every time. If she directed a remark at Peewee alone, it was usually just birdsongs to me—but if it was meant for me, I got it.

Call it telepathy if you like, although it doesn't seem to be what they do at Duke University. I never read her mind and I don't think she read mine. We just talked.

But while I was startled, I minded my manners. I felt the way I do when Mother introduces me to one of her older grande-dame friends. So I bowed and said,

"We're very happy that we've found you, Mother Thing."

It was simple, humble truth. I knew, without explanation, what it was that had made Peewee stubbornly determined to risk recapture rather than give up looking for her—the quality that made her "the Mother Thing."

Peewee has this habit of slapping names on things and her choices aren't always apt, for my taste. But I'll never question this one. The Mother Thing was the Mother Thing because she *was*. Around her you felt happy and safe and warm. You knew that if you skinned your knee and came bawling into the house, she would kiss it well and paint it with merthiolate and everything would be all right. Some nurses have it and some teachers . . . and, sadly, some mothers don't.

But the Mother Thing had it so strongly that I wasn't even worried by Wormface. We had her with us so everything was going to be all right. Logically I knew that she was as vulnerable as we were—I had seen them strike her down. She didn't have my size and strength, she couldn't pilot the ship as Peewee had been able to. It didn't matter.

I wanted to crawl into her lap. Since she was too small and didn't have a lap, I would gratefully hold her in mine, anytime.

I have talked more about my father but that doesn't mean that Mother is less important—just different. Dad is active, Mother is passive; Dad talks, Mother doesn't. But if she died, Dad would wither like an uprooted tree. She makes our world.

The Mother Thing had the effect on me that Mother has, only I'm used to it from Mother. Now I was getting it unexpectedly, far from home, when I *needed* it.

Peewee said excitedly, "Now we can go, Kip. Let's hurry!"

The Mother Thing sang:

("Where are we going, children?")

"To Tombaugh Station, Mother Thing. They'll help us."

The Mother Thing blinked her eyes and looked serenely sad. She had great, soft, compassionate eyes—she looked more like a lemur than anything else but she was not a primate—she wasn't even in our sequence, unearthly. But she had these wonderful eyes and a soft, defenseless mouth out of which music poured. She wasn't as big as Peewee and her hands were tinier still —six fingers, any one of which could oppose the others the way our thumbs can. Her body—well, it never stayed the same shape so it's hard to describe, but it was right for her.

She didn't wear clothes but she wasn't naked; she had soft, creamy fur, sleek and fine as chinchilla. I thought at first she didn't wear anything, but presently I noticed a piece of jewelry, a shiny triangle with a double spiral in each corner. I don't know what made it stick on.

I didn't take all this in at once. At that instant the expression in the Mother Thing's eyes brought a crash of sorrow into the happiness I had been feeling.

Her answer made me realize that she didn't have a miracle ready:

("How are we to fly the ship? They have guarded me most carefully this time.")

Peewee explained eagerly about the space suits and I stood there like a fool, with a lump of ice in my stomach. What had been just a question of using my greater strength to force Peewee to behave was now an unsolvable dilemma. I could no more abandon the Mother Thing than I could have abandoned Peewee ... and there were only two space suits.

Even if she could wear our sort, which looked as practical as roller skates on a snake.

The Mother Thing gently pointed out that her own vacuum gear had been destroyed. (I'm going to quit writing down *all* her songs; I don't remember them exactly anyhow.)

And so the fight began. It was an odd fight, with the Mother Thing gentle and loving and sensible and utterly firm, and Peewee throwing a tearful, bad-little-girl tantrum—and me standing miserably by, not even refereeing.

When the Mother Thing understood the situation, she analyzed it at once to the inevitable answer. Since she had no way to go (and probably couldn't have walked that far anyhow, even if she had had her sort of space suit) the only answer was for us two to leave at once. If we reached safety, then we would, if possible, convince our people of the danger from Wormface & Co.—in which case she might be saved as well ... which would be nice but was not indispensable.

Peewee utterly, flatly, and absolutely refused to listen to any plan which called for leaving the Mother Thing behind. If the Mother Thing couldn't go, she wouldn't budge. "Kip! You go get help! Hurry! I'll stay here."

I stared at her. "Peewee, you know I can't do that."

"You must. You will so! You've *got* to. If you don't, I'll ... I'll never speak to you again!"

"If I did, I'd never speak to myself again. Look, Peewee, it won't wash. You'll have to go—"

"No!"

"Oh, shut up for a change. You go and I stay and guard the door with the shillelagh. I'll hold 'em off while you round up the troops. But tell them to hurry!"

"I—" She stopped and looked very sober and utterly baffled. Then she threw herself on the Mother Thing, sobbing: "Oh, you don't *love* me any more!"

Which shows how far her logic had gone to pot. The Mother Thing sang softly to her while I worried the thought that our last chance was trickling away while we argued. Wormface might come back any second—and while I hoped to slug him a final one if he got in, more likely he had resources to outmaneuver me. Either way, we would not escape.

At last I said, "Look, we'll *all* go."

Peewee stopped sobbing and looked startled. "You know we can't."

The Mother Thing sang: ("How, Kip?")

"Uh, I'll have to show you. Up on your feet, Peewee." We went where the suits were, while Peewee carried Madame Pompadour and half carried the Mother Thing. Lars Eklund, the rigger who had first worn Oscar according to his log, must have weighed about two hundred pounds; in order to wear Oscar I had to strap him tight to keep from bulging. I hadn't considered retailoring him to my size as I was afraid I would never get him gas-tight again. Arm and leg lengths were okay; it was girth that was too big.

There was room inside for both the Mother Thing and me.

I explained, while Peewee looked big-eyed and the Mother Thing sang queries and approvals. Yes, she could hang on piggy-back—and she couldn't fall off, once we were sealed up and the straps cinched.

"All right. Peewee, get into your suit." I went to get

my socks while she started to suit up. When I came back I checked her helmet gauges, reading them backwards through her lens. "We had better give you some air. You're only about half full."

I ran into a snag. The spare bottles I had filched from those ghouls had screw-thread fittings like mine— but Peewee's bottles had bayonet-and-snap joints. Okay, I guess, for tourists, chaperoned and nursed and who might get panicky while bottles were changed unless it was done fast—but not so good for serious work. In my workshop I would have rigged an adapter in twenty minutes. Here, with no real tools—well, that spare air might as well be on Earth for all the good it did Peewee.

For the first time, I thought seriously of leaving them behind while I made a fast forced march for help. But I didn't mention it. I thought that Peewee would rather die on the way than fall back into *his* hands—and I was inclined to agree.

"Kid," I said slowly, "that isn't much air. Not for forty miles." Her gauge was scaled in time as well as pressure; it read just under five hours. Could Peewee move as fast as a trotting horse? Even at lunar gravity? Not likely.

She looked at me soberly. "That's calibrated for full-size people. I'm little—I don't use much air."

"Uh . . . don't use it faster than you have to."

"I won't. Let's go."

I started to close her gaskets. "Hey!" she objected.

"What's the matter?"

"Madame Pompadour! Hand her to me—please. On the floor by my feet."

I picked up that ridiculous dolly and gave it to her. "How much air does *she* take?"

Peewee suddenly dimpled. "I'll caution her not to inhale." She stuffed it inside her shirt, I sealed her up. I sat down in my open suit, the Mother Thing crept up my back, singing reassuringly, and cuddled close. She felt good and I felt that I could hike a hundred miles, to get them both safe.

Getting me sealed in was cumbersome, as the straps had to be let out and then tightened to allow for the Mother Thing, and neither Peewee nor I had bare hands. We managed.

I made a sling from my clothesline for the spare bottles. With them around my neck, with Oscar's weight and the Mother Thing as well, I scaled perhaps fifty pounds at the Moon's one-sixth gee. It just made me fairly sure-footed for the first time.

I retrieved my knife from the air-lock latch and snapped it to Oscar's belt beside the nylon rope and the prospector's hammer. Then we went inside the air lock and closed its inner door. I didn't know how to waste its air to the outside but Peewee did. It started to hiss out.

"You all right, Mother Thing?"

("Yes, Kip.") She hugged me reassuringly.

"Peewee to Junebug," I heard in my phones: "radio check. Alfa, Bravo, Coca, Delta, Echo, Foxtrot—"

"Junebug to Peewee: I read you. Golf, Hotel, India, Juliette, Kilo—"

"I read you, Kip."

"Roger."

"Mind your pressure, Kip. You're swelling up too fast." I kicked the chin valve while watching the gauge —and kicking myself for letting a little girl catch me in a greenhorn trick. But she had used a space suit before, while I had merely pretended to.

I decided this was no time to be proud. "Peewee? Give me all the tips you can. I'm new to this."

"I will, Kip."

The outer door popped silently and swung inward— and I looked out over the bleak bright surface of a lunar plain. For a homesick moment I remembered the trip-to-the-Moon games I had played as a kid and wished I were back in Centerville. Then Peewee touched her helmet to mine. "See anyone?"

"No."

"We're lucky, the door faces away from the other ships. Listen carefully. We won't use radio until we are over the horizon—unless it's a desperate emergency. They listen on our frequencies. I know that for sure. Now see that mountain with the saddle in it? Kip, pay attention!"

"Yes." I had been staring at Earth. She was beautiful even in that shadow show in the control room—but I just hadn't realized. There she was, so close I could almost touch her . . . and so far away that we might never get home. You can't believe what a lovely planet we have, until you see her from outside . . . with clouds girdling her waist and polar cap set jauntily, like a spring hat. "Yes. I see the saddle."

"We head left of there, where you see a pass. Tim and Jock brought me through it in a crawler. Once we pick up its tracks it will be easy. But first we head for those near hills just left of that—that ought to keep this ship between us and the other ships while we get out of sight. I hope."

It was twelve feet or so to the ground and I was prepared to jump, since it would be nothing much in that gravity. Peewee insisted on lowering me by rope. "You'll fall over your feet. Look, Kip, listen to old Aunt Peewee. You don't have Moon legs yet. It's going to be like your first time on a bicycle."

So I let her lower me and the Mother Thing while she snubbed the nylon rope around the side of the lock. Then she jumped with no trouble. I started to loop up the line but she stopped me and snapped the other end to her belt, then touched helmets. "I'll lead. If I go too fast or you need me, tug on the rope. I won't be able to see you."

"Aye aye, Cap'n!"

"Don't make fun of me, Kip. This is serious."

"I wasn't making fun, Peewee. You're boss."

"Let's go. Don't look back, it won't do any good and you might fall. I'm heading for those hills."

Chapter 6

I should have relished the weird, romantic experience,
but I was as busy as Eliza crossing the ice and the things
snapping at my heels were worse than bloodhounds. I
wanted to look back but I was too busy trying to stay
on my feet. I couldn't see my feet; I had to watch
ahead and try to pick my footing—it kept me as busy
as a lumberjack in a logrolling contest. I didn't skid as
the ground was rough—dust or fine sand over raw rock
—and fifty pounds weight was enough for footing. But
I had three hundred pounds mass not a whit reduced
by lowered weight; this does things to lifelong reflex
habits. I had to lean heavily for the slightest turn, lean
back and dig in to slow down, lean far forward to speed
up.

I could have drawn a force diagram, but doing it is
another matter. How long does it take a baby to learn
to walk? This newborn Moon-baby was having to learn
while making a forced march, half blind, at the greatest speed he could manage.

So I didn't have time to dwell on the wonder of it
all.

Peewee moved into a brisk pace and kept stepping
it up. Every little while my leash tightened and I tried
still harder to speed up and not fall down.

The Mother Thing warbled at my spine: ("Are you
all right, Kip? You seem worried.")

"I'm . . . all right! How . . . about . . . *you?*"

("I'm very comfortable. Don't wear yourself out,
dear.")

"Okay!"

Oscar was doing his job. I began to sweat from exer-
tion and naked Sun, but I didn't kick the chin valve

until I saw from my blood-color gauge that I was short on air. The system worked perfectly and the joints, under a four-pound pressure, gave no trouble; hours of practice in the pasture was paying off. Presently my one worry was to keep a sharp eye for rocks and ruts. We were into those low hills maybe twenty minutes after H-hour. Peewee's first swerve as we reached rougher ground took me by surprise; I almost fell.

She slowed down and crept forward into a gulch. A few moments later she stopped; I joined her and she touched helmets with me. "How are you doing?"

"Okay."

"Mother Thing, can you hear me?"

("Yes, dear.")

"Are you comfortable? Can you breathe all right?"

("Yes, indeed. Our Kip is taking good care of me.")

"Good. You behave yourself, Mother Thing. Hear me?"

("I will, dear.") Somehow she put an indulgent chuckle into a birdsong.

"Speaking of breathing," I said to Peewee, "let's check your air." I tried to look into her helmet.

She pulled away, then touched again. "I'm all right!"

"So you say." I held her helmet with both hands, found I couldn't see the dials—with sunlight around us, trying to see in was like peering into a well. "What does it read—and don't fib."

"Don't be nosy!"

I turned her around and read her bottle gauges. One read zero; the other was almost full.

I touched helmets. "Peewee," I said slowly, "how many miles have we come?"

"About three, I think. Why?"

"Then we've got more than thirty to go?"

"At least thirty-five. Kip, quit fretting. I know I've got one empty bottle; I shifted to the full one before we stopped."

"One bottle won't take you thirty-five miles."

"Yes, it will . . . because it's *got* to."

"Look, we've got plenty of air. I'll figure a way to get it to you." My mind was trotting in circles, thinking what tools were on my belt, what else I had.

"Kip, you know you can't hook those spare bottles to my suit—so shut up!"

("What's the trouble, darlings? Why are you quarreling?")

"We aren't fighting, Mother Thing. Kip is a worry wart."

("Now, children—")

I said, "Peewee, I admit I can't hook the spares into your suit . . . but I'll jigger a way to recharge your bottle."

"But— How, Kip?"

"Leave it to me. I'll touch only the empty; if it doesn't work, we're no worse off. If it does, we've got it made."

"How long will it take?"

"Ten minutes with luck. Thirty without."

"No," she decided.

"Now, Peewee, don't be sil—"

"I'm not being silly! We aren't safe until we get into the mountains. I can get that far. Then, when we no longer show up like a bug on a plate, we can rest and recharge my empty bottle."

It made sense. "All right."

"Can you go faster? If we reach the mountains before they miss us, I don't think they'll ever find us. If we don't—"

"I can go faster. Except for these pesky bottles."

"Oh." She hesitated. "Do you want to throw one away?"

"Huh? Oh, no, no! But they throw me off balance. I've just missed a tumble a dozen times. Peewee, can you retie them so they don't swing?"

"Oh. Sure."

I had them hung around my neck and down my

front—not smart but I had been hurried. Now Peewee lashed them firmly, still in front as my own bottles and the Mother Thing were on my back—no doubt she was finding it as crowded as Dollar Day. Peewee passed clothesline under my belt and around the yoke. She touched helmets. "I hope that's okay."

"Did you tie a square knot?"

She pulled her helmet away. A minute later she touched helmets again. "It was a granny," she admitted in a small voice, "but it's a square knot now."

"Good. Tuck the ends in my belt so that I can't trip, then we'll mush. Are you all right?"

"Yes," she said slowly. "I just wish I had salvaged my gum, old and tired as it was. My throat's awful dry."

"Drink some water. Not too much."

"Kip! It's not a nice joke."

I stared. "Peewee—your suit hasn't any *water?*"

"What? Don't be silly."

My jaw dropped. "But, baby," I said helplessly, "why didn't you fill your tank before we left?"

"What are you talking about? Does your suit have a water tank?"

I couldn't answer. Peewee's suit was for tourists—for those "scenic walks amidst incomparable grandeur on the ancient face of the Moon" that the ads promised. Guided walks, of course, not over a half-hour at a time—they wouldn't put in a water tank; some tourist might choke, or bite the nipple off and half drown in his helmet, or some silly thing. Besides, it was cheaper.

I began to worry about other shortcomings that cheapjack equipment might have—with Peewee's life depending on it. "I'm sorry," I said humbly. "Look, I'll try to figure out some way to get water to you."

"I doubt if you can. I can't die of thirst in the time it'll take us to get there, so quit worrying. I'm all right. I just wish I had my bubble gum. Ready?"

"Uh . . . ready."

The hills were hardly more than giant folds in lava; we were soon through them, even though we had to take it cautiously over the very rough ground. Beyond them the ground looked flatter than western Kansas, stretching out to a close horizon, with mountains sticking up beyond, glaring in the Sun and silhouetted against a black sky like cardboard cutouts. I tried to figure how far the horizon was, on a thousand-mile radius and a height of eye of six feet—and couldn't do it in my head and wished for my slipstick. But it was awfully close, less than a mile.

Peewee let me overtake her, touched helmets. "Okay, Kip? All right, Mother Thing?"

"Sure."

("All right, dear.")

"Kip, the course from the pass when they fetched me here was east eight degrees north. I heard them arguing and sneaked a peer at their map. So we go back west eight degrees south—that doesn't count the jog to these hills but it's close enough to find the pass. Okay?"

"Sounds swell." I was impressed. "Peewee, were you an Indian scout once? Or Davy Crockett?"

"Pooh! Anybody can read a map"—she sounded pleased. "I want to check compasses. What bearing do you have on Earth?"

I said silently: Oscar, you've let me down. I've been cussing her suit for not having water—and *you* don't have a compass.

(Oscar protested: "Hey, pal, that's unfair! Why would I need a compass at Space Station Two? Nobody told *me* I was going to the Moon.") I said, "Peewee, this suit is for space station work. What use is a compass in space? Nobody told *me* I was going to the Moon."

"But— Well, don't stop to cry about it. You can get your directions by Earth."

"Why can't I use your compass?"

"Don't be silly; it's built into my helmet. Now just a

moment—" She faced Earth, moved her helmet back and forth. Then she touched helmets again. "Earth is smacko on northwest . . . that makes the course fifty-three degrees left of there. Try to pick it out. Earth is two degrees wide, you know."

"I knew that before you were born."

"No doubt. Some people require a head start."

"Smart aleck!"

"You were rude first!"

"But— Sorry, Peewee. Let's save the fights for later. I'll spot you the first two bites."

"I won't need them! You don't know how nasty I can—"

"I have some idea."

("Children! Children!")

"I'm sorry, Peewee."

"So am I. I'm edgy. I wish we were *there*."

"So do I. Let me figure the course." I counted degrees using Earth as a yardstick. I marked a place by eye, then tried again judging fifty-three degrees as a proportion of ninety. The results didn't agree, so I tried to spot some stars to help me. They say you can see stars from the Moon even when the Sun is in the sky. Well, you can—but not easily. I had the Sun over my shoulder but was facing Earth, almost three-quarters full, and had the dazzling ground glare as well. The polarizer cut down the glare—and cut out the stars, too.

So I split my guesses and marked the spot. "Peewee? See that sharp peak with sort of a chin on its left profile? That ought to be the course, pretty near."

"Let me check." She tried it by compass, then touched helmets. "Nice going, Kip. Three degrees to the right and you've got it."

I felt smug. "Shall we get moving?"

"Right. We go through the pass, then Tombaugh Station is due west."

It was about ten miles to the mountains; we made

short work of it. You can make time on the Moon—*if* it is flat and *if* you can keep your balance. Peewee kept stepping it up until we were almost flying, long low strides that covered ground like an ostrich—and, do you know, it's easier fast than slow. The only hazard, after I got the hang of it, was landing on a rock or hole or something and tripping. But that was hazard enough because I couldn't pick my footing at that speed. I wasn't afraid of falling; I felt certain that Oscar could take the punishment. But suppose I landed on my back? Probably smash the Mother Thing to jelly.

I was worried about Peewee, too. That cut-rate tourist suit wasn't as rugged as Oscar. I've read about explosive decompression—I never want to see it. Especially not a little girl. But I didn't dare use radio to warn her even though we were probably shielded from Wormface—and if I tugged on my leash I might make her fall.

The plain started to rise and Peewee let it slow us down. Presently we were walking, then we were climbing a scree slope. I stumbled but landed on my hands and got up—one-sixth gravity has advantages as well as hazards. We reached the top and Peewee led us into a pocket in the rocks. She stopped and touched helmets. "Anybody home? You two all right?"

("All right, dear.")

"Sure," I agreed. "A little winded, maybe." That was an understatement but if Peewee could take it, I could.

"We can rest," she answered, "and take it easy from here on. I wanted to get us out of the open as fast as possible. They'll never find us here."

I thought she was right. A wormface ship flying over might spot us, if they could see down as well as up—probably just a matter of touching a control. But our chances were better now. "This is the time to recharge your empty bottle."

"Okay."

None too soon—the bottle which had been almost full had dropped by a third, more like half. She couldn't make it to Tombaugh Station on that—simple arithmetic. So I crossed my fingers and got to work. "Partner, will you untie this cat's cradle?"

While Peewee fumbled at knots, I started to take a drink—then stopped, ashamed of myself. Peewee must be chewing her tongue to work up saliva by now—and I hadn't been able to think of *any* way to get water to her. The tank was inside my helmet and there was no way to reach it without making me—and Mother Thing —dead in the process.

If I ever lived to be an engineer I'd correct that!

I decided that it was idiotic not to drink because she couldn't; the lives of all of us might depend on my staying in the best condition I could manage. So I drank and ate three malted milk tablets and a salt tablet, then had another drink. It helped a lot but I hoped Peewee hadn't noticed. She was busy unwinding clothesline—anyhow it was hard to see into a helmet.

I took Peewee's empty bottle off her back, making darn sure to close her outside stop valve first—there's supposed to be a one-way valve where an air hose enters a helmet but I no longer trusted her suit; it might have more cost-saving shortcomings. I laid the empty on the ground by a full one, looked at, straightened up and touched helmets. "Peewee, disconnect the bottle on the left side of my back."

"Why, Kip?"

"Who's doing this job?" I had a reason but was afraid she might argue. My lefthand bottle held pure oxygen; the others were oxy-helium. It was full, except for a few minutes of fiddling last night in Centerville. Since I couldn't possibly give her bottle a full charge, the next best thing was to give her a half-charge of straight oxygen.

She shut up and removed it.

I set about trying to transfer pressure between bottles whose connections didn't match. There was no way to do it properly, short of tools a quarter of a million miles away—or over in Tombaugh Station which was just as bad. But I did have adhesive tape.

Oscar's manual called for two first-aid kits. I didn't know what was supposed to be in them; the manual had simply given USAF stock numbers. I hadn't been able to guess what would be useful in an outside kit— a hypodermic needle, maybe, sharp enough to stab through and give a man morphine when he needed it terribly. But since I didn't know, I had stocked inside and outside with bandage, dressings, and a spool of surgical tape.

I was betting on the tape.

I butted the mismatched hose connections together, tore off a scrap of bandage and wrapped it around the junction—I didn't want sticky stuff on the joint; it could foul the operation on a suit. Then I taped the junction, wrapping tightly, working very painstakingly and taping three inches on each side as well as around the joint—if tape could restrain that pressure a few moments, there would still be one deuce of a force trying to drag that joint apart. I didn't want it to pull apart at the first jolt. I used the entire roll.

I motioned Peewee to touch helmets. "I'm about to open the full bottle. The valve on the empty is already open. When you see me start to close the valve on the full one, you close the other one—*fast!* Got it?"

"Close the valve when you do, quickly. Roger."

"Stand by. Get your hand on the valve." I grabbed that lump of bandaged joint in one fist, squeezed as hard as I could, and put my other hand on the valve. If that joint let go, maybe my hand would go with it—but if the stunt failed, little Peewee didn't have long to live. So I really gripped.

Watching both gauges, I barely cracked the valve.

The hose quivered; the needle gauge that read "empty" twitched. I opened the valve wide.

One needle swung left, the other right. Quickly they approached half-charge. "Now!" I yelled uselessly and started closing the valve.

And felt that patchwork joint start to give.

The hoses squeezed out of my fist but we lost only a fraction of gas. I found that I was trying to close a valve that was closed tight. Peewee had hers closed. The gauges each showed just short of half full—there was air for Peewee.

I sighed and found I had been holding my breath.

Peewee put her helmet against mine and said very soberly, "Thanks, Kip."

"Charton Drugs service, ma'am—no tip necessary. Let me tidy this mess, you can tie me and we'll go."

"You won't have to carry but one extra bottle now."

"Wrong, Peewee. We may do this stunt five or six times until there's only a whisper left"—or until the tape wears out, I added to myself. The first thing I did was to rewrap the tape on its spool—and if you think that is easy, wearing gloves and with the adhesive drying out as fast as you wind it, try it.

In spite of the bandage, sticky stuff had smeared the connections when the hoses parted. But it dried so hard that it chipped off the bayonet-and-snap joint easily. I didn't worry about the screw-thread joint; I didn't expect to use it on a suit. We mounted Peewee's recharged bottle and I warned her that it was straight oxygen. "Cut your pressure and feed from both bottles. What's your blood color reading?"

"I've been carrying it low on purpose."

"Idiot! You want to keel over? Kick your chin valve! Get into normal range!"

We mounted one bottle I had swiped on my back, tied the other and the oxy bottle on my front, and were on our way.

Earth mountains are predictable; lunar mountains aren't, they've never been shaped by water. We came to a hole too steep to go down other than by rope and a wall beyond I wasn't sure we could climb. With pitons and snap rings and no space suits it wouldn't have been hard in the Rockies—but not the way we were. Peewee reluctantly led us back. The scree slope was worse going down—I backed down on hands and knees, with Peewee belaying the line above me. I wanted to be a hero and belay for her—we had a brisk argument. "Oh, quit being big and male and gallantly stupid, Kip! You've got four big bottles and the Mother Thing and you're topheavy and I climb like a goat."

I shut up.

At the bottom she touched helmets. "Kip," she said worriedly, "I don't know what to do."

"What's the trouble?"

"I kept a little south of where the crawler came through. I wanted to avoid crossing right where the crawler crossed. But I'm beginning to think there isn't any other way."

"I wish you had told me before."

"But I didn't want them to find us! The way the crawler came is the first place they'll look."

"Mmm . . . yes." I looked up at the range that blocked us. In pictures, the mountains of the Moon look high and sharp and rugged; framed by the lens of a space suit they look simply impossible.

I touched helmets again. "We might find another way —if we had time and air and the resources of a major expedition. We've got to take the route the crawler did. Which way?"

"A little way north . . . I think."

We tried to work north along the foothills but it was slow and difficult. Finally we backed off to the edge of the plain. It made us jumpy but it was a chance we had to take. We walked, briskly but not running, for we didn't dare miss the crawler's tracks. I counted paces and when I reached a thousand I tugged the line; Peewee stopped and we touched helmets. "We've come half a mile. How much farther do you think it is? Or could it possibly be behind us?"

Peewee looked up at the mountains. "I don't know," she admitted. "Everything looks different."

"We're lost?"

"Uh . . . it *ought* to be ahead somewhere. But we've come pretty far. Do you want to turn around?"

"Peewee, I don't even know the way to the post office."

"But what should we *do?*"

"I think we ought to keep going until you are absolutely certain the pass can't be any farther. You watch for the pass and I'll watch for crawler tracks. Then, when you're *certain* that we've come too far, we'll turn back. We can't afford to make short casts like a dog trying to pick up a rabbit's scent."

"All right."

I had counted two thousand more paces, another mile, when Peewee stopped. "Kip? It can't be ahead of us. The mountains are higher and solider than ever."

"You're sure? Think hard. Better to go another five miles than to stop too short."

She hesitated. She had her face pushed up close to her lens while we touched helmets and I could see her frown. Finally she said, "It's not up ahead, Kip."

"That settles it. To the rear, march! 'Lay on, Macduff, and curs'd be him who first cries, "Hold, enough!" ' "

"King Lear."

"Macbeth. Want to bet?"

Those tracks were only half a mile behind us—I had missed them. They were on bare rock with only the lightest covering of dust; the Sun had been over my shoulder when we first crossed them, and the caterpillar-tread marks hardly showed—I almost missed them going back.

They led off the plain and straight up into the mountains.

We couldn't possible have crossed those mountains without following the crawler's trail; Peewee had had the optimism of a child. It wasn't a road; it was just something a crawler on caterpillar treads could travel. We saw places that even a crawler hadn't been able to go until whoever pioneered it set a whopping big blast, backed off and waited for a chunk of mountain to get out of the way. I doubt if Skinny and Fatty carved that goat's path; they didn't look fond of hard work. Probably one of the exploration parties. If Peewee and I had attempted to break a new trail, we'd be there yet, relics for tourists of future generations.

But where a tread vehicle can go, a man can climb. It was no picnic; it was trudge, trudge, trudge, up and up and up—watch for loose rock and mind where you put your feet. Sometimes we belayed with the line. Nevertheless it was mostly just tedious.

When Peewee had used that half-charge of oxygen, we stopped and I equalized pressure again, this time being able to give her only a quarter-charge—like Achilles and the tortoise. I could go on indefinitely giving her half of what was left—if the tape held out. It was in bad shape but the pressure was only half as great and I managed to keep the hoses together until we closed valves.

I should say that I had it fairly easy. I had water, food, pills, dexedrine. The last was enormous help, any time I felt fagged I borrowed energy with a pep-pill. Poor Peewee had nothing but air and courage.

She didn't even have the cooling I had. Since she was on a richer mix, one bottle being pure oxygen, it did not take as much flow to keep up her blood-color index—and I warned her not to use a bit more than necessary; she could not afford air for cooling, she had to save it to breathe.

"I know, Kip," she answered pettishly. "I've got the needle jiggling the red light right now. Think I'm a fool?"

"I just want to keep you alive."

"All right, but quit treating me as a child. You put one foot in front of the other. I'll make it."

"Sure you will!"

As for the Mother Thing she always *said* she was all right and she was breathing the air I had (a trifle used), but I didn't know what was hardship to her. Hanging by his heels all day would kill a man; to a bat it is a nice rest—yet bats are our cousins.

I talked with her as we climbed. It didn't matter what; her songs had the effect on me that it has to have your own gang cheering. Poor Peewee didn't even have that comfort, except when we stopped and touched helmets—we still weren't using radio; even in the mountains we were fearful of attracting attention.

We stopped again and I gave Peewee one-eighth of a charge. The tape was in very poor shape afterwards; I doubted if it would serve again. I said, "Peewee, why don't you run your oxy-helium bottle dry while I carry this one? It'll save your strength."

"I'm all right."

"Well, you won't use air so fast with a lighter load."

"You have to have your arms free. Suppose you slip?"

"Peewee, I won't carry it in my arms. My righthand backpack bottle is empty; I'll chuck it. Help me make the change and I'll still be carrying only four—just balanced evenly."

"Sure, I'll help. But I'll carry two bottles. Honest, Kip, the weight isn't anything. But if I run the oxy-helium bottle dry, what would I breathe while you're giving me my next charge?"

I didn't want to tell her that I had doubts about another charge, even in those ever smaller amounts. "Okay, Peewee."

She changed bottles for me; we threw the dead one down a black hole and went on. I don't know how far we climbed nor how long; I know that it seemed like days—though it couldn't have been, not on that much air. During mile after mile of trail we climbed at least eight thousand feet. Heights are hard to guess—but I've seen mountains I knew the heights of. Look it up yourself—the first range east of Tombaugh Station.

There's a lot of climbing, even at one-sixth gee.

It seemed endless because I didn't know how far it was nor how long it had been. We both had watches—under our suits. A helmet ought to have a built-in watch. I should have read Greenwich time from the face of Earth. But I had no experience and most of the time I couldn't see Earth because we were deep in mountains—anyhow I didn't know what time it had been when we left the ship.

Another thing space suits should have is rear-view mirrors. While you are at it, add a window at the chin so that you can see where you step. But of the two, I would take a rear-view mirror. You can't glance behind you; you have to turn your entire body. Every few seconds I wanted to see if they were following us—and I couldn't spare the effort. All that nightmare trek I kept imagining them on my heels, expecting a wormy hand on my shoulder. I listened for footsteps which couldn't be heard in vacuum anyhow.

When you buy a space suit, make them equip it with a rear-view mirror. You won't have Wormface on your trail but it's upsetting to have even your best friend sneak up behind you. Yes, and if you are coming to the Moon, bring a sunshade. Oscar was doing his best and York had done an honest job on the air conditioning—but the untempered Sun is hotter than you would believe and I didn't dare use air just for cooling, any more than Peewee could.

It got hot and stayed hot and sweat ran down and I itched all over and couldn't scratch and sweat got into my eyes and burned. Peewee must have been parboiled. Even when the trail wound through deep gorges lighted only by reflection off the far wall, so dark that we turned on headlamps, I still was hot—and when we curved back into naked sunshine, it was almost unbearable. The temptation to kick the chin valve, let air pour in and cool me, was almost too much. The desire to be cool seemed more important than the need to breathe an hour hence.

If I had been alone, I might have done it and died. But Peewee was worse off than I was. If she could stand it, I *had* to.

I had wondered how we could be so lost so close to human habitation—and how crawly monsters could hide a base only forty miles from Tombaugh Station. Well, I had time to think and could figure it out because I could see the Moon around me.

Compared with the Moon the Arctic is swarming with people. The Moon's area is about equal to Asia—with fewer people than Centerville. It might be a century before anyone explored that plain where Wormface was based. A rocket ship passing over wouldn't notice anything even if camouflage hadn't been used; a man in a space suit would never go there; a man in a crawler would find their base only by accident even if he took the pass we were in and ranged around that plain. The lunar mapping satellite could photograph it and rephotograph, then a technician in London might note a tiny difference on two films. Maybe. Years later somebody might check up—if there wasn't something more urgent to do in a pioneer outpost where *everything* is new and urgent.

As for radar sightings—there were unexplained radar sightings before I was born.

Wormface could sit there, as close to Tombaugh Station as Dallas is to Fort Worth, and not fret, snug as a snake under a house. Too many square miles, not enough people.

Too incredibly many square miles. . . . Our whole world was harsh bright cliffs and dark shadows and black sky, and endless putting one foot in front of the other.

But eventually we were going downhill oftener than up and at weary last we came to a turn where we could see out over a hot bright plain. There were mountains awfully far away; even from our height, up a thousand feet or so, they were beyond the horizon. I looked out over that plain, too dead beat to feel triumphant, then glanced at Earth and tried to estimate due west.

Peewee touched her helmet to mine. "There it is, Kip."

"Where?" She pointed and I caught a glint on a silvery dome.

The Mother Thing trilled at my spine ("What is it, children?")

"Tombaugh Station, Mother Thing."

Her answer was wordless assurance that we were good children and that she had known that we could do it.

The station may have been ten miles away. Distances were hard to judge, what with that funny horizon and never anything for comparison—I didn't even know how big the dome was. "Peewee, do we dare use radio?"

She turned and looked back. I did also; we were about as alone as could be. "Let's risk it."

"What frequency?"

"Same as before. Space operations. I think."

So I tried. "Tombaugh Station. Come in, Tombaugh

Station. Do you read me?" Then Peewee tried. I listened up and down the band I was equipped for. No luck.

I shifted to horn antenna, aiming at the glint of light. No answer.

"We're wasting time, Peewee. Let's start slogging."

She turned slowly away. I could feel her disappointment—I had trembled with eagerness myself. I caught up with her and touched helmets. "Don't let it throw you, Peewee. They can't listen all day for us to call. We see it, now we'll walk it."

"I know," she said dully.

As we started down we lost sight of Tombaugh Station, not only from twists and turns but because we dropped it below the horizon. I kept calling as long as there seemed any hope, then shut it off to save breath and battery.

We were about halfway down the outer slope when Peewee slowed and stopped—sank to the ground and sat still.

I hurried to her. "Peewee!"

"Kip," she said faintly, "could you go get somebody? Please? You know the way now. I'll wait here. Please, Kip?"

"Peewee!" I said sharply. "Get up! You've got to keep moving."

"I c- c- can't!" She began to cry. "I'm so thirsty . . . and my legs—" She passed out.

"Peewee!" I shook her shoulder. "You *can't* quit now! Mother Thing!—you tell her!"

Her eyelids fluttered. "Keep telling her, Mother Thing!" I flopped Peewee over and got to work. Hypoxia hits as fast as a jab on the button. I didn't need to see her blood-color index to know it read DANGER; the gauges on her bottles told me. The oxygen bottles showed empty, the oxy-helium tank was practically so. I closed her exhaust valves, overrode her chin valve with the outside valve and let what was left in the oxy-helium bottle flow into her suit. When it started to swell I cut back the flow and barely cracked one exhaust valve. Not until then did I close stop valves and remove the empty bottle.

I found myself balked by a ridiculous thing.

Peewee had tied me too well; I couldn't reach the knot! I could feel it with my left hand but couldn't get my right hand around; the bottle on my front was in the way—and I couldn't work the knot loose with one hand.

I made myself stop panicking. My knife—of course, my knife! It was an old scout knife with a loop to hang it from a belt, which was where it was. But the map hooks on Oscar's belt were large for it and I had had to force it on. I twisted it until the loop broke.

Then I couldn't get the little blade open. Space-suit gauntlets don't have thumb nails.

I said to myself: Kip, quit running in circles. This is easy. All you have to do is open a knife—and you've *got* to . . . because Peewee is suffocating. I looked around for a sliver of rock, anything that could pinch-hit for a thumb nail. Then I checked my belt.

The prospector's hammer did it, the chisel end of the head was sharp enough to open the blade. I cut the clothesline away.

I was still blocked. I wanted very badly to get at a bottle on my back. When I had thrown away that empty and put the last fresh one on my back, I had started feeding from it and saved the almost-half-charge in the other one. I meant to save it for a rainy day and split it with Peewee. Now was the time—she was out of air, I was practically so in one bottle but still had that half-charge in the other—plus an eighth of a charge or less in the bottle that contained straight oxygen (the best I could hope for in equalizing pressures), I had planned to surprise her with a one-quarter charge of oxy-helium, which would last longer and give more cooling.

A real knight-errant plan, I thought. I didn't waste two seconds discarding it.

I *couldn't* get that bottle off my back!

Maybe if I hadn't modified the backpack for non-regulation bottles I could have done it. The manual says: "Reach over your shoulder with the opposite arm, close stop valves at bottle and helmet, disconnect the shackle—" My pack didn't have shackles; I had substituted straps. But I still don't think you can reach over your shoulder in a pressurized suit and do anything effective. I think that was written by a man at a desk. Maybe he had seen it done under favorable conditions. Maybe he had done it, but was one of those freaks who can dislocate both shoulders. But I'll bet a full charge of oxygen that the riggers around Space Station Two did it for each other as Peewee and I had, or went inside and deflated.

If I ever get a chance, I'll change that. *Everything* you have to do in a space suit should be arranged to do in *front*—valves, shackles, everything, even if it is to affect something in back. We aren't like Wormface, with eyes all around and arms that bend in a dozen places; we're built to work in *front* of us—that goes triple in a space suit.

You need a chin window to let you see what you're doing, too! A thing can look fine on paper and be utterly crumby in the field.

But I didn't waste time moaning; I had a one-eighth charge of oxygen I could reach. I grabbed it.

That poor, overworked adhesive tape was a sorry mess. I didn't bother with bandage; if I could get the tape to stick at all I'd be happy. I handled it as carefully as gold leaf, trying to get it tight, and stopped in the middle to close Peewee's exhaust entirely when it looked as if her suit was collapsing. I finished with trembling fingers.

I didn't have Peewee to close a valve. I simple gripped that haywired joint in one hand, opened Peewee's empty bottle with the other, swung over fast and opened the oxygen bottle wide—jerked my hand across and grabbed the valve of Peewee's bottle and watched those gauges.

The two needles moved toward each other. When they slowed down I started closing her bottle—and the taped joint blew out.

I got that valve closed in a hurry; I didn't lose much gas from Peewee's bottle. But what was left on the supply side leaked away. I didn't stop to worry; I peeled away a scrap of adhesive, made sure the bayonet-and-snap joint was clean, got that slightly recharged bottle back on Peewee's suit, opened stop valves.

Her suit started to distend. I opened one exhaust valve a crack and touched helmets. "Peewee! Peewee! Can you hear me? Wake up, baby! Mother Thing!—make her wake up!"

"Peewee!"

"Yes, Kip?"

"Wake up! On your feet, Champ! Get up! Honey, *please* get up."

"Huh? Help me get my helmet off . . . I can't *breathe*."

"Yes, you can. Kick your chin valve—feel it, taste it. Fresh air!"

She tried, feebly; I gave her a quick strong shot, over-riding her chin valve from outside. *"Oh!"*

"See? You've got air. You've got lots of air. Now get up."

"Oh, *please*, just let me lie here."

"No, you don't! You're a nasty, mean, spoiled little brat—and if you don't get up, nobody will love you. The Mother Thing won't love you. Mother Thing!—tell her!"

("Stand up, daughter!")

Peewee tried. I helped her, once she was trying. She trembled and clung to me and I kept her from falling. "Mother Thing?" she said faintly. "I did it. You . . . still love me?"

("Yes, darling!")

"I'm dizzy . . . and I don't think I . . . can walk."

"You don't have to, honey," I said gently and picked her up in my arms. "You don't have to walk any farther."

She didn't weigh anything.

The trail disappeared when we were down out of the foothills but the crawler's tracks were sharp in the dust and led due west. I had my air trimmed down until the needle of the blood-color indicator hung at the edge of the danger sector. I held it there, kicking my chin valve only when it swung past into DANGER. I figured that the designer must have left some leeway, the way they do with gasoline gauges. I had long since warned Peewee never to take her eyes off her own indicator and hold it at the danger limit. She promised and I kept reminding her. I pressed her helmet against the yoke of mine, so that we could talk.

I counted paces and every half-mile I told Peewee to call Tombaugh Station. It was over the horizon but they might have a high mast that could "see" a long way.

The Mother Thing talked to her, too—anything to keep her from slipping away again. It saved my strength to have the Mother Thing talk and was good for all of us.

After a while I noticed that my needle had drifted into the red again. I kicked the valve and waited. Nothing happened. I kicked it again and the needle drifted slowly toward the white. "How you fixed for air, Peewee?"

"Just fine, Kip, just fine."

Oscar was yelling at me. I blinked and noticed that my shadow had disappeared. It had been stretched out ahead at an angle to the tracks. The tracks were there but my shadow was not. That made me sore, so I turned around and looked for it. It was behind me.

The darn thing had been hiding. Games!

("That better!" said Oscar.)

"It's hot in here, Oscar."

("You think it's cool out here? Keep your eye on that shadow, bud—and on those tracks.")

"All right, all right! Quit pestering me." I made up my mind that I wouldn't let that shadow get away again. Games it wanted to play, huh?

"There's darn little air in here, Oscar."

("Breathe shallow, chum. We can make it.")

"I'm breathing my socks, now."

("So breathe your shirt.")

"Did I see a ship pass over?"

("How should I know? You're the one with the blinkers.")

"Don't get smart. I'm in no mood to joke."

I was sitting on the ground with Peewee across my knees and Oscar was really shouting—and so was the Mother Thing. ("Get up, you big ape! Get up and *try*.") ("Get up, Kip dear! Only a little way now.")

"I just want to get my wind."

("All right, you've got it. Call Tombaugh Station.")

I said, "Peewee, call Tombaugh Station."

She didn't answer. That scared me and I snapped out of it. "Tombaugh Station, come in! Come in!" I got to my knees and then to my feet. "Tombaugh Station, do you read me? Help! Help!"

A voice answered, "I read you."

"Help! *M'aidez!* I've got a little girl dying! Help!"

Suddenly it sprang up in front of my eyes—great shiny domes, tall towers, radio telescopes, a giant Schmidt camera. I staggered toward it. "*May Day!*"

An enormous lock opened and a crawler came toward me. A voice in my phones said, "We're coming. Stay where you are. Over and out."

A crawler stopped near me. A man got out, came over and touched helmets. I gasped: "Help me get her inside."

I got back: "You've given me trouble, bub. I don't like people who give me trouble." A bigger, fatter man got out behind him.

The smaller man raised a thing like a camera and aimed it at me. That was the last I knew.

Chapter 7

I don't know if they took us all that weary way back in the crawler, or if Wormface sent a ship. I woke up being slapped and was inside, lying down. The skinny one was slapping me—the man the fat one called "Tim." I tried to fight back and found that I couldn't. I was in a straitjacket thing that held me as snugly as a wrapped mummy. I let out a yelp.

Skinny grabbed my hair, jerked my head up, tried to put a big capsule into my mouth.

I tried to bite him.

He slapped me harder and offered me the capsule again. His expression didn't change—it stayed mean.

I heard: "Take it, boy," and turned my eyes. The fat one was on the other side. "Better swallow it," he said. "You got five bad days ahead."

I took it. Not because of the advice but because a hand held my nose and another popped the pill into my mouth when I gasped. Fatty held a cup of water for me to wash it down; I didn't resist that, I needed it.

Skinny stuck a hypodermic needle big enough for a horse into my shoulder. I told him what I thought of him, using words I hardly ever use. The skinny one could have been deaf; the fat one chuckled. I rolled my eyes at him. "You, too," I added weakly. "Squared."

Fatty clucked reprovingly. "You ought to be glad we saved your life." He added, "Though it wasn't my idea, you strike me as a sorry team. *He* wanted you alive."

"Shaddap," Skinny said. "Strap his head."

"Let him break his neck. We better fix our ownselves. *He* won't wait." But he started to obey.

Skinny glanced at his watch. "Four minutes."

The fat one hastily tightened a strap across my fore-

109

head, then both moved very fast, swallowing capsules, giving each other hypos. I watched as best I could.

I was back in the ship. The ceiling glowed the same way, the walls looked the same. It was the room the two men used; their beds were on each side and I was strapped to a soft couch between them.

Each hurriedly got on his bed, began zipping up a tight wrapping like a sleeping bag. Each strapped his head in place before completing the process. I was not interested in them. "Hey! What did you do with Peewee?"

The fat man chuckled. "Hear that, Tim? That's a good one."

"Shaddap."

"You—" I was about to sum up Fatty's character but my thoughts got fuzzy and my tongue was thick. Besides, I wanted to ask about the Mother Thing, too.

I did not get out another word. Suddenly I was incredibly heavy and the couch was rock hard.

For a long, long time I wasn't awake or truly asleep. At first I couldn't feel anything but that terrible weight, then I hurt all over and wanted to scream. I didn't have the strength for it.

Slowly the pain went away and I stopped feeling anything. I wasn't a body—just me, no attachments. I dreamed a lot and none of it made sense; I seemed to be stuck in a comic book, the sort P.T.A. meetings pass resolutions against, and the baddies were way ahead no matter what I did.

Once the couch gave a twisting lurch and suddenly I had a body, one that was dizzy. After a few ages I realized vaguely that I had gone through a skew-flip turn-over. I had known, during lucid moments, that I was going somewhere, very fast, at terribly high acceleration. I decided solemnly that we must be halfway and tried to figure out how long two times eternity was. It kept coming out eighty-five cents plus sales tax; the cash register rang "NO SALE" and I would start over.

Fats was undoing my head strap. It stuck and skin came away. "Rise and shine, bub. Time's awastin'."

A croak was all I managed. The skinny one was unwrapping me. My legs sagged apart and hurt. "Get up!"

I tried and didn't make it. Skinny grabbed one of my legs and started to knead it.

I screamed.

"Here, lemme do that," said Fatty. "I used to be a trainer."

Fats did know something about it. I gasped when his thumbs dug into my calves and he stopped. "Too rough?" I couldn't answer. He went on massaging me and said almost jovially, "Five days at eight gravities ain't no joy ride. But you'll be okay. Got the needle, Tim?"

The skinny one jabbed me in my left thigh. I hardly felt it. Fats pulled me to a sitting position and handed me a cup. I thought it was water; it wasn't and I choked and sprayed. Fats waited, then gave it to me again. "Drink some, this time." I did.

"Okay, up on your feet. Vacation is over."

The floor swayed and I had to grab him until it stopped. "Where are we?" I said hoarsely.

Fats grinned, as if he knew an enormously funny joke. "Pluto, of course. Lovely place, Pluto. A summer resort."

"Shaddap. Get him moving."

"Shake it up, kid. You don't want to keep *him* waiting."

Pluto! It couldn't be; nobody could get that far. Why, they hadn't even attempted Jupiter's moons yet. Pluto was so much farther that—

My brain wasn't working. The experience just past

had shaken me so badly that I couldn't accept the fact that the experience itself proved that I was wrong.

But Pluto!

I wasn't given time to wonder; we got into space suits. Although I hadn't known, Oscar was there, and I was so glad to see him that I forgot everything else. He hadn't been racked, just tossed on the floor. I bent down (discovering charley horses in every muscle) and checked him. He didn't seem hurt.

"Get in it," Fats ordered. "Quit fiddlin'."

"All right," I answered almost cheerfully. Then I hesitated. "Say—I haven't any air."

"Take another look," said Fats. I looked. Charged oxyhelium bottles were on the backpack. "Although," he continued, "if we didn't have orders from *him*, I wouldn't give you a whiff of Limburger. You made us for two bottles—*and* a rock hammer—*and* a line that cost four ninety-five, earthside. Sometime," he stated without rancor, "I'm gonna take it out of your hide."

"Shaddap," said Skinny. "Get going."

I spread Oscar open, wriggled in, clipped on the blood-color reader, and zipped the gaskets. Then I stood up, clamped my helmet, and felt better just to be inside. "Tight?"

("Tight!" Oscar agreed.)

"We're a long way from home."

("But we got air! Chin up, pal.")

Which reminded me to check the chin valve. Everything was working. My knife was gone and so were the hammer and line, but those were incidentals. We were tight.

I followed Skinny out with Fats behind me. We passed Wormface in the corridor—or a wormface—but while I shuddered, I had Oscar around me and felt that he couldn't get at me. Another creature joined us in the air lock and I had to look twice to realize that it was a wormface in a space suit. The material was smooth and did not bulge the way ours did. It looked like a dead tree trunk with bare branches and heavy roots, but the supreme improvement was its "helmet"—a glassy smooth dome. One-way glass, I suppose; I couldn't see in. Cased that way, a wormface was grotesquely ridiculous rather than terrifying. But I stood no closer than I had to.

Pressure was dropping and I was busy wasting air to keep from swelling up. It reminded me of what I wanted most to know: what had happened to Peewee and the Mother Thing. So I keyed my radio and announced: "Radio check. Alfa, Bravo, Coca—"

"Shaddap that nonsense. We want you, we'll tell you."

The outer door opened and I had my first view of Pluto.

I don't know what I expected. Pluto is so far out that they can't get decent photographs even at Luna Observatory. I had read articles in the *Scientific American* and seen pictures in *LIFE,* bonestelled to look like photographs, and remembered that it was approaching its summer—if "summer" is the word for warm enough to melt air. I recalled that because they had announced that Pluto was showing an atmosphere as it got closer to the Sun.

But I had never been much interested in Pluto—too few facts and too much speculation, too far away and not desirable real estate. By comparison the Moon was a choice residential suburb. Professor Tombaugh (the one the station was named for) was working on a giant electronic telescope to photograph it, under a Guggenheim grant, but he had a special interest; he discovered Pluto years before I was born.

The first thing I noticed as the door was opening was *click . . . click . . . click*—and a fourth click, in my helmet, as Oscar's heating units all cut in.

The Sun was in front of me—I didn't realize what it was at first; it looked no bigger than Venus or Jupiter does from Earth (although much brighter). With no disc you could be sure of, it looked like an electric arc.

Fats jabbed me in the ribs. "Snap out of your hop."

A drawbridge joined the door to an elevated roadway that led into the side of a mountain about two hundred yards away. The road was supported on spidery legs two or three feet high up to ten or twelve, depending on the lay of the land. The ground was covered with snow, glaringly white even under that pinpoint Sun. Where the stilts were longest, about halfway, the viaduct crossed a brook.

What sort of "water" was that? Methane? What was the "snow"? Solid ammonia? I didn't have tables to tell me what was solid, what was liquid, and what was gas at whatever hellish cold Pluto enjoyed in the "summer." All I knew was that it got so cold in its winter that it didn't have any gas or liquid—just vacuum, like the Moon.

I was glad to hurry. A wind blew from our left and was not only freezing that side of me in spite of Oscar's best efforts, it made the footing hazardous—I decided it would be far safer to do that forced march on the Moon again than to fall into that "snow." Would a man struggle before he shattered himself and his suit, or would he die as he hit?

Adding to hazard of wind and no guard rail was traffic, space-suited wormfaces. They moved at twice our speed and shared the road the way a dog does a bone. Even Skinny resorted to fancy footwork and I had three narrow squeaks.

The way continued into a tunnel; ten feet inside a panel snapped out of the way as we got near it. Twenty feet beyond was another; it did the same and closed behind us. There were about two dozen panels, each behaving like fast-acting gate valves, and the pressure was a little higher after each. I couldn't see what operated them although it was light in the tunnel from glowing ceilings. Finally we passed through a heavy-duty air lock, but the pressure was already taken care of and its doors stood open. It led into a large room.

Wormface was inside. *The* Wormface, I think, because he spoke in English: "Come!" I heard it through my helmet. But I couldn't be sure it was he as there were others around and I would have less trouble telling wart hogs apart.

Wormface hurried away. He was not wearing a space suit and I was relieved when he turned because I could no longer see his squirming mouth; but it was only a slight improvement as it brought into sight his rear-view eye.

We were hard put to keep up. He led us down a corridor, to the right through another open double set of doors, and finally stopped suddenly just short of a hole in the floor about like a sewer manhole. "Undress it!" he commanded.

Fats and Skinny had their helmets open, so I knew it was safe, in one way. But in every other way I wanted to stay inside Oscar—as long as Wormface was around.

Fats unclamped my helmet. "Out of that skin, bub. Snap it up!" Skinny loosened my belt and they quickly had the suit off even though I hindered.

Wormface waited. As soon as I was out of Oscar he pointed at the hole. "Down!"

I gulped. That hole looked as deep as a well and less inviting.

"Down," he repeated. "Now."

"Do it, bub," Fats advised. "Jump or be pushed. Get down that hole before he gets annoyed."

I tried to run.

Wormface was around me and chivvying me back before I was well started. I slammed on the brakes and backed up—glanced behind just in time to turn a fall into a clumsy jump.

It was a long way to the bottom. Landing did not hurt the way it would have on Earth, but I turned an ankle. That didn't matter; I wasn't going anywhere; the hole in the ceiling was the only exit.

My cell was about twenty feet square. It was, I suppose, carved out of solid rock, although there was no way to tell as the walls and floor and ceiling were the same elephant hide used in the ship. A lighting panel covered half the ceiling and I could have read if I'd had anything to read. The only other detail was a jet of water that splashed out of a hole in the wall, landed in a depression the size of a washtub, and departed for parts unknown.

The place was warm, which was well as there was nothing resembling bed or bedclothes. I had already concluded that I might be here quite a while and was wondering about eating and sleeping.

I decided I was tired of this nonsense. I had been minding my own business, out back of my own house. Everything else was Wormface's fault! I sat down on the floor and thought about slow ways to kill him.

I finally gave up that foolishness and wondered about Peewee and the Mother Thing. Were they here? Or were they dead somewhere between the mountains and Tombaugh Station? Thinking it over glumly, I decided that poor little Peewee was best off if she had never wakened from that second coma. I wasn't sure about the Mother Thing because I didn't know enough about her—but in Peewee's case I was sure.

Well, there was a certain appropriateness to the fix I was in; a knight-errant usually lands in a dungeon at some point. But by rights, the maiden fair ought to be imprisoned in a tower in the same castle. Sorry, Peewee; as a knight-errant, I'm a good soda jerk. Or jerk. "His strength is as the strength of ten because his heart is pure."

It wasn't funny.

I got tired of punishing myself and looked to see what time it was—not that it mattered. But a prisoner is traditionally expected to scratch marks on the wall, tallying the days he's been in, so I thought I might as well start. My watch was on my wrist but not running and I couldn't start it. Maybe eight gees was too much for it, even though it was supposed to be shockproof, waterproof, magnetism-proof, and immune to un-American influences.

After a while I lay down and went to sleep.

I was awakened by a clatter.

It was a ration can hitting the floor and the fall hadn't helped it, but the key was on it and I got it open—corned beef hash and very good, too. I used the empty can to drink from—the water might be poisoned, but did I have a choice?—and then washed the can so that it wouldn't smell.

The water was warm. I took a bath.

I doubt if many American citizens during the past twenty years have ever needed a bath as much as I did. Then I washed my clothes. My shirt, shorts, and socks were wash-and-wear synthetics; my slacks were denim and took longer to dry, but I didn't mind: I just wished that I had one of the two hundred bars of Skyway Soap that were home on the floor of my closet. If I had known I was coming to Pluto, I would have brought one.

Washing clothes caused me to take inventory. I had a handkerchief, sixty-seven cents in change, a dollar bill so sweat-soaked and worn that it was hard to make out Washington's picture, a mechanical pencil stamped "Jay's Drive-In—the thickest malts in town!"—a canard; *I* make the thickest—and a grocery list I should have taken care of for Mother but hadn't because of that silly air conditioner in Charton's Drugstore. It wasn't as bedraggled as the dollar bill because it had been in my shirt pocket.

I lined up my assets and looked at them. They did not look like a collection that could be reworked into a miracle weapon with which I would blast my way out, steal a ship, teach myself to pilot it, and return triumphantly to warn the President and save the country. I rearranged them and they still didn't.

I was correct. They weren't.

I woke up from a terrible nightmare, remembered where I was, and wished I were back in the nightmare. I lay there feeling sorry for myself and presently tears started welling out of my eyes while my chin trembled. I had never been badgered "not to be a crybaby"; Dad says there is nothing wrong with tears; it's just that they are socially not acceptable—he says that in some cultures weeping is a social grace. But in Horace Mann Grammar School being a crybaby was no asset; I gave it up years ago. Besides, it's exhausting and gets you nowhere. I shut off the rain and took stock.

My action list ran like this:

1. Escape from this cell.
2. Find Oscar, suit up.
3. Go outdoors, steal a ship, head home—if I could figure out how to gun it.
4. Figure out a weapon or stratagem to fight off the wormfaces or keep them busy while I sneaked out and grabbed a ship. Nothing to it. Any superman capable of teleportation and other assorted psionic tricks could do it. Just be sure the plan is foolproof and that your insurance is paid up.
5. Crash priority: make sure, before bidding farewell to the romantic shores of exotic Pluto and its friendly colorful natives, that neither Peewee nor the Mother Thing is here—if they are, take them along—because, contrary to some opinions, it is better to be a dead hero than a live louse. Dying is messy and incon-

venient but even a louse dies someday no matter what he will do to stay alive and he is forever having to explain his choice. The gummed-up spell that I had had at the hero business had shown that it was undesirable work but the alternative was still less attractive.

The fact that Peewee knew how to gun those ships, or that the Mother Thing could coach me, did not figure. I can't prove that, but *I* know.

Footnote: after I learned to run one of their ships, could I do so at eight gravities? That may simply call for arch supports for a wormface but I knew what eight gees did to me. Automatic pilot? If so, would it have directions on it, in English? (Don't be silly, Clifford!)

Subordinate footnote: how long would it take to get home at *one* gravity? The rest of the century? Or just long enough to starve to death?

6. Occupational therapy for the lulls when I went stale on the problems. This was important in order to avoid coming apart at the seams. O. Henry wrote stories in prison, St. Paul turned out his strongest epistles incarcerated in Rome, Hitler wrote *Mein Kampf* in jail—next time I would bring a typewriter and paper. This time I could work out magic squares and invent chess problems. Anything was better than feeling sorry for myself. Lions put up with zoos and wasn't I smarter than a lion? Some, anyhow?

And so to work— One: how to get out of this hole? I came up with a straight-forward answer: there wasn't any way. The cell was twenty feet on a side with a ceiling twelve feet high; the walls were as smooth as a baby's cheek and as impervious as a bill collector. The other features were the hole in the ceiling, which ran about six feet still higher, the stream of water and its catch basin, and a glowing area in the ceiling. For tools I had the stuff previously listed (a few

119

ounces of nothing much, nothing sharp, nor explosive, nor corrosive), my clothes, and an empty tin can.

I tested how high I could jump. Even a substitute guard needs springs in his legs—I touched the ceiling. That meant a gravity around one-half gee—I hadn't been able to guess, as I had spent an endless time under one-sixth gravity followed by a few eons at eight gees; my reflexes had been mistreated.

But, although I could touch the ceiling, I could neither walk on it nor levitate. I could get that high, but there was nothing a mouse could cling to.

Well, I could rip my clothes and braid a rope. Was there anything near the hole on which to catch it? All I could recall was smooth floor. But suppose it did catch? What next? Paddle around in my skin until Wormface spotted me and herded me back down, this time with no clothes? I decided to postpone the rope trick until I worked out that next step which would confound Wormface and his tribe.

I sighed and looked around. All that was left was that jet of water and the floor basin that caught it.

There is a story about two frogs trapped in a crock of cream. One sees how hopeless it is, gives up and drowns. The other is too stupid to know he's licked; he keeps on paddling. In a few hours he has churned so much butter that it forms an island, on which he floats, cool and comfortable, until the milkmaid comes and chucks him out.

That water spilled in and ran out. Suppose it didn't run out?

I explored the bottom of the catch basin. The drain was large by our standards, but I thought I could plug it. Could I stay afloat while the room filled up, filled the hole above, and pushed me out the spout? Well, I could find out, I had a can.

The can looked like a pint and a "pint's a pound the world 'round" and a cubic foot of water weighs (on

Earth) a little over sixty pounds. But I had to be sure. My feet are eleven inches long; they've been that size since I was ten—I took a lot of ribbing until I grew up to them. I marked eleven inches on the floor with two pennies. It turns out that a dollar bill is two and a half inches wide and quarter is a smidgeon under an inch. Shortly I knew the dimensions of room and can pretty accurately.

I held the can under the stream, letting it fill and dumping it fast, while I ticked of cans of water on my left hand and counted seconds. Eventually I calculated how long it would take to fill the room. I didn't like the answer, so I did it over.

It would take fourteen hours to fill the room and the hole above, plus an hour to allow for crude methods. Could I stay afloat that long?

You're darn tootin' I could!—if I had to. And I had to. There isn't any limit to how long a man can float if he doesn't panic.

I balled my slacks and stuffed them in the drain. I almost lost them, so I wrapped them around the can and used the bundle as a cork. It stayed put and I used the rest of my clothes to caulk it. Then I waited, feeling cocky. Maybe the flood would create the diversion I needed for the rest of the caper. Slowly the basin filled.

The water got about an inch below floor level and stopped.

A pressure switch, I suppose. I should have known that creatures who could build eight-gee, constant-boost ships would design plumbing to "fail-safe." I wish we could.

I recovered my clothes, all but one sock, and spread them to dry. I hoped the sock would foul a pump or something but I doubted it; they were good engineers.

I never really believed that story about the frogs.

Another can was tossed down—roast beef and soggy potatoes. It was filling but I began to long for peaches. The can was stenciled "Available for subsidized resale on Luna" which made it possible that Skinny and Fatty had come by this food honestly. I wondered how they liked sharing their supplies? No doubt they did so only because Wormface had twisted their arms. Which made me wonder why Wormface wanted me alive? I was in favor of it but couldn't see why he was. I decided to call each can a "day" and let the empties be my calendar.

Which reminded me that I had not worked out how long it would take to get home on a one-gee boost, if it turned out that I could not arrange automatic piloting at eight gees. I was stymied on getting out of the cell, I hadn't even nibbled at what I would do if I did get out (correction: *when* I got out), but I could work ballistics.

I didn't need books. I've met people, even in this day and age, who can't tell a star from a planet and who think of astronomical distances simply as "big." They remind me of those primitives who have just four numbers: one, two, three, and "many." But any tenderfoot Scout knows the basic facts and a fellow bitten by the space bug (such as myself) usually knows a number of figures.

"Mother very thoughtfully made a jelly sandwich under no protest." Could you forget that after saying it a few times? Okay, lay it out so:

Mother	MERCURY	$.39
Very	VENUS	$.72
Thoughtfully	TERRA	$1.00
Made	MARS	$1.50
A	ASTEROIDS	(assorted prices, unimportant)

Jelly	JUPITER	$5.20
Sandwich	SATURN	$9.50
Under	URANUS	$19.00
No	NEPTUNE	$30.00
Protest	PLUTO	$39.50

The "prices" are distances from the Sun in astronomical units. An A.U. is the mean distance of Earth from Sun, 93,000,000 miles. It is easier to remember one figure that everybody knows and some little figures than it is to remember figures in millions and billions. I use dollar signs because a figure has more flavor if I think of it as money—which Dad considers deplorable. Some way you must remember them, or you don't know your own neighborhood.

Now we come to a joker. The list says that Pluto's distance is thirty-nine and a half times Earth's distance. But Pluto and Mercury have very eccentric orbits and Pluto's is a dilly; its distance varies almost *two billion* miles, more than the distance from the Sun to Uranus. Pluto creeps to the orbit of Neptune and a hair inside, then swings way out and stays there a couple of centuries—it makes only four round trips in a thousand years.

But I had seen that article about how Pluto was coming into its "summer." So I knew it was close to the orbit of Neptune now, and would be for the rest of my life—my life expectancy in Centerville; I didn't look like a preferred risk here. That gave an easy figure—30 astronomical units.

Acceleration problems are simple $s = \frac{1}{2} at^2$; distance equals half the acceleration times the square of elapsed time. If astrogation were that simple any sophomore could pilot a rocket ship—the complications come from gravitational fields and the fact that everything moves fourteen directions at once. But I could disregard gravitational fields and planetary motions; at the speeds a wormface ship makes neither factor matters until you are very close. I wanted a rough answer.

I missed my slipstick. Dad says that anyone who can't use a slide rule is a cultural illiterate and should not be allowed to vote. Mine is a beauty—a K&E 20″ Log-log Duplex Decitrig. Dad surprised me with it after I mastered a ten-inch polyphase. We ate potato soup that week—but Dad says you should always budget luxuries first. I knew where it was. Home on my desk.

No matter. I had figures, formula, pencil and paper.

First a check problem. Fats had said "Pluto," "five days," and "eight gravities."

It's a two-piece problem; accelerate for half time (and half distance); do a skew-flip and decelerate the other half time (and distance). You can't use the whole distance in the equation, as "time" appears as a square—it's a parabolic.

Was Pluto in opposition? Or quadrature? Or conjunction? Nobody looks at Pluto—so why remember where it is on the ecliptic? Oh, well, the average distance was 30 A.U.s—that would give a close-enough answer.

Half that distance, in feet, is: ½ X 30 X 93,000,000 X 5280.

Eight gravities is: 8 X 32.2 ft./sec./sec.—speed increases by 258 feet per second every second up to skew-flip and decreases just as fast thereafter. So—

$$\tfrac{1}{2} \text{ X } 30 \text{ X } 93{,}000{,}000 \text{ X } 5280 = \tfrac{1}{2} \text{ X } 8 \text{ X } 32.2 \text{ X } t^2$$

—and you wind up with the time for half the trip, in seconds. Double that for full trip. Divide by 3600 to get hours; divide by 24 and you have days. On a slide rule such a problem takes forty seconds, most of it to get your decimal point correct. It's as easy as computing sales tax.

It took me at least an hour and almost as long to

prove it, using a different sequence—and a third time, because the answers didn't match (I had forgotten to multiply by 5280, and had "miles" on one side and "feet" on the other—a no-good way to do arithmetic)—then a fourth time because my confidence was shaken. I tell you, the slide rule is the greatest invention since girls.

But I got a proved answer. Five and a half days. I was on Pluto.

Or maybe Neptune—

No, on Neptune I would not be able to jump to a twelve-foot ceiling; Pluto alone matched all facts. So I erased and computed the trip at one gravity, with turnover.

Fifteen days.

It seemed to me that it ought to take at least eight times as long at one gee as at eight—more likely sixty-four. Then I was glad I had bulled my way through analytical geometry, for I made a rough plot and saw the trouble. Squared time *cut down* the advantage—because the more boost, the shorter the trip, and the shorter the trip the less time in which to use the built-up speed. To cut time in half, you need four times as much boost; to cut it to a quarter, you need *sixteen* times the boost, and so on. This way lies bankruptcy.

To learn that I could get home in about two weeks at one gravity cheered me. I couldn't starve in two weeks. If I could steal a ship. If I could run it. If I could climb out of this hole. If—

Not "if," but "when!" I was too late for college this year; fifteen more days wouldn't matter.

I had noticed, in the first problem, the speed we had been making at skew-flip. More than eleven thousand miles per second. That's a nice speed, even in space. It made me think. Consider the nearest star, Proxima Centauri, four and three-tenths light-years away, the distance you hear so often on quiz shows. How long at eight gees?

The problem was the same sort but I had to be careful about decimal points; the figures mount up. A light-year is—I had forgotten. So multiply 186,000 miles per second (the speed of light) by the seconds in a year (365.25 X 24 X 3600) and get—5,880,000,000,000 miles
—multiply that by 4.3 and get—
25,284,000,000,000

Call it twenty-five trillion miles. Whew!

It works out to a year and five months—not as long as a trip around the Horn only last century.

Why, these monsters had star travel!

I don't know why I was surprised; it had been staring me in the face. I had assumed that Wormface had taken me to his home planet, that he was a Plutonian, or Plutocrat, or whatever the word is. But he *couldn't* be.

He breathed air. He kept his ship warm enough for me. When he wasn't in a hurry, he cruised at one gee, near enough. He used lighting that suited my eyes. Therefore he came from the sort of planet I came from.

Proxima Centauri is a double star, as you know if you do crossword puzzles, and one is a twin for our own Sun—size, temperature, special pattern. Is it a fair guess that it has a planet like Earth? I had a dirty hunch that I knew Wormface's home address.

I knew where he *didn't* come from. Not from a planet that runs a couple of centuries in utter airlessness with temperatures pushing absolute zero, followed by a "summer" in which some gases melt but water is solid rock and even Wormface has to wear a space suit. Nor from anywhere in our system, for I was sure as taxes that Wormface felt at home only on a planet like ours. Never mind the way he looked; spiders don't look like us but they like the things we like—there must be a thousand spiders in our houses for every one of us.

Wormface and his kin would like Earth. My fear was that they liked it too much.

I looked at that Proxima Centauri problem and saw something else. The turn-over speed read 1,110,000 miles per second, six times the speed of light. Relativity theory says that's impossible.

I wanted to talk to Dad about it. Dad reads everything from *The Anatomy of Melancholy* to *Acta Mathematica* and *Paris-Match* and will sit on a curbstone separating damp newspapers wrapped around garbage in order to see continued-on-page-eight. Dad would haul down a book and we'd look it up. Then he would try four or five more with other opinions. Dad doesn't hold with the idea that it-must-be-true-or-they-wouldn't-have-printed-it; he doesn't consider *any* opinion sacred —it shocked me the first time he took out a pen and changed something in one of my math books.

Still, even if speed-of-light was a limit, four or five years wasn't impossible, or even impractical. We've been told for so long that star trips, even to the nearest stars, would take generations that we may have a wrong slant. A mile of lunar mountains is a long way but a trillion miles in empty space may not be.

But what was Wormface doing on Pluto?

If you were invading another solar system, how would you start? I'm not joking; a dungeon on Pluto is no joke and I never laughed at Wormface. Would you just barge in, or toss your hat in first? They seemed far ahead of us in engineering but they couldn't have known that ahead of time. Wouldn't it be smart to build a supply base in that system in some spot nobody ever visited?

Then you could set up advance bases, say on an airless satellite of a likely-looking planet, from which you could scout the surface of the target planet. If you lost your scouting base, you would pull back to main base and work out a new attack.

Remember that while Pluto is a long way off to us, it was only five days from Luna for Wormface. Think about World War II, back when speeds were slow. Main Base is safely out of reach (U.S.A./Pluto) but only about five days from advance base (England/The Moon) which is three hours from theater-of-operations (France-Germany/Earth). That's a slow way to operate but it worked for the Allies in World War II.

I just hoped it would not work for Wormface's gang. Though I didn't see anything to prevent it.

Somebody chucked down another can—spaghetti and meat balls. If it had been canned peaches, I might not have had the fortitude to do what I did next, which was to use it for a hammer before I opened it. I beat an empty can into a flat narrow shape and beat a point on it, which I sharpened on the edge of the catch basin. When I was through, I had a dagger—not a good one, but it made me feel less helpless.

Then I ate. I felt sleepy and went to sleep in a warm glow. I was still a prisoner but I had a weapon of sorts and I believed that I had figured out what I was up against. Getting a problem analyzed is two-thirds of solving it. I didn't have nightmares.

The next thing tossed down the hole was Fats.

Skinny landed on him seconds later. I backed off and held my dagger ready. Skinny ignored me, picked himself up, looked around, went to the water spout and got a drink. Fats was in no shape to do anything; his breath was knocked out.

I looked at him and thought what a nasty parcel he was. Then I thought, oh, what the deuce!—he had massaged me when I needed it. I heaved him onto his stomach and began artificial respiration. In four or five pushes his motor caught and he was able to breathe. He gasped, "That's enough!"

I backed off, got my knife out. Skinny was sitting

against a wall, ignoring us. Fats looked at my feeble weapon and said, "Put that away, kid. We're bosom buddies now."

"We are?"

"Yeah. Us human types had better stick together." He sighed wretchedly. "After all we done for him! That's gratitude."

"What do you mean?" I demanded.

"Huh?" said Fats. "Just what I said. *He* decided he could do without us. So Annie doesn't live here any more."

"Shaddap," the skinny one said flatly.

Fats screwed his face into a pout. "*You* shaddap," he said peevishly. "I'm tired of that. It's shaddap here, shaddap there, all day long—and look where we are."

"Shaddap, I said."

Fats shut up. I never did find out what had happened, because Fats seldom gave the same explanation twice. The older man never spoke except for that tiresome order to shut up, or in monosyllables even less helpful. But one thing was clear: they had lost their jobs as assistant gangsters, or fifth columnists, or whatever you call a human being who would stooge against his own race. Once Fats said, "Matter of fact, it's *your* fault."

"Mine?" I dropped my hand to my tin-can knife.

"Yours. If you hadn't butted in, *he* wouldn't have got sore."

"I didn't do anything."

"Says you. You swiped his two best prizes, that's all, and held *him* up when *he* planned to high-tail it back here."

"Oh. But that wasn't your fault."

"So I told him. *You* try telling him. Take your hand away from that silly nail file." Fats shrugged. "Like I always say, let bygones be bygones."

I finally learned the thing I wanted most to know.

About the fifth time I brought up the matter of Peewee, Fats said, "What d'you want to know about the brat for?"

"I just want to know whether she's alive or dead."

"Oh, she's alive. Leastwise she was last time I seen her."

"When was that?"

"You ask too many questions. Right here."

"She's *here?*" I said eagerly.

"That's what I said, wasn't it? Around everywhere and always underfoot. Living like a princess, if you ask me." Fats picked his teeth and frowned. "Why *he* should make a pet out of her and treat us the way he did, beats me. It ain't right."

I didn't think so, either, but for another reason. The idea that gallant little Peewee was the spoiled darling of Wormface I found impossible to believe. There was some explanation—or Fats was lying. "You mean he doesn't have her locked up?"

"What's it get him? Where's she gonna go?"

I pondered that myself. Where *could* you go?—when to step outdoors was suicide. Even if Peewee had her space suit (and that, at least, was probably locked up), even if a ship was at hand and empty when she got outside, even if she could get into it, she still wouldn't have a "ship's brain," the little gadget that served as a lock. "What happened to the Mother Thing?"

"The what?"

"The—" I hesitated. "Uh, the non-human who was in my space suit with me. You must know, you were there. Is she alive? Is she here?"

But Fats was brooding. "Them bugs don't interest me none," he said sourly and I could get no more out of him.

But Peewee was alive (and a hard lump in me was suddenly gone). She was here! Her chances, even as a prisoner, had been enormously better on the Moon; nevertheless I felt almost ecstatic to know that she was near. I began thinking about ways to get a message to her.

As for Fats' insinuation that she was playing footy with Wormface, it bothered me not at all. Peewee was unpredictable and sometimes a brat and often exasperating, as well as conceited, supercilious, and downright childish. But she would be burned alive rather than turn traitor. Joan of Arc had not been made of sterner stuff.

We three kept uneasy truce. I avoided them, slept with one eye open, and tried not to sleep unless they were asleep first, and I always kept my dagger at hand. I did not bathe after they joined me; it would have put me at a disadvantage. The older one ignored me, Fats was almost friendly. He pretended not to be afraid of my puny weapon, but I think he was. The reason I think so comes from the first time we were fed. Three cans dropped from the ceiling; Skinny picked up one, Fats got one, but when I circled around to take the third, Fats snatched it.

I said, "Give me that, please."

Fats grinned. "What makes you think this is for you, sonny boy?"

"Uh, three cans, three people."

"So what? I'm feeling a mite hungry. I don't hardly think I can spare it."

"I'm hungry, too. Be reasonable."

"Mmmm—" He seemed to consider it. "Tell you what. I'll sell it to you."

I hesitated. It had a shifty logic; Wormface couldn't walk into Lunar Base commissary and buy these rations; probably Fats or his partner had bought them. I wouldn't mind signing I.O.U.s—a hundred dollars a meal, a thousand, or a million; money no longer meant anything. Why not humor him?

No! If I gave in, if I admitted I had to dicker with

him for my prison rations, he would own me. I'd wait on him hand and foot, do anything he told me, just to eat.

I let him see my tin dagger. "I'll fight you for it."

Fats glanced at my hand and grinned broadly. "Can't you take a joke?" He tossed me the, can. There was no trouble at feeding times after that.

We lived like that "Happy Family" you sometimes see in traveling zoos: a lion caged with a lamb. It is a startling exhibit but the lamb has to be replaced frequently. Fats liked to talk and I learned things from him, when I could sort out truth from lies. His name—so he said—was Jacques de Barre de Vigny ("Call me 'Jock.' ") and the older man was Timothy Johnson—but I had a hunch that their real names could be learned only by inspecting post office bulletin boards. Despite Jock's pretense of knowing everything, I soon decided that he knew nothing about Wormface's origin and little about his plans and purposes. Wormface did not seem the sort to discuss things with "lower animals"; he would simply make use of them, as we use horses.

Jock admitted one thing readily. "Yeah, we put the snatch on the brat. There's no uranium on the Moon; those stories are just to get suckers. We were wasting our time—and a man's got to eat, don't he?"

I didn't make the obvious retort; I wanted information. Tim said, "Shaddap!"

"Aw, what of it, Tim? You worried about the F.B.I.? You think the Man can put the arm on you—*here?*"

"Shaddap, I said."

"Happens I feel like talking. So blow it." Jock went on, "It was easy. The brat's got more curiosity than seven cats. *He* knew she was coming and when." Jock looked thoughtful. "*He* always knows—he's got lots of people working for him, some high up. All I had to do was be in Luna City and get acquainted—I made the contact because Tim here ain't the fatherly type, the way I am.

I get to talking with her, I buy her a coke, I tell her about the romance of hunting uranium on the Moon and similar hogwash. Then I sigh and say it's too bad I can't show her the mine of my partner and I. That's all it took. When the tourist party visited Tombaugh Station, she got away and sneaked out the lock—she worked that part out her ownself. She's sly, that one. All we had to do was wait where I told her—didn't even have to be rough with her until she got worried about taking longer for the crawler to get to our mine than I told her." Jock grinned. "She fights pretty well for her weight. Scratched me some."

Poor little Peewee! Too bad she hadn't drawn and quartered him! But the story sounded true for it was the way Peewee would behave—sure of herself, afraid of no one, unable to resist any "educational" experience.

Jock went on, "It wasn't the brat *he* wanted. *He* wanted her old man. Had some swindle to get him to the Moon, didn't work." Jock grinned sourly. "That was a bad time, things ain't good when *he* don't have his own way. But he had to settle for the brat. Tim here pointed out to him he could trade."

Tim chucked in one word which I took as a general denial. Jock raised his eyebrows. "Listen to vinegar puss. Nice manners, ain't he?"

Maybe I should have kept quiet since I was digging for facts, not philosophy. But I've got Peewee's failing myself; when I don't understand, I have an unbearable itch to know why. I didn't (and don't) understand what made Jock tick. "Jock? Why did you do it?"

"Huh?"

"Look, you're a human being." (At least he looked like one.) "As you pointed out, we humans had better stick together. How could you bring yourself to kidnap a little girl—and turn her over to *him?*"

"Are you crazy, boy?"

"I don't think so."

"You talk crazy. Have you ever tried not doing something *he* wanted? Try it some time."

I saw his point. Refusing Wormface would be like a rabbit spitting in a snake's eye—as I knew too well. Jock went on, "You got to understand the other man's viewpoint. Live and let live, I always say. We got grabbed while we were messin' around, lookin' for carnotite—and after that, we never stood no chance. You can't fight City Hall, that gets you nowhere. So we made a dicker —we run his errands, he pays us in uranium."

My faint sympathy vanished. I wanted to throw up. "And you got paid?"

"Well . . . you might say we got time on the books."

I looked around our cell. "You made a bad deal."

Jock grimaced, looking like a sulky baby. "Maybe so. But be reasonable, kid. You got to cooperate with the inevitable. These boys are moving in—they got what it takes. You seen that yourself. Well, a man's got to look out for number one, don't he? It's a cinch nobody else will. Now I seen a case like this when I was no older than you and it taught me a lesson. Our town had run quietly for years, but the Big Fellow was getting old and losing his grip . . . whereupon some boys from St. Louis moved in. Things were confused for a while. A man had to know which way to jump—else he woke up wearing a wooden overcoat, like as not. Those that seen the handwriting made out; those that didn't . . . well, it don't do no good to buck the current, I always say. That makes sense, don't it?"

I could follow his "logic"—provided you accepted his "live louse" standard. But he had left out a key point. "Even so, Jock, I don't see how you could do that to a little girl."

"Huh? I just explained how we couldn't help it."

"But you *could*. Even allowing how hard it is to face up to *him* and refuse orders, you had a perfect chance to duck out."

"Wha' d'you mean?"

"He sent you to Luna City to find her, you said so. You've got a return-fare benefit—I know you have, I know the rules. All you had to do was sit tight, where *he* couldn't reach you—and take the next ship back to Earth. You didn't have to do his dirty work."

"But—"

I cut him off. "Maybe you couldn't help yourself, out in a lunar desert. Maybe you wouldn't feel safe even inside Tombaugh Station. But when he sent you into Luna City, you had your chance. You didn't have to steal a little girl and turn her over to a—a bug-eyed *monster!*"

He looked baffled, then answered quickly. "Kip, I like you. You're a good boy. But you ain't smart. You don't understand."

"I think I do!"

"No, you don't." He leaned toward me, started to put a hand on my knee; I drew back. He went on, "There's something I didn't tell you . . . for fear you'd think I was a—well, a zombie, or something. They operated on us."

"Huh?"

"They operated on us," he went on glibly. "They planted bombs in our heads. Remote control, like a missile. A man gets out of line . . . *he* punches a button—*blooie!* Brains all over the ceiling." He fumbled at the nape of his neck. "See the scar? My hair's getting kind o' long . . . but if you look close I'm sure you'll see it; it can't 'ave disappeared entirely. See it?"

I started to look. I might even have been sold on it— I had been forced to believe less probable things lately. Tim cut short my suspended judgment with one explosive word.

Jock flinched, then braced himself and said, "Don't pay any attention to *him!*"

I shrugged and moved away. Jock didn't talk the rest of that "day." That suited me.

The next "morning" I was roused by Jock's hand on my shoulder. "Wake up, Kip! Wake up!"

I groped for my toy weapon. "It's over there by the wall," Jock said, "but it ain't ever goin' to do you any good *now*."

I grabbed it. "What do you mean? Where's Tim?"

"You didn't wake up?"

"Huh?"

"This is what I've been scared of. Cripes, boy! I just had to talk to somebody. You slept through it?"

"Through what? And where's Tim?"

Jock was shivering and sweating. "They blue-lighted us, that's what. They took Tim." He shuddered. "I'm glad it was him. I thought—well, maybe you've noticed I'm a little stout . . . they like fat."

"What do you mean? What have they done with him?"

"Poor old Tim. He had his faults, like anybody, but— He's soup, by now . . . that's what." He shuddered again. "They like soup—bones and all."

"I don't believe it. You're trying to scare me."

"So?" He looked me up and down. "They'll probably take you next. Son, if you're smart, you'll take that letter opener of yours over to that horse trough and open your veins. It's better that way."

I said, "Why don't you? Here, I'll lend it to you."

He shook his head and shivered. "I ain't smart."

I don't know what became of Tim. I don't know whether the wormfaces ate people, or not. (You can't say "cannibal." We may be mutton, to them.) I wasn't especially scared because I had long since blown all fuses in my "scare" circuits.

What happens to my body after I'm through with it doesn't matter to me. But it did to Jock; he had a phobia about it. I don't think Jock was a coward; cowards don't even try to become prospectors on the Moon. He believed his theory and it shook him. He halfway admitted that he had more reason to believe it than I had known. He had been to Pluto once before, so he said, and other men who had come along, or been dragged, on that trip hadn't come back.

When feeding time came—two cans—he said he wasn't hungry and offered me his rations. That "night" he sat up and kept himself awake. Finally I just had to go to sleep before he did.

I awoke from one of those dreams where you can't move. The dream was correct; sometime not long before, I had surely been blue-lighted.

Jock was gone.

I never saw either of them again.

Somehow I missed them . . . Jock at least. It was a relief not to have to watch all the time, it was luxurious to bathe. But it gets mighty boring, pacing your cage alone.

I have no illusions about them. There must be well over three billion people I would rather be locked up with. But they were *people*.

Tim didn't have anything else to recommend him; he was as coldly vicious as a guillotine. But Jock had some slight awareness of right and wrong, or he wouldn't have tried to justify himself. You might say he was just weak.

But I don't hold with the idea that to understand all is to forgive all; you follow that and first thing you know you're sentimental over murderers and rapists and kidnappers and forgetting their victims. That's wrong. I'll weep over the likes of Peewee, not over criminals whose victims they are. I missed Jock's talk but if there were some way to drown such creatures at birth, I'd take my turn as executioner. That goes double for Tim.

If they ended up as soup for hobgoblins, I couldn't

honestly be sorry—even though it might be my turn tomorrow.

As soup, they probably had their finest hour.

Chapter 8

I was jarred out of useless brain-cudgeling by an explosion, a sharp *crack*—a bass rumble—then a *whoosh!* of reduced pressure. I bounced to my feet—anyone who has ever depended on a space suit is never again indifferent to a drop in pressure.

I gasped, "What the deuce!"

Then I added, "Whoever is on watch had better get on the ball—or we'll *all* be breathing thin cold stuff." No oxygen outside, I was sure—or rather the astronomers were and I didn't want to test it.

Then I said, "Somebody bombing us? I hope.

"Or was it an earthquake?"

This was not an idle remark. That *Scientific American* article concerning "summer" on Pluto had predicted "sharp isostatic readjustments" as the temperature rose —which is a polite way of saying, "Hold your hats! Here comes the chimney!"

I was in an earthquake once, in Santa Barbara; I didn't need a booster shot to remember what every Californian knows and others learn in one lesson: when the ground does a jig, *get outdoors!*

Only I couldn't.

I spent two minutes checking whether adrenalin had given me the strength to jump eighteen feet instead of twelve. It hadn't. That was all I did for a half-hour, if you don't count nail biting.

Then I heard my name! "Kip! Oh, Kip!"

"Peewee!" I screamed. "Here! *Peewee!*"

Silence for an eternity of three heartbeats— "Kip?"

"Down HERE!"

"Kip? Are you down this hole?"

"*Yes!* Can't you see me?" I saw her head against the light above.

"Uh, I can now. Oh, Kip, I'm so *glad!*"

"Then why are you crying? So am I!"

"I'm not crying," she blubbered. "Oh Kip . . . *Kip.*"

"Can you get me out?"

"Uh—" She surveyed that drop. "Stay where you are."

"*Don't go 'way!*" She already had.

She wasn't gone two minutes; it merely seemed like a week. Then she was back and the darling had a nylon rope!

"Grab on!" she shrilled.

"Wait a sec. How is it fastened?"

"I'll pull you up."

"No, you won't—or we'll *both* be down here. Find somewhere to belay it."

"I can lift you."

"Belay it! *Hurry!*"

She left again, leaving an end in my hands. Shortly I heard very faintly: "*On belay!*"

I shouted, "Testing!" and took up the slack. I put my weight on it—it held. "*Climbing!*" I yelled, and followed the final "g" up the hole and caught it.

She flung herself on me, an arm around my neck, one around Madame Pompadour, and both of mine around her. She was even smaller and skinnier than I remembered. "Oh, Kip, it's been *just awful.*"

I patted her bony shoulder blades. "Yeah, I know. What do we do now? Where's W—"

I started to say, "Where's Wormface?" but she burst into tears.

"Kip—I think she's *dead!*"

My mind skidded—I was a bit stir-crazy anyhow. "Huh? Who?"

She looked as amazed as I was confused. "Why, the Mother Thing."

"Oh." I felt a flood of sorrow. "But, honey, are you *sure?* She was talking to me all right up to the last—and *I* didn't die."

"What in the world are you talk— Oh. I don't mean *then*, Kip; I mean *now*."

"Huh? She was *here?*"

"Of course. Where else?"

Now that's a silly question, it's a big universe. I had decided long ago that the Mother Thing couldn't be here—because Jock had brushed off the subject. I reasoned that Jock would either have said that she was here or have invented an elaborate lie, for the pleasure of lying. Therefore she wasn't on his list—perhaps he had never seen her save as a bulge under my suit.

I was so sure of my "logic" that it took a long moment to throw off prejudice and accept fact. "Peewee," I said, gulping, "I feel like I'd lost my own mother. Are you sure?"

" 'Feel as if,' " she said automatically. "I'm not *sure* sure . . . but she's outside—so she *must* be dead."

"Wait a minute. If she's outside, she's wearing a space suit? Isn't she?"

"No, no! She hasn't had one—not since they destroyed her ship."

I was getting more confused. "How did they bring her in here?"

"They just sacked her and sealed her and carried her in. Kip—*what do we do now?*"

I knew several answers, all of them wrong—I had already considered them during my stretch in jail. "Where is Wormface? Where are all the wormfaces?"

"Oh. All dead. I think."

"I hope you're right." I looked around for a weapon and never saw a hallway so bare. My toy dagger was only eighteen feet away but I didn't feel like going back down for it. "What makes you think so?"

Peewee had reason to think so. The Mother Thing didn't look strong enough to tear paper but what she lacked in beef she made up in brains. She had done what I had tried to do: reasoned out a way to take them all on. She had not been able to hurry because her plan had many factors all of which had to mesh at once and many of them she could not influence; she had to wait for the breaks.

First, she needed a time when there were few wormfaces around. The base was indeed a large supply dump and space port and transfer point, but it did not need a large staff. It had been unusually crowded the few moments I had seen it, because our ship was in.

Second, it also had to be when no ships were in because she couldn't cope with a ship—she couldn't get at it.

Third, H-Hour had to be while the wormfaces were feeding. They all ate together when there were few enough not to have to use their mess hall in relays—crowded around one big tub and sopping it up, I gathered—a scene out of Dante. That would place all her enemies on one target, except possibly one or two on engineering or communication watches.

"Wait a minute!" I interrupted. "You said they were *all* dead?"

"Well . . . I don't know. I haven't seen any."

"Hold everything until I find something to fight with."

"But—"

"First things first, Peewee."

Saying that I was going to find a weapon wasn't finding one. That corridor had nothing but more holes like the one I had been down—which was why Peewee had looked for me there; it was one of the few places where she had not been allowed to wander at will. Jock had been correct on one point: Peewee—and the Mother Thing—had been star prisoners, allowed all privileges except freedom . . . whereas Jock and Tim and myself had been third-class prisoners and/or soup bones. It fitted the theory that Peewee and the Mother Thing were hostages rather than ordinary P.W.s.

I didn't explore those holes after I looked down one

and saw a human skeleton—maybe they got tired of tossing food to him. When I straightened up Peewee said, "What are you shaking about?"

"Nothing. Come on."

"I want to see."

"Peewee, every second counts and we've done nothing but yak. Come on. Stay behind me."

I kept her from seeing the skeleton, a major triumph over that little curiosity box—although it probably would not have affected her much; Peewee was sentimental only when it suited her.

"Stay behind me" had the correct gallant sound but it was not based on reason. I forgot that attack could come from the rear—I should have said: "Follow me and watch behind us."

She did anyway. I heard a squeal and whirled around to see a wormface with one of those camera-like things aimed at me. Even though Tim had used one on me I didn't realize what it was; for a moment I froze.

But not Peewee. She launched herself through the air, attacking with both hands and both feet in the gallant audacity and utter recklessness of a kitten.

That saved me. Her attack would not have hurt anything but another kitten but it mixed him up so that he didn't finish what he was doing, namely paralyzing or killing me; he tripped over her and went down.

And I stomped him. With my bare feet I stomped him, landing on that lobster-horror head with both feet.

His head *crunched*. It felt awful.

It was like jumping on a strawberry box. It splintered and crunched and went to pieces. I cringed at the feel, even though I was in an agony to fight, to kill. I trampled worms and hopped away, feeling sick. I scooped up Peewee and pulled her back, as anxious to get clear as I had been to join battle seconds before.

I hadn't killed it. For an awful moment I thought I

was going to have to wade back in. Then I saw that while it was alive, it did not seem aware of us. It flopped like a chicken freshly chopped, then quieted and began to move purposefully.

But it couldn't see. I had smashed its eyes and maybe its ears—but certainly those terrible eyes.

It felt around the floor carefully, then got to its feet, still undamaged except that its head was a crushed ruin. It stood still, braced tripod-style by that third appendage, and felt the air. I pulled us back farther.

It began to walk. Not toward us or I would have screamed. It moved away, ricocheted off a wall, straightened out, and went back the way we had come.

It reached one of those holes they used for prisoners, walked into it and dropped.

I sighed, and realized that I had been holding Peewee too tightly to breathe. I put her down.

"There's your weapon," she said.

"Huh?"

"On the floor. Just beyond where I dropped Madame Pompadour. The gadget." She went over, picked up her dolly, brushed away bits of ruined wormface, then took the camera-like thing and handed it to me. "Be careful. Don't point it toward you. Or me."

"Peewee," I said faintly, "don't you ever have an attack of nerves?"

"Sure I do. When I have leisure for it. Which isn't now. Do you know how to work it?"

"No. Do you?"

"I think so. I've seen them and the Mother Thing told me about them." She took it, handling it casually but not pointing it at either of us. "These holes on top—uncover one of them, it stuns. If you uncover them all, it kills. To make it work you push it *here*." She did and a bright blue light shot out, splashed against the wall. "The light doesn't do anything," she added. "It's for aiming. I hope there wasn't anybody on the other side of that wall. No, I hope there was. You know what I mean."

It looked like a cockeyed 35 mm. camera, with a lead lens—one built from an oral description. I took it, being very cautious where I pointed it, and looked at it. Then I tried it—full power, by mistake.

The blue light was a shaft in the air and the wall where it hit glowed and began to smoke. I shut it off.

"You wasted power," Peewee chided. "You may need it later."

"Well, I had to try it. Come on, let's go."

Peewee glanced at her Mickey Mouse watch—and I felt irked that it had apparently stood up when my fancy one had not. "There's very little time, Kip. Can't we assume that only this one escaped?"

"What? We certainly *cannot!* Until we're sure that all of them are dead, we can't do *anything* else. Come on."

"But— Well, I'll lead. I know my way around, you don't."

"No."

"Yes!"

So we did it her way; she led and carried the blue-light projector while I covered the rear and wished for a third eye, like a wormface. I couldn't argue that my reflexes were faster when they weren't, and she knew more than I did about our weapon.

But it's graveling, just the same.

The base was huge; half that mountain must have been honeycombed. We did it at a fast trot, ignoring things as complicated as museum exhibits and twice as interesting, simply making sure that no wormface was anywhere. Peewee ran with the weapon at the ready, talking twenty to the dozen and urging me on.

Besides an almost empty base, no ships in, and the wormfaces feeding, the Mother Thing's plan required that all this happen shortly before a particular hour of the Plutonian night.

"Why?" I panted.

"So she could signal her people, of course."

"But—" I shut up. I had wondered about the Mother Thing's people but didn't even know as much about her as I did about Wormface—except that she was everything that made her the Mother Thing. Now she was dead—Peewee said that she was outside without a space suit, so she was surely dead; that little soft warm thing wouldn't last two seconds in that ultra-arctic weather. Not to mention suffocation and lung hemorrhage. I choked up.

Of course, Peewee might be wrong. I had to admit that she rarely was—but this might be one of the times . . . in which case we would find her. But if we didn't find her, she was outside and— "Peewee, do you know where my space suit is?"

"Huh? Of course. Right next to where I got this." She patted the nylon rope, which she had coiled around her waist and tied with a bow.

"Then the second we are sure that we've cleaned out the wormfaces I'm going outside and look for her!"

"Yes, yes! But we've got to find *my* suit, too. I'm going with you."

No doubt she would. Maybe I could persuade her to wait in the tunnel out of that bone-freezing wind. "Peewee, why did she have to send her message at night? To a ship in a rotation-period orbit? Or is there—"

My words were chopped off by a rumble. The floor shook in that loose-bearing vibration that frightens people and animals alike. We stopped dead. "What was that?" Peewee whispered.

I swallowed. "Unless it's part of this rumpus the Mother Thing planned—"

"It isn't. I think."

"It's a quake."

"An earthquake?"

"A Pluto quake. Peewee, we've got to get out of here!" I wasn't thinking about *where*—you don't in a quake.

Peewee gulped. "We can't bother with earthquakes; we haven't time. Hurry, Kip, hurry!" She started to run and I followed, gritting my teeth. If Peewee could ignore a quake, so could I—though it's like ignoring a rattlesnake in bed.

"Peewee . . . Mother Thing's people . . . is their ship in orbit around Pluto?"

"What? Oh, no, no! They're not in a ship."

"Then why at night? Something about the Heaviside layers here? How far away is their base?" I was wondering how far a man could walk here. We had done almost forty miles on the Moon. Could we do forty blocks here? Or even forty yards? You could insulate your feet, probably. But that wind— "Peewee, they don't *live* here, do they?"

"What? Don't be silly! They have a nice planet of their own. Kip, if you keep asking foolish questions, we'll be too late. Shut up and listen."

I shut up. What follows I got in snatches as we ran, and some of it later. When the Mother Thing had been captured, she had lost ship, space clothing, communicator, everything; Wormface had destroyed it all. There had been treachery, capture through violation of truce while parleying. "He grabbed her when they were supposed to be under a King's 'X' " was Peewee's indignant description, "and that's not fair! He had promised."

Treachery would be as natural in Wormface as venom in a Gila monster; I was surprised that the Mother Thing had risked a palaver with him. It left her a prisoner of ruthless monsters equipped with ships that made ours look like horseless carriages, weapons which started with a "death ray" and ended heaven knows where, plus bases, organization, supplies.

She had only her brain and her tiny soft hands.

Before she could use the rare combination of circumstances necessary to have any chance at all she had to replace her communicator (I think of it as her "radio" but it was more than that) and she had to have weapons. The only way she could get them was to build them.

She had nothing, not a bobby pin—only that triangular ornament with spirals engraved on it. To build anything she had to gain access to a series of rooms which I would describe as electronics labs—not that they looked like the bench where I jiggered with electronics, but electron-pushing has its built-in logic. If electrons are to do what you want them to, components have to look pretty much a certain way, whether built by humans, wormfaces, or the Mother Thing. A wave guide gets its shape from the laws of nature, an inductance has its necessary geometry, no matter who the technician is.

So it looked like an electronics lab—a very good one. It had gear I did not recognize, but which I felt I could understand if I had time. I got only a glimpse.

The Mother Thing spent many, many hours there. She would not have been permitted there, even though she was a prisoner-at-large with freedom in most ways and anything she wanted, including private quarters with Peewee. I think that Wormface was afraid of her, even though she was a prisoner—he did not want to offend her unnecessarily.

She got the run of their shops by baiting their cupidity. Her people had many things that wormfaces had not —gadgets, inventions, conveniences. She began by inquiring why they did a thing this way rather than another way which was so much more efficient? A tradition? Or religious reasons?

When asked what she meant she looked helpless and protested that she couldn't *explain*—which was a shame because it was simple and so easy to build, too.

Under close chaperonage she built something. The gadget worked. Then something else. Presently she was in the labs daily, making things for her captors, things that delighted them. She always delivered; the privilege depended on it.

But each gadget involved parts she needed herself.

"She sneaked bits and pieces into her pouch," Peewee told me. "They never knew exactly what she was doing. She would use five of a thing and the sixth would go into her pouch."

"Her pouch?"

"Of course. That's where she hid the 'brain' the time she and I swiped the ship. Didn't you know?"

"I didn't know she had a pouch."

"Well, neither did they. They watched to see she didn't carry anything out of the shop—and she never did. Not where it showed."

"Uh, Peewee, is the Mother Thing a marsupial?"

"Huh? Like possums? You don't have to be a marsupial to have a pouch. Look at squrrels, they have pouches in their cheeks."

"Mmm, yes."

"She sneaked a bit now and a bit then, and I swiped things, too. During rest time she worked on them in our room."

The Mother Thing had not slept all the time we had been on Pluto. She worked long hours publicly, making things for wormfaces—a stereotelephone no bigger than a pack of cigarettes, a tiny beetle-like arrangement that crawled all over anything it was placed on and integrated the volume, many other things. But during hours set apart for rest she worked for herself, usually in darkness, those tiny fingers busy as a blind watchmaker's.

She made two bombs and a long-distance communicator-and-beacon.

I didn't get all this tossed over Peewee's shoulder while we raced through the base; she simply told me that the Mother Thing had managed to build a radio-beacon and had been responsible for the explosion I had felt. And that we must hurry, hurry, *hurry!*

"Peewee," I said, panting. "What's the rush? If the Mother Thing is outside, I want to bring her in—her body, I mean. But you act as if we had a deadline."

"We do!"

The communicator-beacon had to be placed outside at a particular local time (the Plutonian day is about a week—the astronomers were right again) so that the planet itself would not blanket the beam. But the Mother Thing had no space suit. They had discussed having Peewee suit up, go outside, and set the beacon—it had been so designed that Peewee need only trigger it. But that depended on locating Peewee's space suit, then breaking in and getting it after the wormfaces were disposed of.

They had never located it. The Mother Thing had said serenely, singing confident notes that I could almost hear ringing in my head: ("Never mind, dear. I can go out and set it myself.")

"Mother Thing! You *can't!*" Peewee had protested. "It's *cold* out there."

("I shan't be long.")

"You won't be able to *breathe.*"

("It won't be necessary, for so short a time.")

That settled it. In her own way, the Mother Thing was as hard to argue with as Wormface.

The bombs were built, the beacon was built, a time approached when all factors would match—no ship expected, few wormfaces, Pluto faced the right way, feeding time for the staff—and they still did not know where Peewee's suit was—if it had not been destroyed. The Mother Thing resolved to go ahead.

"But she told me, just a few hours ago when she let me know that today was the day, that if she did not come back in ten minutes or so, that she hoped I could find my suit and trigger the beacon—if she hadn't been able to." Peewee started to cry. "That was the f- f- first time she admitted that she wasn't sure she could do it!"

"Peewee! Stop it! Then what?"

"I waited for the explosions—they came, right together —and I started to search, places I hadn't been allowed to go. But I *couldn't* find my suit! Then I found you and —oh, Kip, she's been out there almost an hour!" She looked at her watch. "There's only about twenty minutes left. If the beacon isn't triggered by then, she's had all her trouble and died for n- n- nothing! She wouldn't *like* that."

"Where's my suit!"

We found no more wormfaces—apparently there was only one on duty while the others fed. Peewee showed me a door, air-lock type, behind which was the feeding chamber—the bomb may have cracked that section for gas-tight doors had closed themselves when the owners were blown to bits. We hurried past.

Logical as usual, Peewee ended our search at my space suit. It was one of more than a dozen human-type suits—I wondered how much soup those ghouls ate. Well, they wouldn't eat again! I wasted no time; I simply shouted, "Hi, Oscar!" and started to suit up.

("Where you been, chum?")

Oscar seemed in perfect shape. Fats' suit was next to mine and Tim's next to it; I glanced at them as I stretched Oscar out, wondering whether they had equipment I could use. Peewee was looking at Tim's suit. "Maybe I can wear this."

It was much smaller than Oscar, which made it only nine sizes too big for Peewee. "Don't be silly! It'd fit you like socks on a rooster. Help me. Take off that rope, coil it and clip it to my belt."

"You won't need it. The Mother Thing planned to take the beacon out the walkway about a hundred yards and sit it down. If she didn't manage it, that's all you do. Then twist the stud on top."

"Don't argue! How much time?"

"Yes, Kip. Eighteen minutes."

"Those winds are strong," I added. "I may need the line." The Mother Thing didn't weigh much. If she had been swept off, I might need a rope to recover her body. "Hand me that hammer off Fats' suit."

"Right away!"

I stood up. It felt good to have Oscar around me. Then I remembered how *cold* my feet got, walking in from the ship. "I wish I had asbestos boots."

Peewee looked startled. "Wait right here!" She was gone before I could stop her. I went on sealing up while I worried—she hadn't even stopped to pick up the projector weapon. Shortly I said, "Tight, Oscar?"

("Tight, boy!")

Chin valve okay, blood-color okay, radio—I wouldn't need it—water— The tank was dry. No matter, I wouldn't have time to grow thirsty. I worked the chin valve, making the pressure low because I knew that pressure outdoors was quite low.

Peewee returned with what looked like ballet slippers for a baby elephant. She leaned close to my face plate and shouted, "They wear these. Can you get them on?" It seemed unlikely, but I forced them over my feet like badly fitting socks. I stood up and found that they improved traction; they were clumsy but not hard to walk in.

A minute later we were standing at the exit of the big room I had first seen. Its air-lock doors were closed now as a result of the Mother Thing's other bomb, which she had placed to blow out the gate-valve panels in the tunnel beyond. The bomb in the feeding chamber had been planted by Peewee who had then ducked back to their room. I don't know whether the Mother Thing timed the two bombs to go off together, or triggered them by remote-control—nor did it matter; they had made a shambles of Wormface's fancy base.

Peewee knew how to waste air through the air lock. When the inner door opened I shouted, "Time?"

"Fourteen minutes." She held up her watch.

"Remember what I said, just stay here. If anything moves, blue-light it first and ask questions afterwards."

"I remember."

I stepped in and closed the inner door, found the valve in the outer door, waited for pressure to equalize.

The two or three minutes it took that big lock to bleed off I spent in glum thought. I didn't like leaving Peewee alone. I *thought* all wormfaces were dead, but I wasn't sure. We had searched hastily; one could have zigged when we zagged—they were so fast.

Besides that, Peewee had said, "I remember," when she should have said, "Okay, Kip, I will." A slip of the tongue? That flea-hopping mind made "slips" only when it wanted to. There is a world of difference between "Roger" and "Wilco."

Besides I was doing this for foolish motives. Mostly I was going out to recover the Mother Thing's body—folly, because after I brought her in, she would spoil. It would be kinder to leave her in natural deep-freeze.

But I couldn't bear that—it was cold out there and I couldn't leave her out in the cold. She had been so little and warm . . . so alive. I had to bring her in where she could get warm.

You're in bad shape when your emotions force you into acts which you know are foolish.

Worse still, I was doing this in a reckless rush because the Mother Thing had wanted that beacon set before a certain second, now only twelve minutes away, maybe ten. Well, I'd do it, but what sense was it? Say her home star is close by—oh, say it's Proxima Centauri and the wormfaces came from somewhere farther. Even if her beacon works—it still takes over four years for her S.O.S. to reach her friends!

This might have been okay for the Mother Thing. I had an impression that she lived a very long time; waiting a few years for rescue might not bother her. But Peewee and I were not creatures of her sort. We'd be dead before that speed-of-light message crawled to Proxima Centauri. I was glad that I had seen Peewee again, but I knew what was in store for us. Death, in days, weeks, or months at most, from running out of air, or water, or food—or a wormface ship might land before we died—which meant one unholy sabbat of a fight in which, if we were lucky, we would die quickly.

No matter how you figured, planting that beacon was merely "carrying out the deceased's last wishes"— words you hear at funerals. Sentimental folly.

The outer door started to open. *Ave,* Mother Thing! *Nos morituri—*

It was *cold* out there, biting cold, even though I was not yet in the wind. The glow panels were still working and I could see that the tunnel was a mess; the two dozen fractional-pressure stops had ruptured like eardrums. I wondered what sort of bomb could be hay-wired from stolen parts, kept small enough to conceal two in a body pouch along with some sort of radio rig, and nevertheless have force enough to blow out those panels. The blast had rattled my teeth, several hundred feet away in solid rock.

The first dozen panels were blown inwards. Had she set it off in the middle of the tunnel? A blast that big would fling her away like a feather! She must have planted it there, then come inside and triggered it—then gone back through the lock just as I had. That was the only way I could see it.

It got colder every step. My feet weren't too cold yet,

those clumsy mukluks were okay; the wormfaces understood insulation. "Oscar, you got the fires burning?"

("Roaring, chum. It's a cold night.")

"You're telling me!"

Just beyond the outermost burst panel, I found her. She had sunk forward, as if too tired to go on. Her arms stretched in front of her and, on the floor of the tunnel not quite touched by her tiny fingers, was a small round box about the size ladies keep powder in on dressing tables.

Her face was composed and her eyes were open except that nictitating membranes were drawn across as they had been when I had first seen her in the pasture back of our house, a few days or weeks or a thousand years ago. But she had been hurt then and looked it; now I half expected her to draw back those inner lids and sing a welcome.

I touched her.

She was hard as ice and much colder.

I blinked back tears and wasted not a moment. She wanted that little box placed a hundred yards out on the causeway and the bump on top twisted—and she wanted it done in the next six or seven minutes. I scooped it up. "Righto, Mother Thing! On my way!"

("Get cracking, chum!")

("Thank you, dear Kip. . . .")

I don't believe in ghosts. I had heard her sing thank-you so many times that the notes echoed in my head.

A few feet away at the mouth of the tunnel, I stopped. The wind hit me and was so cold that the deathly chill in the tunnel seemed summery. I closed my eyes and counted thirty seconds to give time to adjust to starlight while I fumbled on the windward side of the tunnel at a slanting strut that anchored the causeway to the mountain, tied my safety line by passing it around the strut and snapping it back on itself. I had known that it was night outside and I expected the causeway to stand out as a black ribbon against the white "snow" glittering under a skyful of stars. I thought I would be safer on that windswept way if I could see its edges—which I couldn't by headlamp unless I kept swinging my shoulders back and forth—clumsy and likely to throw me off balance or slow me down.

I had figured this carefully; I didn't regard this as a stroll in the garden—not at night, not on Pluto! So I counted thirty seconds and tied my line while waiting for eyes to adjust to starlight. I opened them.

And I couldn't see a darned thing!

Not a star. Not even the difference between sky and ground. My back was to the tunnel and the helmet shaded my face like a sunbonnet; I should have been able to see the walkway. Nothing.

I turned the helmet and saw something that accounted both for black sky and the quake we had felt—an active volcano. It may have been five miles away or fifty, but I could not doubt what it was—a jagged, angry red scar low in the sky.

But I didn't stop to stare. I switched on the headlamp, splashed it on the righthand windward edge, and started a clumsy trot, keeping close to that side, so that if I stumbled I would have the entire road to recover in before the wind could sweep me off. That wind scared me. I kept the line coiled in my left hand and paid it out as I went, keeping it fairly taut. The coil felt stiff in my fingers.

The wind not only frightened me, it *hurt*. It was a cold so intense that it felt like flame. It burned and blasted, then numbed. My right side, getting the brunt of it, began to go and then my left side hurt more than the right.

I could no longer feel the line. I stopped, leaned forward and got the coil in the light from the headlamp—that's another thing that needs fixing! the headlamp should swivel.

The coil was half gone, I had come a good fifty yards. I was depending on the rope to tell me; it was a hundred-meter climbing line, so when I neared its end I would be as far out as the Mother Thing had wanted. Hurry, Kip!

("Get cracking, boy! It's cold out here.")

I stopped again. *Did I have the box?*

I couldn't feel it. But the headlamp showed my right hand clutched around it. Stay there, fingers! I hurried on, counting steps. One! Two! Three! Four! ...

When I reached forty I stopped and glanced over the edge, saw that I was at the highest part where the road crossed the brook and remembered that it was about midway. That brook—methane, was it?—was frozen solid, and I *knew* that the night was cold.

There were a few loops of line on my left arm—close enough. I dropped the line, moved cautiously to the middle of the way, eased to my knees and left hand, and started to put the box down.

My fingers wouldn't unbend.

I forced them with my left hand, got the box out of my fist. That diabolical wind caught it and I barely saved it from rolling away. With both hands I set it carefully upright.

("Work your fingers, bud. Pound your hands together!")

I did so. I could tighten the muscles of my forearms, though it was tearing agony to flex fingers. Clumsily steadying the box with my left hand, I groped for the little knob on top.

I couldn't feel it but it turned easily once I managed to close my fingers on it; I could see it turn.

It seemed to come to life, to purr. Perhaps I heard vibration, through gloves and up my suit; I certainly couldn't have felt it, not the shape my fingers were in. I hastily let go, got awkwardly to my feet and backed up, so that I could splash the headlamp on it without leaning over.

I was through, the Mother Thing's job was done, and (I hoped) before deadline. If I had had as much sense as the ordinary doorknob, I would have turned and hurried into the tunnel faster than I had come out.

But I was fascinated by what it was doing.

It seemed to shake itself and three spidery little legs grew out the bottom. It raised up until it was standing on its own little tripod, about a foot high. It shook itself again and I thought the wind would blow it over. But the spidery legs splayed out, seemed to bite into the road surface and it was rock firm.

Something lifted and unfolded out the top.

It opened like a flower, until it was about eight inches across. A finger lifted (an antenna?), swung as if hunting, steadied and pointed at the sky.

Then the beacon switched on. I'm sure that is what happened although all I saw was a flash of light—parasitic it must have been, for light alone would not have served even without that volcanic overcast. It was probably some harmless side effect of switching on an enormous pulse of power, something the Mother Thing hadn't had time, or perhaps equipment or materials, to eliminate or shield. It was about as bright as a peanut photoflash.

But I was looking at it. Polarizers can't work that fast. It blinded me.

I thought my headlamp had gone out, then I realized that I simply couldn't see through a big greenish-purple disc of dazzle.

("Take it easy, boy. It's just an after-image. Wait and it'll go away.")

"I can't wait! I'm freezing to death!"

("Hook the line with your forearm, where it's clipped to your belt. Pull on it.")

I did as Oscar told me, found the line, turned around, started to wind it on both forearms.

It shattered.

It did not break as you expect rope to break; it shattered like glass. I suppose that is what it was by then—glass, I mean. Nylon and glass are super-cooled liquids.

Now I know what "super-cooled" means.

But all I knew then was that my last link with life had gone. I couldn't see, I couldn't hear, I was all alone on a bare platform, billions of miles from home, and a wind out of the depths of a frozen hell was bleeding the last life out of a body I could barely feel—and where I *could* feel, it hurt like fire.

"Oscar!"

("I'm here, bud. You can make it. Now—can you see anything?")

"No!"

("Look for the mouth of the tunnel. It's got light in it. Switch off your headlamp. Sure, you can—it's just a toggle switch. Drag your hand back across the right side of our helmet.")

I did.

("See anything?")

"Not yet."

("Move your head. Try to catch it in the corner of your eye—the dazzle stays in front, you know. Well?")

"I caught something that time!"

("Reddish, wasn't it? Jagged, too. The volcano. Now we know which way we're facing. Turn slowly and catch the mouth of the tunnel as it goes by.")

Slowly was the only way I could turn. "There it is!"

("Okay, you're headed home. Get down on your hands and knees and crab slowly to your left. Don't turn—because you want to hang onto that edge and *crawl.* Crawl toward the tunnel.")

I got down. I couldn't feel the surface with my hands but I felt pressure on my limbs, as if all four were artificial. I found the edge when my left hand slipped over it and I almost fell off. But I recovered. "Am I headed right?"

("Sure you are. You haven't turned. You've just moved sideways. Can you lift your head to see the tunnel?")

"Uh, not without standing up."

("Don't do that! Try the headlamp again. Maybe your eyes are okay now.")

I dragged my hand forward against the right side of the helmet. I must have hit the switch, for suddenly I saw a circle of light, blurred and cloudy in the middle. The edge of the walkway sliced it on the left.

("Good boy! No, don't get up; you're weak and dizzy and likely to fall. Start crawling. Count 'em. Three hundred ought to do it.")

I started crawling, counting.

"It's a long way, Oscar. You think we can make it?"

("Of course we can! You think I want to be left out *here?*")

"I'd be with you."

("Knock off the chatter. You'll make me lose count. Thirty-six . . . thirty-seven . . . thirty-eight—")

We crawled.

("That's a hundred. Now we double it. Hundred one . . . hundred two . . . hundred three—")

"I'm feeling better, Oscar. I think it's getting warmer."

("*WHAT!*")

"I said I'm feeling a little warmer."

("You're not warmer, you blistering idiot! That's freeze-to-death you're feeling! Crawl faster! Work your chin valve. Get more air. Le' me hear that chin valve click!")

I was too tired to argue; I chinned the valve three or four times, felt a blast blistering my face.

("I'm stepping up the stroke. Warmer indeed! Hund'd *nine* . . . hund'd *ten* . . . hun'*leven* . . . hun'-*twelve*—pick it up!")

At two hundred I said I would just have to rest.

("No, you don't!")

"But I've *got* to. Just a little while."

("Like that, uh? You know what happens. What's Peewee goin' to do? She's in there, waiting. She's already scared because you're late. What's she goin' to *do?* Answer me!")

"Uh . . . she's going to try to wear Tim's suit."

("Right! In case of duplicate answers the prize goes to the one postmarked first. How far will she get? *You* tell *me*.")

"Uh . . . to the mouth of the tunnel, I guess. Then the wind will get her."

("My opinion exactly. Then we'll have the whole family together. You, me, the Mother Thing, Peewee. Cozy. A family of stiffs.")

"But—"

("So start slugging, brother. Slug . . . slug . . . slug . . . slug . . . tw'und'd *five* . . . two'und'd *six* . . . tw'und'd *sev'n'—*")

I don't remember falling off. I don't even know what the "snow" felt like. I just remember being glad that the dreadful counting was over and I could rest.

But Oscar wouldn't let me. ("Kip! *Kip!* Get up! Climb back on the straight and narrow.")

"Go 'way."

("I *can't* go away. I wish I could. Right in front of you. Grab the edge and scramble up. It's only a little farther now.")

I managed to raise my head, saw the edge of the walkway in the light of my headlamp about two feet above my head. I sank back. "It's too high," I said listlessly. "Oscar, I think we've had it."

He snorted. ("So? Who was it, just the other day, cussed out a little bitty girl who was too tired to get up? 'Commander Comet,' wasn't it? Did I get the name right? The 'Scourge of the Spaceways' . . . the no-good lazy sky tramp. 'Have Space Suit—Will Travel.' Before you go to sleep, Commander, can I have your autograph! I've never met a real live space pirate before . . . one that goes around hijacking ships and kidnapping little girls.")

"That's not fair!"

("Okay, okay, I know when I'm not wanted. But just one thing before I leave: she's got more guts in her little finger than you have in your whole body—you lying, fat, lazy swine! Good-bye. Don't wait up.")

"Oscar! Don't leave me!"

("Eh? You want help?")

"Yes!"

("Well, if it's too high to reach, grab your hammer and hook it over the edge. Pull yourself up.")

I blinked. Maybe it would work. I reached down, decided I had the hammer even though I couldn't feel it, got it loose. Using both hands I hooked it over the edge above me. I pulled.

That silly hammer broke just like the line. Tool steel—and it went to pieces as if it had been cast out of type slugs.

That made me mad. I heaved myself to a sitting position, got both elbows on the edge, and struggled and groaned and burst into fiery sweat—and rolled over onto the road surface.

("That's my boy! Never mind counting, just crawl toward the light!")

The tunnel wavered in front of me. I couldn't get my breath, so I kicked the chin valve.

Nothing happened.

"Oscar! The chin valve is stuck!" I tried again.

Oscar was very slow in answering. ("No, pal, the valve isn't stuck. Your air hoses have frozen up. I guess that last batch wasn't as dry as it could have been.")

"I haven't any *air!*"

Again he was slow. But he answered firmly, ("Yes,

you have. You've got a whole suit full. Plenty for the few feet left.")

"I'll never make it."

("A few feet, only. There's the Mother Thing, right ahead of you. Keep moving.")

I raised my head and, sure enough, there she was. I kept crawling, while she got bigger and bigger. Finally I said, "Oscar . . . this is as far as I go."

("I'm afraid it is. I've let you down . . . but thanks for not leaving me outside there.")

"You didn't let me down . . . you were *swell*. I just didn't quite make it."

("I guess we both didn't quite make it . . . but we sure let 'em know that we tried! So long, partner.")

"So long. *¡Hasta la vista, amigo!*" I managed to crawl two short steps and collapsed with my head near the Mother Thing's head.

She was smiling. ("Hello, Kip my son.")

"I didn't . . . quite make it, Mother Thing. I'm sorry."

("Oh, but you *did* make it!")

"Huh?"

("Between us, we've both made it.")

I thought about that for a long time. "And Oscar."

("And Oscar, of course.")

"And Peewee."

("And always Peewee. We've all made it. Now we can rest, dear.")

"G'night . . . Mother Thing."

It was a darn short rest. I was just closing my eyes, feeling warm and happy that the Mother Thing thought that I had done all right—when Peewee started shaking my shoulder. She touched helmets. "Kip! *Kip!* Get up. *Please* get up."

"Huh? Why?"

"Because I can't *carry* you! I tried, but I can't do it. You're just *too big!*"

I considered it. Of course she couldn't carry me—where did she get the silly notion that she could? I was twice her size. I'd carry her . . . just as soon as I caught my breath.

"*Kip! Please* get up." She was crying now, blubbering.

"Why, sure, honey," I said gently, "if that's what you want." I tried and had a clumsy bad time of it. She almost picked me up, she helped a lot. Once up, she steadied me.

"Turn around. Walk."

She almost did carry me. She got her shoulders under my right arm and kept pushing. Every time we came to one of those blown-out panels she either helped me step over, or simply pushed me through and helped me up again.

At last we were in the lock and she was bleeding air from inside to fill it. She had to let go of me and I sank down. She turned when the inner door opened, started to say something—then got my helmet off in a hurry.

I took a deep breath and got very dizzy and the lights dimmed.

She was looking at me. "You all right now?"

"Me? Sure! Why shouldn't I be?"

"Let me help you inside."

I couldn't see why, but she did help and I needed it. She sat me on the floor near the door with my back to the wall—I didn't want to lie down. "Kip, I was so scared!"

"Why?" I couldn't see what she was worried about. Hadn't the Mother Thing said that we had all done all right?

"Well, I was. I shouldn't have let you go out."

"But the beacon had to be set."

"Oh, but— You set it?"

"Of course. The Mother Thing was pleased."

"I'm sure she would have been," she said gravely.

"She was."

"Can I do anything? Can I help you out of your suit?"

"Uh . . . no, not yet. Could you find me a drink of water?"

"Right away!"

She came back and held it for me—I wasn't as thirsty as I had thought; it made me a bit ill. She watched me for some time, then said, "Do you mind if I'm gone a little while? Will you be all right?"

"Me? Certainly." I didn't feel well, I was beginning to hurt, but there wasn't anything she could do.

"I won't be long." She began clamping her helmet and I noticed with detached interest that she was wearing her own suit—somehow I had had the impression that she had been wearing Tim's.

I saw her head for the lock and realized where she was going and why. I wanted to tell her that the Mother Thing would rather not be inside here, where she might . . . where she might—I didn't want to say "spoil" even to myself.

But Peewee was gone.

I don't think she was away more than five minutes. I had closed my eyes and I am not sure. I noticed the inner door open. Through it stepped Peewee, carrying the Mother Thing in her arms like a long piece of firewood. She didn't bend at all.

Peewee put the Mother Thing on the floor in the same position I had last seen her, then unclamped her helmet and bawled.

I couldn't get up. My legs hurt too much. And my arms. "Peewee . . . please, honey. It doesn't do any good."

She raised her head. "I'm all through. I won't cry any more."

And she didn't.

We sat there a long time. Peewee again offered to

help me out of my suit, but when we tried it, I hurt so terribly, especially my hands and my feet, that I had to ask her to stop. She looked worried. "Kip . . . I'm afraid you froze them."

"Maybe. But there's nothing to do about it now." I winced and changed the subject. "Where did you find your suit?"

"Oh!" She looked indignant, then almost gay. "You'd *never* guess. Inside Jock's suit."

"No, I guess I wouldn't. 'The Purloined Letter.'"

"The what?"

"Nothing. I hadn't realized that old Wormface had a sense of humor."

Shortly after that we had another quake, a bad one. Chandeliers would have jounced if the place had had any and the floor heaved. Peewee squealed. "Oh! That was almost as bad as the last one."

"A lot worse, I'd say. That first little one wasn't anything."

"No, I mean the one while you were outside."

"Was there one then?"

"Didn't you feel it?"

"No." I tried to remember. "Maybe that was when I fell off in the snow."

"You fell off? Kip!"

"It was all right. Oscar helped me."

There was another ground shock. I wouldn't have minded, only it shook me up and made me hurt worse. I finally came out of the fog enough to realize that I didn't have to hurt.

Let's see, medicine pills were on the right and the codeine dispenser was farthest back— "Peewee? Could I trouble you for some water again?"

"Of course!"

"I'm going to take codeine. It may make me sleep. Do you mind?"

"You ought to sleep if you can. You need it."

"I suppose so. What time is it?"

She told me and I couldn't believe it. "You mean it's been more than twelve hours?"

"Huh? Since what?"

"Since this started."

"I don't understand, Kip." She stared at her watch. "It has been exactly an hour and a half since I found you—not quite two hours since the Mother Thing set off the bombs."

I couldn't believe that, either. But Peewee insisted that she was right.

The codeine made me feel much better and I was beginning to be drowsy, when Peewee said, "Kip, do you smell anything?"

I sniffed. "Something like kitchen matches?"

"That's what I mean. I think the pressure is dropping, too. Kip . . . I think I had better close your helmet—if you're going to sleep."

"All right. You close yours, too?"

"Yes. Uh, I don't think this place is tight any longer."

"You may be right." Between explosions and quakes, I didn't see how it could be. But, while I knew what that meant, I was too weary and sick—and getting too dreamy from the drug—to worry. Now, or a month from now—what did it matter? The Mother Thing had said everything was okay.

Peewee clamped us in, we checked radios, and she sat down facing me and the Mother Thing. She didn't say anything for a long time. Then I heard: "Peewee to Junebug—"

"I read you, Peewee."

"Kip? It's been fun, mostly. Hasn't it?"

"Huh?" I glanced up, saw that the dial said I had about four hours of air left. I had had to reduce pressure twice, since we closed up, to match falling pressure in the room. "Yes, Peewee, it's been swell. I wouldn't have missed it for the world."

She sighed. "I just wanted to be sure you weren't blaming me. Now go to sleep."

I did almost go to sleep, when I saw Peewee jump up and my phones came to life. "Kip! Something's coming in the door!"

I came wide awake, realized what it meant. Why couldn't they have let us be? A few hours, anyhow? "Peewee. Don't panic. Move to the far side of the door. You've got your blue-light gadget?"

"Yes."

"Pick them off as they come in."

"You've got to move, Kip. You're right where they will come!"

"I can't get up." I hadn't been able to move, not even my arms, for quite a while. "Use low power, then if you brush me, it won't matter. Do what I say! *Fast!*"

"Yes, Kip." She got where she could snipe at them sideways, raised her projector and waited.

The inner door opened, a figure came in. I saw Peewee start to nail it—and I called into my radio: *"Don't shoot!"*

But she was dropping the projector and running forward even as I shouted.

They were "mother thing" people.

It took six of them to carry me, only two to carry the Mother Thing. They sang to me soothingly all the time they were rigging a litter. I swallowed another codeine tablet before they lifted me, as even with their gentleness any movement hurt. It didn't take long to get me into their ship, for they had landed almost at the tunnel mouth, no doubt crushing the walkway—I hoped so.

Once I was safely inside Peewee opened my helmet and unzipped the front of my suit. "Kip! Aren't they *wonderful?*"

"Yes." I was getting dizzier from the drug but was feeling better. "When do we raise ship?"

"We've already started."

"They're taking us home?" I'd have to tell Mr. Charton what a big help the codeine was.

"Huh? Oh, my, no! We're headed for Vega."

I fainted.

Chapter 9

I had been dreaming that I was home; this awoke me with a jerk. "Mother Thing!"

("Good morning, my son. I am happy to see that you are feeling better.")

"Oh, I feel fine. I've had a good night's rest—" I stared, then blurted: "—you're *dead!*" I couldn't stop it.

Her answer sounded warmly, gently humorous, the way you correct a child who has made a natural mistake. ("No, dear, I was merely frozen. I am not as frail as you seem to think me.")

I blinked and looked again. "Then it wasn't a dream?"

("No, it was not a dream.")

"I thought I was home and—" I tried to sit up, managed only to raise my head. "I *am* home!" *My* room! Clothes closet on the left—hall door behind the Mother Thing—my desk on the right, piled with books and with a Centerville High pennant over it—window beyond it, with the old elm almost filling it—sun-speckled leaves stirring in a breeze.

My slipstick was where I had left it.

Things started to wobble, then I figured it out. I had dreamed only the silly part at the end. Vega—I had been groggy with codeine. "You brought me *home.*"

("We brought you home . . . to your other home. My home.")

The bed started to sway. I clutched at it but my arms didn't move. The Mother Thing was still singing. ("You needed your own nest. So we prepared it.")

"Mother Thing, I'm confused."

("We know that a bird grows well faster in its own nest. So we built yours.") "Bird" and "nest" weren't what she sang, but an Unabridged won't give anything closer.

I took a deep breath to steady down. I understood her—that's what she was best at, making you understand. This wasn't my room and I wasn't home; it simply looked like it. But I was still terribly confused.

I looked around and wondered how I could have been mistaken.

The light slanted in the window from a wrong direction. The ceiling didn't have the patch in it from the time I built a hide-out in the attic and knocked plaster down by hammering. It wasn't the right shade, either.

The books were too neat and clean; they had that candy-box look. I couldn't recognize the bindings. The over-all effect was mighty close, but details were not right.

("I like this room,") the Mother Thing was singing. ("It looks like you, Kip.")

"Mother Thing," I said weakly, "*how* did you do it?"

("We asked you. And Peewee helped.")

I thought, "But Peewee has never seen my room either," then decided that Peewee had seen enough American homes to be a consulting expert. "Peewee is here?"

("She'll be in shortly.")

With Peewee and the Mother Thing around things couldn't be too bad. Except— "Mother Thing, I can't move my arms and legs."

She put a tiny, warm hand on my forehead and leaned over me until her enormous, lemur-like eyes blanked out everything else. ("You have been damaged. Now you are growing well. Do not worry.")

When the Mother Thing tells you not to worry, you don't. I didn't want to do handstands anyhow; I was satisfied to look into her eyes. You could sink into them, you could have dived in and swum around. "All right, Mother Thing." I remembered something else. "Say ... you *were* frozen? Weren't you?"

("Yes.")

"But— Look, when water freezes it ruptures living cells. Or so they say."

She answered primly, ("My body would never permit *that!*")

"Well—" I thought about it. "Just don't dunk *me* in liquid air! I'm not built for it."

Again her song held roguish, indulgent humor. ("We shall endeavor not to hurt you.") She straightened up and grew a little, swaying like a willow. ("I sense Peewee.")

There was a knock—another discrepancy; it didn't sound like a knock on a light-weight interior door—and Peewee called out, "May I come in?" She didn't wait (I wondered if she ever did) but came on in. The bit I could see past her looked like our upper hall; they'd done a thorough job.

("Come in, dear.")

"Sure, Peewee. You *are* in."

"Don't be captious."

"Look who's talking. Hi, kid!"

"Hi yourself."

The Mother Thing glided away. ("Don't stay long, Peewee. You are not to tire him.")

"I won't, Mother Thing."

(" 'Bye, dears.")

I said, "What are the visiting hours in this ward?"

"When *she* says, of course." Peewee stood facing me, fists on hips. She was really clean for the first time in our acquaintance—cheeks pink with scrubbing, hair fluffy—maybe she would be pretty, in about ten years. She was dressed as always but her clothes were fresh, all buttons present, and tears invisibly mended.

"Well," she said, letting out her breath, "I guess you're going to be worth keeping, after all."

"Me? I'm in the pink. How about yourself?"

She wrinkled her nose. "A little frost nip. Nothing. But you were a *mess.*"

"I was?"

"I can't use adequate language without being what Mama calls 'unladylike.' "

"Oh, we wouldn't want you to be *that.*"

"Don't be sarcastic. You don't do it well."

"You won't let me practice on you?"

She started to make a Peewee retort, stopped suddenly, smiled and came close. For a nervous second I thought she was going to kiss me. But she just patted the bedclothes and said solemnly, "You bet you can, Kip. You can be sarcastic, or nasty, or mean, or scold me, or anything, and I won't let out a peep. Why, I'll bet you could even talk back to the Mother Thing."

I couldn't imagine wanting to. I said, "Take it easy, Peewee. Your halo is showing."

"I'd have one if it weren't for you. Or flunked my test for it, more likely."

"So? I seem to remember somebody about your size lugging me indoors almost piggy-back. How about that?"

She wriggled. "That wasn't anything. *You* set the beacon. That was *everything.*"

"Uh, each to his own opinion. It was cold out there." I changed the subject; it was embarrassing us. Mention of the beacon reminded me of something else. "Peewee? Where are we?"

"Huh? In the Mother Thing's home, of course." She looked around and said, "Oh, I forgot. Kip, this isn't really your—"

"I know," I said impatiently. "It's a fake. Anybody can see that."

"They can?" She looked crestfallen. "I thought we had done a perfect job."

"It's an incredibly good job. I don't see how you did it."

"Oh, your memory is most detailed. You must have a camera eye."

—and I must have spilled my guts, too! I added to myself. I wondered what else I had said—with Peewee listening. I was afraid to ask; a fellow ought to have privacy.

"But it's still a fake," I went on. "I know we're in the Mother Thing's home. But *where's that?*"

"Oh." She looked round-eyed. "I told you. Maybe you don't remember—you were sleepy."

"I remember," I said slowly, "something. But it didn't make sense. I thought you said we were going to *Vega.*"

"Well, I suppose the catalogs will list it as Vega Five. But they call it—" She threw back her head and vocalized; it recalled to me the cockcrow theme in *Le Coq d'Or.* "—but I couldn't say *that.* So I told you Vega, which is close enough."

I tried again to sit up, failed. "You mean to stand there and tell me we're on *Vega?* I mean, a 'Vegan planet'?"

"Well, you haven't asked me to sit down."

I ignored the Peeweeism. I looked at "sunlight" pouring through the window. "That light is from *Vega?*"

"That stuff? That's artificial sunlight. If they had used real, bright, Vega light, it would look ghastly. Like a bare arc light. Vega is 'way up the Russell diagram, you know."

"It is?" I didn't know the spectrum of Vega; I had never expected to *need* to know it.

"Oh, yes! You be careful, Kip—when you're up, I mean. In ten seconds you can get more burn than all winter in Key West—and ten minutes would kill you."

I seemed to have a gift for winding up in difficult

climates. What star class was Vega? "A," maybe? Probably "B." All I knew was that it was big and bright, bigger than the Sun, and looked pretty set in Lyra.

But *where* was it? How in the name of Einstein did we get here? "Peewee? How far is Vega? No, I mean, 'How far is the Sun?' You wouldn't happen to know?"

"Of course," she said scornfully. "Twenty-seven light-years."

Great Galloping Gorillas! "Peewee—get that slide rule. You know how to push one? I don't seem to have the use of my hands."

She looked uneasy. "Uh, what do you want it for?"

"I want to see what that comes to in miles."

"Oh. I'll figure it. No need for a slide rule."

"A slipstick is faster and more accurate. Look, if you don't know how to use one, don't be ashamed—I didn't, at your age. I'll show you."

"Of course I can use one!" she said indignantly. "You think I'm a stupe? But I'll work it out." Her lips moved silently. "One point five nine times ten to the fourteenth miles."

I had done that Proxima Centauri problem recently; I remembered the miles in a light-year and did a rough check in my head—uh, call it six times twenty-five makes a hundred and fifty—and where was the decimal point? "Your answer sounds about right." 159,000,-000,000,000 weary miles! Too many zeroes for comfort.

"Of course I'm right!" she retorted. "I'm *always* right."

"Goodness me! The handy-dandy pocket encyclopedia."

She blushed. "I can't help being a genius."

Which left her wide open and I was about to rub her nose in it—when I saw how unhappy she looked.

I remembered hearing Dad say: "Some people insist that 'mediocre' is better than 'best.' They delight in clipping wings because they themselves can't fly. They despise brains because they have none. Pfah!"

"I'm sorry, Peewee," I said humbly. "I know you can't. And I can't help not being one . . . any more than you can help being little, or I can help being big."

She relaxed and looked solemn. "I guess I was being a show-off again." She twisted a button. "Or maybe I assumed that you understand me—like Daddy."

"I feel complimented. I doubt if I do—but from now on I'll try."

She went on worrying the button. "You're pretty smart yourself, Kip. You know that, don't you?"

I grinned. "If I were smart, would I be *here?* All thumbs and my ears rub together. Look, honey, would you mind if we checked you on the slide rule? I'm really interested." Twenty-seven light-years—why, you wouldn't be able to *see* the Sun. It isn't any great shakes as a star.

But I had made her uneasy again. "Uh, Kip, that isn't much of a slide rule."

"What? Why, that's the best that money can—"

"Kip, please! It's part of the desk. It's not a slide rule."

"Huh?" I looked sheepish. "I forgot. Uh, I suppose that hall out there doesn't go very far?"

"Just what you can see. Kip, the slide rule would have been real—if we had had time enough. They understand logarithms. Oh, indeed they do!"

That was bothering me—"time enough" I mean. "Peewee, how long did it take us to get here?" Twenty-seven light-years! Even at speed-of-light—well, maybe the Einstein business would make it seem like a quick trip to me—but not to Centerville. Dad could be dead! Dad was older than Mother, old enough to be my grandfather, really. Another twenty-seven years back— Why, that would make him well over a hundred. Even Mother might be dead.

"Time to get here? Why, it didn't take *any*."

"No, no. I know it feels that way. You're not any older, I'm still laid up by frostbite. But it took at least twenty-seven years. Didn't it?"

"What are you talking about, Kip?"

"The relativity equations, of course. You've heard of them?"

"Oh, *those!* Certainly. But they don't apply. It didn't take *time*. Oh, fifteen minutes to get out of Pluto's atmosphere, about the same to cope with the atmosphere here. But otherwise, *pht!* Zero."

"At the speed of light you would think so."

"No, Kip." She frowned, then her face lighted up. "How long was it from the time you set the beacon till they rescued us?"

"Huh?" It hit me. Dad wasn't dead! Mother wouldn't even have gray hair. "Maybe an hour."

"A little over. It would have been less if they had had a ship ready . . . then they might have found you in the tunnel instead of me. No time for the message to reach here. Half an hour frittered away getting a ship ready—the Mother Thing was *vexed*. I hadn't known she could be. You see, a ship is supposed to be *ready*."

"Any time she wants one?"

"Any and all the time—the Mother Thing is *important*. Another half-hour in atmosphere maneuvering—and that's all. *Real* time. None of those funny contractions."

I tried to soak it up. They take an hour to go twenty-seven light-years—and get bawled out for dallying. Dr. Einstein must be known as "Whirligig Albert" among his cemetery neighbors. "But *how?*"

"Kip, do you know any geometry? I don't mean Euclid—I mean *geometry*."

"Mmm . . . I've fiddled with open and closed curved spaces—and I've read Dr. Bell's popular books. But you couldn't say I know any geometry."

"At least you won't boggle at the idea that a straight line is not necessarily the shortest distance between two points." She made motions as if squeezing a grapefruit in both hands. "Because it's not. Kip—it all *touches*. You could put it in a bucket. In a thimble if you folded it so that spins matched."

I had a dizzying picture of a universe compressed into a teacup, nucleons and electrons packed solidly—really *solid* and not the thin mathematical ghost that even the uranium nucleus is said to be. Something like the "primal atom" that some cosmogonists use to explain the expanding universe. Well, maybe it's both—packed and expanding. Like the "wavicle" paradox. A particle isn't a wave and a wave can't be a particle—yet everything is *both*. If you believe in wavicles, you can believe in anything—and if you don't, then don't bother to believe at all. Not even in yourself, because that's what you are—wavicles. "How many dimensions?" I said weakly.

"How many would you like?"

"Me? Uh, twenty, maybe. Four more for each of the first four, to give some looseness on the corners."

"Twenty isn't a starter. I don't know, Kip; I don't know geometry, either—I just thought I did. So I've pestered them."

"The Mother Thing?"

"Her? Oh, heavens, no! She doesn't know geometry. Just enough to pilot a ship in and out of the folds."

"Only that much?" I should have stuck to advanced finger-painting and never let Dad lure me into trying for an education. There isn't any end—the more you learn, the more you need to learn. "Peewee, you knew what that beacon was for, didn't you?"

"Me?" She looked innocent. "Well . . . yes."

"You knew we were going to Vega."

"Well . . . if the beacon worked. If it was set in time."

"Now the prize question. Why didn't you tell me?"

"Well—" Peewee was going to twist that button off. "I wasn't sure how much math you knew and—you might have gone all masculine and common-sensical and father-knows-best. Would you have believed me?"

("I told Orville and I told Wilbur and now I'm telling you—that contraption will never work!") "Maybe not, Peewee. But next time you're tempted not to tell me something 'for my own good,' will you take a chance that I'm not wedded to my own ignorance? I know I'm not a genius but I'll try to keep my mind open—and I might be able to help, if I knew what you were up to. Quit twisting that button."

She let go hastily. "Yes, Kip. I'll remember."

"Thanks. Another thing is fretting me. I was pretty sick?"

"Huh? You certainly were!"

"All right. They've got these, uh, 'fold ships' that go anywhere in no time. Why didn't you ask them to bounce me home and pop me into a hospital?"

She hesitated. "How do you feel?"

"Huh? I feel fine. Except that I seem to be under spinal anesthesia, or something."

"Or something," she agreed. "But you feel as if you are getting well?"

"Shucks, I feel *well*."

"You aren't. But you're going to be." She looked at me closely. "Shall I put it bluntly, Kip?"

"Go ahead."

"If they had taken you to Earth to the best hospital we have, you'd be a 'basket case.' Understand me? No arms, no legs. As it is, you are getting completely well. No amputations, not even a toe."

I think the Mother Thing had prepared me. I simply said, "You're sure?"

"Sure. Sure both. You're going to be *all right*." Suddenly her face screwed up. "Oh, you were a mess! I *saw*."

"Pretty bad?"

"Awful. I have nightmares."

"They shouldn't have let you look."

"They couldn't stop me. I was next of kin."

"Huh? You told them you were my sister or something?"

"What? I *am* your next of kin."

I was about to say she was cockeyed when I tripped over my tongue. We were the only humans for a hundred and sixty trillion miles. As usual, Peewee was right.

"So I had to grant permission," she went on.

"For what? What did they do to me?"

"Uh, first they popped you into liquid helium. They left you there and the past month they have been using me as a guinea pig. Then, three days ago—three of ours—they thawed you out and got to work. You've been getting well ever since."

"What shape am I in now?"

"Uh . . . well, you're growing back. Kip, this isn't a bed. It just looks like it."

"What is it, then?"

"We don't have a name for it and the tune is pitched too high for me. But everything from here on down—" She patted the spread. "—on into the room below, does things for you. You're wired like a hi-fi nut's basement."

"I'd like to see it."

"I'm afraid you can't. You don't *know*, Kip. They had to cut your space suit off."

I felt more emotion at that than I had at hearing what a mess I had been. "Huh? Where is Oscar? Did they ruin him? My space suit, I mean."

"I know what you mean. Every time you're delirious you talk to 'Oscar'—and you answer back, too. Sometimes I think you're schizoid, Kip."

"You've mixed your terms, runt—that'ud make me a

180

split personality. All right, but you're a paranoid yourself."

"Oh, I've known that for a long time. But I'm a very well adjusted one. You want to see Oscar? The Mother Thing said that you would want him near when you woke up." She opened the closet.

"Hey! You said he was all cut up!"

"Oh, they repaired him. Good as new. A little better than new."

("Time, dear! Remember what I said.")

"Coming, Mother Thing! 'Bye, Kip. I'll be back soon, and real often."

"Okay. Leave the closet open so I can see Oscar."

Peewee did come back, but not "real often." I wasn't offended, not much. She had a thousand interesting and "educational" things to poke her ubiquitous nose into, all new and fascinating—she was as busy as a pup chewing slippers. She ran our hosts ragged. But I wasn't bored. I was getting well, a full-time job and not boring if you are happy—which I was.

I didn't see the Mother Thing often. I began to realize that she had work of her own to do—even though she came to see me if I asked for her, with never more than an hour's delay, and never seemed in a hurry to leave.

She wasn't my doctor, nor my nurse. Instead I had a staff of veterinarians who were alert to supervise every heartbeat. They didn't come in unless I asked them to (a whisper was as good as a shout) but I soon realized that "my" room was bugged and telemetered like a ship in flight test—and my "bed" was a mass of machinery, gear that bore the relation to our own "mechanical hearts" and "mechanical lungs" and "mechanical kidneys" that a Lockheed ultrasonic courier does to a baby buggy.

I never saw that gear (they never lifted the spread, unless it was while I slept), but I know what they were doing. They were encouraging my body to repair itself—not scar tissue but the way it had been. Any lobster can do this and starfish do it so well that you can chop them to bits and wind up with a thousand brand-new starfish.

This is a trick any animal should do, since its gene pattern is in every cell. But a few million years ago we lost it. Everybody knows that science is trying to recapture it; you see articles—optimistic ones in *Reader's Digest,* discouraged ones in *The Scientific Monthly,* wildly wrong ones in magazines whose "science editors" seem to have received their training writing horror movies. But we're working on it. Someday, if anybody dies an accidental death, it will be because he bled to death on the way to the hospital.

Here I was with a perfect chance to find out about it—and I didn't.

I tried. Although I was unworried by what they were doing (the Mother Thing had told me not to worry and every time she visited me she looked in my eyes and repeated the injunction), nevertheless like Peewee, I like to *know.*

Pick a savage so far back in the jungle that they don't even have installment-plan buying. Say he has an I.Q. of 190 and Peewee's yen to understand. Dump him into Brookhaven Atomic Laboratories. How much will he learn? With all possible help?

He'll learn which corridors lead to what rooms and he'll learn that a purple trefoil means: "Danger!"

That's all. Not because he *can't;* remember he's a supergenius—but he needs twenty years schooling before he can ask the right questions and understand the answers.

I asked questions and always got answers and formed notions. But I'm not going to record them; they are as confused and contradictory as the notions a savage would form about design and operation of atomic equipment. As they say in radio, when noise level reaches a certain value, no information is transmitted. All I got was "noise."

Some of it was literally "noise." I'd ask a question and one of the therapists would answer. I would understand part, then as it reached the key point, I would hear nothing but birdsongs. Even with the Mother Thing as an interpreter, the parts I had no background for would turn out to be a canary's cheerful prattle.

Hold onto your seats; I'm going to explain something I don't understand: how Peewee and I could talk with the Mother Thing even though her mouth could not shape English and we couldn't sing the way she did and had not studied her language. The Vegans—(I'll call them "Vegans" the way we might be called "Solarians"; their real name sounds like a wind chime in a breeze. The Mother Thing had a real name, too, but I'm not a coloratura soprano. Peewee used it when she wanted to wheedle her—fat lot of good it did her.) The Vegans have a supreme talent to understand, to put themselves in the other person's shoes. I don't think it was telepathy, or I wouldn't have gotten so many wrong numbers. Call it empathy.

But they have it in various degrees, just as all of us drive cars but only a few are fit to be racing drivers. The Mother Thing had it the way Novaës understands a piano. I once read about an actress who could use Italian so effectively to a person who did not understand Italian that she always made herself understood. Her name was "Duce." No, a "duce" is a dictator. Something like that. She must have had what the Mother Thing had.

The first words I had with the Mother Thing were things like "hello" and "good-bye" and "thank you" and "where are we going?" She could project her meaning with those—shucks, you can talk to a strange dog that much. Later I began to understand her speech as *speech.* She picked up meanings of English words even faster; she had this great talent, and she and Peewee had talked for days while they were prisoners.

But while this is easy for "you're welcome" and "I'm hungry" and "let's hurry," it gets harder for ideas like "heterodyning" and "amino acid" even when both are familiar with the concept. When one party doesn't even have the concept, it breaks down. That's the trouble I had understanding those veterinarians. If we had all spoken English I still would not have understood.

An oscillating circuit sending out a radio signal produces dead silence unless there is another circuit capable of oscillating in the same way to receive it. I wasn't on the right frequency.

Nevertheless I understood them when the talk was not highbrow. They were nice people; they talked and laughed a lot and seemed to like each other. I had trouble telling them apart, except the Mother Thing. (I learned that the only marked difference to them between Peewee and myself was that I was ill and she wasn't.) They had no trouble telling each other apart; their conversations were interlarded with musical names, until you felt that you were caught in *Peter and the Wolf* or a Wagnerian opera. They even had a leit-motif for me. Their talk was cheerful and gay, like the sounds of a bright summer dawn.

The next time I meet a canary I'll know what he is saying even if he doesn't.

I picked up some of this from Peewee—a hospital bed is not a good place from which to study a planet. Vega Five has Earth-surface gravity, near enough, with an oxygen, carbon dioxide, and water life cycle. The planet would not suit humans, not only because the noonday "sun" would strike you dead with its jolt of ultraviolet but also the air has poisonous amounts of ozone—a trace of ozone is stimulating but a trifle more

—well, you might as well sniff prussic acid. There was something else, too, nitrous oxide I think, which was ungood for humans if breathed too long. My quarters were air-conditioned; the Vegans could breathe what I used but they considered it tasteless.

I learned a bit as a by-product of something else; the Mother Thing asked me to dictate how I got mixed up in these things. When I finished, she asked me to dictate everything I knew about Earth, its history, and how we work and live together. This is a tall order—I'm not still dictating because I found out I don't know much. Take ancient Babylonia—how is it related to early Egyptian civilizations? I had only vague notions.

Maybe Peewee did better, since she remembers everything she has heard or read or seen the way Dad does. But they probably didn't get her to hold still long, whereas I had to. The Mother Thing wanted this for the reasons we study Australian aborigines and also as a record of our language. There was another reason, too.

The job wasn't easy but there was a Vegan to help me whenever I felt like it, willing to stop if I tired. Call him Professor Josephus Egghead; "Professor" is close enough and his name can't be spelled. I called him Joe and he called me the leitmotif that meant "Clifford Russell, the monster with the frostbite." Joe had almost as much gift for understanding as the Mother Thing. But how do you put over ideas like "tariffs" and "kings" to a person whose people have never had either? The English words were just noise.

But Joe knew histories of many peoples and planets and could call up scenes, in moving stereo and color, until we agreed on what I meant. We jogged along, with me dictating to a silvery ball floating near my mouth and with Joe curled up like a cat on a platform raised to my level, while he dictated to another microphone, making running notes on what I said. His mike had a gimmick that made it a hush-phone; I did not hear him unless he spoke to me.

Then we would stumble. Joe would stop and throw me a sample scene, his best guess of what I meant. The pictures appeared in the air, positioned for my comfort—if I turned my head, the picture moved to accommodate me. The pix were color-stereo-television with perfect life and sharpness—well, give us another twenty years and we'll have them as realistic. It was a good trick to have the projector concealed and to force images to appear as if they were hanging in air, but those are just gimmicks of stereo optics; we can do them anytime we really want to—after all, you can pack a lifelike view of the Grand Canyon into a viewer you hold in your hand.

The thing that did impress me was the organization behind it. I asked Joe about it. He sang to his microphone and we went on a galloping tour of their "Congressional Library."

Dad claims that library science is the foundation of all sciences just as math is the key—and that we will survive or founder, depending on how well the librarians do their jobs. Librarians didn't look glamorous to me but maybe Dad had hit on a not very obvious truth.

This "library" had hundreds, maybe thousands, of Vegans viewing pictures and listening to sound tracks, each with a silvery sphere in front of him. Joe said they were "telling the memory." This was equivalent to typing a card for a library's catalog, except that the result was more like a memory path in brain cells—ninetenths of that building was an electronic brain.

I spotted a triangular sign like the costume jewelry worn by the Mother Thing, but the picture jumped quickly to something else. Joe also wore one (and others did not) but I did not get around to asking about it, as the sight of that incredible "library" brought up the word "cybernetics" and we went on a detour. I decided later that it might be a lodge pin, or like a Phi Beta Kappa key—the Mother Thing was smart even for a Vegan and Joe was not far behind.

Whenever Joe was sure that he understood some English word, he would wriggle with delight like a puppy being tickled. He was very dignified, but this is not undignified for a Vegan. Their bodies are so fluid and mobile that they smile and frown with the whole works. A Vegan holding perfectly still is either displeased or extremely worried.

The sessions with Joe let me tour places from my bed. The difference between "primary school" and "university" caused me to be shown examples. "A "kindergarten" looked like an adult Vegan being overwhelmed by babies; it had the innocent rowdiness of a collie pup stepping on his brother's face to reach the milk dish. But the "university" was a place of quiet beauty, strange-looking trees and plants and flowers among buildings of surrealistic charm unlike any architecture I have ever seen—I suppose I would have been flabbergasted if they had looked familiar. Parabolas were used a lot and I think all the "straight" lines had that swelling the Greeks called "entasis"—delicate grace with strength.

Joe showed up one day simply undulating with pleasure. He had another silvery ball, larger than the other two. He placed it in front of me, then sang to his own. ("I want you to hear this, Kip!")

As soon as he ceased the larger sphere spoke in English: "I want you to hear this, Kip!"

Squirming with delight, Joe swapped spheres and told me to say something.

"What do you want me to say?" I asked.

("What do you want me to say?") the larger sphere sang in Vegan.

That was my last session with Prof Joe.

Despite unstinting help, despite the Mother Thing's

ability to make herself understood, I was like the Army mule at West Point: an honorary member of the student body but not prepared for the curriculum. I never did understand their government. Oh, they *had* government, but it wasn't any system I've heard of. Joe knew about democracies and representation and voting and courts of law; he could fish up examples from many planets. He felt that democracy was "a very good system, for beginners." It would have sounded patronizing, except that is not one of their faults.

I never met one of their young. Joe explained that children should not see "strange creatures" until they had learned to feel understanding sympathy. That would have offended me if I hadn't been learning some "understanding sympathy" myself. Matter of fact, if a human ten-year-old saw a Vegan, he would either run, or poke it with a stick.

I tried to learn about their government from the Mother Thing, in particular how they kept the peace—laws, crimes, punishments, traffic regulations, etc.

It was as near to flat failure as I ever had with her. She pondered a long time, then answered: ("How could one possibly act against one's own nature?")

I guess their worst vice was that they didn't have any. This can be tiresome.

The medical staff were interested in the drugs in Oscar's helmet—like our interest in a witch doctor's herbs, but that is not idle interest; remember digitalis and curare.

I told them what each drug did and in most cases I knew the Geneva name as well as the commercial one. I knew that codeine was derived from opium, and opium from poppies. I knew that dexedrine was a sulphate but that was all. Organic chemistry and biochemistry are not easy even with no language trouble. We got together on what a benzene ring was, Peewee drawing it and sticking in her two dollars' worth, and we managed to agree on "element," "isotope," "half life," and the periodic table. I should have drawn structural formulas, using Peewee's hands—but neither of us had the slightest idea of the structural formula for codeine and couldn't do it even when supplied with kindergarten toys which stuck together only in the valences of the elements they represented.

Peewee had fun, though. They may not have learned much from her; she learned a lot from them.

I don't know when I became aware that the Mother Thing was not, or wasn't quite, a female. But it didn't matter; being a mother is an attitude, not a biological relation.

If Noah launched his ark on Vega Five, the animals would come in by twelves. That makes things complicated. But a "mother thing" is one who takes care of others. I am not sure that all mother things were the same gender; it may have been a matter of temperament.

I met one "father thing." You might call him "governor" or "mayor," but "parish priest" or "scoutmaster" is closer, except that his prestige dominated a continent. He breezed in during a session with Joe, stayed five minutes, urged Joe to do a good job, told me to be a good boy and get well, and left, all without hurrying. He filled me with the warm self-reliance that Dad does—I didn't need to be told that he was a "father thing." His visit had a flavor of "royalty visiting the wounded" without being condescending—no doubt it was hard to work me into a busy schedule.

Joe neither mothered nor fathered me; he taught me and studied me—"a professor thing."

Peewee showed up one day full of bubbles. She posed like a mannequin. "Do you like my new spring outfit?"

She was wearing silvery tights, plus a little hump like

a knapsack. She looked cute but not glamorous, for she was built like two sticks and this get-up emphasized it.

"Very fancy," I said. "Are you learning to be an acrobat?"

"Don't be silly, Kip; it's my new space suit—a *real* one."

I glanced at Oscar, big and bulky and filling the closet and said privately, "Hear that, chum?"

("It takes all kinds to make a world.")

"Your helmet won't fit it, will it?"

She giggled. "I'm wearing it."

"You are? 'The Emperor's New Clothes'?"

"Pretty close. Kip, disconnect your prejudices and listen. This is like the Mother Thing's suit except that it's tailored for me. My old suit wasn't much good—and that *cold* cold about finished it. But you'll be amazed at this one. Take the helmet. It's there, only you can't see it. It's a field. Gas can't go in or out." She came close. "Slap me."

"With what?"

"Oh. I forgot. Kip, you've got to get well and up off that bed. I want to take you for a walk."

"I'm in favor. They tell me it won't be long now."

"It had better not be. Here, I'll show you." She hauled off and slapped herself. Her hand smacked into something inches from her face.

"Now watch," she went on. She moved her hand very slowly; it sank through the barrier, she thumbed her nose at me and giggled.

This impressed me—a space suit you could reach into! Why, I would have been able to give Peewee water and dexedrine and sugar pills when she needed them. "I'll be darned! What does it?"

"A power pack on my back, under the air tank. The tank is good for a week, too, and hoses can't give trouble because there aren't any."

"Uh, suppose you blow a fuse. There you are, with a lungful of vacuum."

"The Mother Thing says that can't happen."

Hmm—I had never known the Mother Thing to be wrong when she made a flat statement.

"That's not all," Peewee went on. "It feels like skin, the joints aren't clumsy, and you're never hot or cold. It's like street clothes."

"Uh, you risk a bad sunburn, don't you? Unhealthy, you tell me. Unhealthy even on the Moon."

"Oh, no! The field polarizes. That's what the field is, sort of. Kip, get them to make you one—we'll go places!"

I glanced at Oscar. ("Please yourself, pal," he said distantly. "I'm not the jealous type.")

"Uh, Peewee, I'll stick to one I understand. But I'd like to examine that monkey suit of yours."

"Monkey suit indeed!"

I woke up one morning, turned over, and realized that I was hungry.

Then I sat up with a jerk. I had *turned over in bed.*

I had been warned to expect it. The "bed" was a bed and my body was back under my control. Furthermore, I was hungry and I hadn't been hungry the whole time I had been on Vega Five. Whatever that machinery was, it included a way to nourish me without eating.

But I didn't stop to enjoy the luxury of hunger; it was too wonderful to be a body again, not just a head. I got out of bed, was suddenly dizzy, recovered and grinned. Hands! *Feet!*

I examined those wonderful things. They were unchanged and unhurt.

Then I looked more closely. No, not quite unchanged. I had had a scar on my left shin where I had been spiked in a close play at second; it was gone. I once had "Mother" tattooed on my left forearm at a carnival. Mother had been distressed and Dad disgusted, but he had said to leave it as a reminder not to be a witling. It was gone.

There was not a callus on hand or foot.

I used to bite my nails. My nails were a bit long but perfect. I had lost the nail from my right little toe years ago through a slip with a hatchet. It was back.

I looked hastily for my appendectomy scar—found it and felt relieved. If it had been missing, I would have wondered if I was me.

There was a mirror over the chest of drawers. It showed me with enough hair to warrant a guitar (I wear a crew cut) but somebody had shaved me.

On the chest was a dollar and sixty-seven cents, a mechanical pencil, a sheet of paper, my watch, and a handkerchief. The watch was running. The dollar bill, the paper, and the handkerchief had been laundered.

My clothes, spandy clean and invisibly repaired, were on the desk. The socks weren't mine; the material was more like felt, if you will imagine felted material no thicker than Kleenex which stretches instead of tearing. On the floor were tennis shoes, like Peewee's even to a "U.S. Rubber" trademark, but in my size. The uppers were heavier felted material. I got dressed.

I was wearing the result when Peewee kicked the door. "Anybody home?" She came in, bearing a tray. "Want breakfast?"

"Peewee! Look at me!"

She did. "Not bad," she admitted, "for an ape. You need a haircut."

"Yes, but isn't it *wonderful!* I'm all together again!"

"You never were apart," she answered, "except in spots—I've had daily reports. Where do you want this?" She put the tray on the desk.

"Peewee," I asked, rather hurt, "don't you care that I'm well?"

"Of course I do. Why do you think I made 'em let me carry in your breakfast? But I knew last night that they were going to uncork you. Who do you think cut your nails and shaved you? That'll be a dollar, please. Shaves have gone up."

I got that tired dollar and handed it to her.

She didn't take it. "Aw, can't you take a joke?"

" 'Neither a borrower nor a lender be.' "

"Polonius. He was a stupid old bore. Honest, Kip, I wouldn't take your last dollar."

"Now who can't take a joke?"

"Oh, eat your breakfast. That purple juice," she said, "tastes like orange juice—it's very nice. The stuff that looks like scrambled eggs is a fair substitute and I had 'em color it yellow—the eggs here are *dreadful,* which wouldn't surprise you if you knew where they get them. The buttery stuff is vegetable fat and I had them color it, too. The bread is bread, I toasted it myself. The salt is salt and it surprises them that we eat it—they think it's poison. Go ahead; I've guinea-pigged everything. No coffee."

"I won't miss it."

"I never touch the stuff—I'm trying to grow. Eat. Your sugar count has been allowed to drop so that you will enjoy it."

The aroma was wonderful. "Where's your breakfast, Peewee?"

"I ate hours ago. I'll watch and swallow when you do."

The tastes were odd but it was just what the doctor ordered—literally, I suppose. I've never enjoyed a meal so much.

Presently I slowed down to say, "Knife and fork? Spoons?"

"The only ones on—" She vocalized the planet's name. "I got tired of fingers and I play hob using what they use. So I drew pictures. This set is mine but we'll order more."

There was even a napkin, more felted stuff. The water tasted distilled and not aerated. I didn't mind. "Pee-wee, how did you shave me? Not even a nick."

"Little gismo that beats a razor all hollow. I don't know what they use it for, but if you could patent it, you'd make a fortune. Aren't you going to finish that toast?"

"Uh—" I had thought that I could eat the tray. "No, I'm full."

"Then I will." She used it to mop up the "butter," then announced, "I'm off!"

"Where?"

"To suit up. I'm going to take you for a walk!" She was gone.

The hall outside did not imitate ours where it could not be seen from the bed, but a door to the left was a bathroom, just where it should have been. No attempt had been made to make it look like the one at home, and valving and lighting and such were typically Vegan. But everything worked.

Peewee returned while I was checking Oscar. If they had cut him off me, they had done a marvelous job of repairing; even the places I had patched no longer showed. He had been cleaned so thoroughly that there was no odor inside. He had three hours of air and seemed okay in every way. "You're in good shape, partner."

("In the pink! The service is excellent here.")

"So I've noticed." I looked up and saw Peewee; she was already in her "spring outfit."

"Peewee, do we need space suits just for a walk?"

"No. You could get by with a respirator, sun glasses, and a sun shade."

"You've convinced me. Say, where's Madame Pompadour? How do you get her inside that suit?"

"No trouble at all, she just bulges a little. But I left her in my room and told her to behave herself."

"Will she?"

"Probably not. She takes after me."

"Where is your room?"

"Next door. This is the only part of the house which is Earth-conditioned."

I started to suit up. "Say, has that fancy suit got a radio?"

"All that yours has and then some. Did you notice the change in Oscar?"

"Huh? What? I saw that he was repaired and cleaned up. What else have they done?"

"Just a little thing. One more click on the switch that changes antennas and you can talk to people around you who aren't wearing radios without shouting."

"I didn't see a speaker."

"They don't believe in making everything big and bulky."

As we passed Peewee's room I glanced in. It was not decorated Vegan style; I had seen Vegan interiors through stereo. Nor was it a copy of her own room—not if her parents were sensible. I don't know what to call it—"Moorish harem" style, perhaps, as conceived by Mad King Ludwig, with a dash of Disneyland.

I did not comment. I had a hunch that Peewee had been given a room "just like her own" because I had one; that fitted the Mother Thing's behavior—but Peewee had seen a golden chance to let her overfertile imagination run wild. I doubt if she fooled the Mother Thing one split second. She had probably let that indulgent overtone come into her song and had given Peewee what she wanted.

The Mother Thing's home was smaller than our state capitol but not much; her family seemed to run dozens, or hundreds—"family" has a wide meaning under their complex interlinkage. We didn't see any young ones on our floor and I knew that they were being kept away from the "monsters." The adults all greeted me, inquired as to my health, and congratulated me on my recovery; I was kept busy saying "Fine, thank you! Couldn't be better."

They all knew Peewee and she could sing their names.

I thought I recognized one of my therapists, but the Mother Thing, Prof Joe and the boss veterinarian were the only Vegans I was sure of and we did not meet them.

We hurried on. The Mother Thing's home was typical —many soft round cushions about a foot thick and four in diameter, used as beds or chairs, floor bare, slick and springy, most furniture on the walls where it could be reached by climbing, convenient rods and poles and brackets a person could drape himself on while using the furniture, plants growing unexpectedly here and there as if the jungle were moving in—delightful, and as useful to me as a corset.

Through a series of parabolic arches we reached a balcony. It was not railed and the drop to a terrace below was about seventy-five feet; I stayed back and regretted again that Oscar had no chin window. Peewee went to the edge, put an arm around a slim pillar and leaned out. In the bright outdoor light her "helmet" became an opalescent sphere. "Come see!"

"And break my neck? Maybe you'd like to belay me?"

"Oh, pooh! Who's afraid of heights?"

"I am when I can't see what I'm doing."

"Well, for goodness' sakes, take my hand and grab a post."

I let her lead me to a pillar, then looked out.

It was a city in a jungle. Thick dark green, so tangled that I could not tell trees from vine and bush, spread out all around but was broken repeatedly by buildings as large and larger than the one we were in. There were no roads; their roads are underground in cities and sometimes outside the cities. But there was air traffic—individual fliers supported by contrivances even less substantial than our own one-man 'copter harnesses or flying carpets. Like birds they launched themselves from and landed in balconies such as the one we stood in.

There were real birds, too, long and slender and brilliantly colored, with two sets of wings in tandem—which looked aerodynamically unsound but seemed to suit them.

The sky was blue and fair but broken by three towering cumulous anvils, blinding white in the distance.

"Let's go on the roof," said Peewee.

"How?"

"Over here."

It was a scuttle hole reached by staggered slender brackets the Vegans use as stairs. "Isn't there a ramp?"

"Around on the far side, yes."

"I don't think those things will hold me. And that hole looks small for Oscar."

"Oh, don't be a sissy." Peewee went up like a monkey. I followed like a tired bear. The brackets were sturdy despite their grace; the hole was a snug fit.

Vega was high in the sky. It appeared to be the angular size of our Sun, which fitted since we were much farther out than Terra is from the Sun, but it was too bright even with full polarization. I looked away and presently eyes and polarizers adjusted until I could see again. Peewee's head was concealed by what appeared to be a polished chrome basketball. I said, "Hey, are you still there?"

"Sure," she answered. "I can see out all right. It's a grand view. Doesn't it remind you of Paris from the top of the Arc de Triomphe?"

"I don't know, I've never done any traveling."

"Except no boulevards, of course. Somebody is about to land here."

I turned the way she was pointing—she could see in all directions while I was hampered by the built-in tunnel vision of my helmet. By the time I was turned around the Vegan was coming in beside us.

("Hello, children!")

"Hi, Mother Thing!" Peewee threw her arms around her, picking her up.

("Not so hasty, dear. Let me shed this.") The Mother Thing stepped out of her harness, shook herself in ripples, folded the flying gear like an umbrella and hung it over an arm. ("You're looking fit, Kip.")

"I feel fine, Mother Thing! Gee, it's nice to have you back."

("I wished to be back when you got out of bed. However, your therapists have kept me advised every minute.") She put a little hand against my chest, growing a bit to do so, and placed her eyes almost against my face plate. ("You are well?")

"I couldn't be better."

"He really is, Mother Thing!"

("Good. You agree that you are well, I sense that you are, Peewee is sure that you are and, most important, your leader therapist assures me that you are. We'll leave at once.")

"What?" I asked. "Where, Mother Thing?"

She turned to Peewee. ("Haven't you told him, dear?")

"Gee, Mother Thing, I haven't had a *chance*."

("Very well.") She turned to me. ("Dear Kip, we must now attend a gathering. Questions will be asked and answered, decisions will be made.") She spoke to us both. ("Are you ready to leave?")

"Now?" said Peewee. "Why, I guess so—except that I've got to get Madame Pompadour."

("Fetch her, then. And you, Kip?")

"Uh—" I couldn't remember whether I had put my watch back on after I washed and I couldn't tell because I can't feel it through Oscar's thick hide. I told her so.

("Very well. You children run to your rooms while I have a ship fetched. Meet me here and don't stop to admire flowers.")

We went down by ramp. I said, "Peewee, you've been holding out on me again."

"Why, I have not!"

"What do you call it?"

"Kip—please listen! I was *told* not to tell you while you were ill. The Mother Thing was very firm about it. You were not to be *disturbed*—that's what she said!—while you were growing well."

"Why should I feel disturbed? What is all this? What gathering? What questions?"

"Well . . . the gathering is sort of a court. A criminal court, you might say."

"Huh?" I took a quick look at my conscience. But I hadn't had any chance to do anything wrong—I had been helpless as a baby up to two hours ago. That left Peewee. "Runt," I said sternly, "what have you done now?"

"Me? Nothing."

"Think hard."

"No, Kip. Oh, I'm sorry I didn't tell you at breakfast! But Daddy says never to break any news until after his second cup of coffee and I thought how nice it would be to take a little walk before we had any worries and I was going to tell you—"

"Make it march."

"—as soon as we came down. *I* haven't done anything. But there's old Wormface."

"What? I thought he was dead."

"Maybe so, maybe not. But, as the Mother Thing says, there are still questions to be asked, decisions to be made. He's up for the limit, is my guess."

I thought about it as we wound our way through strange apartments toward the air lock that led to our Earth-conditioned rooms. High crimes and misdemeanors . . . skulduggery in the spaceways—yes, Wormface was probably in for it. If the Vegans could catch him. "Had caught him" apparently, since they were going to try him. "But where do we come in? As witnesses?"

"I suppose you could call it that."

What happened to Wormface was no skin off my nose —and it would be a chance to find out more about the Vegans. Especially if the court was some distance away, so that we would travel and see the country.

"But that isn't all," Peewee went on worriedly.

"What else?"

She sighed. "This is why I wanted us to have a nice sight-see first. Uh . . ."

"Don't chew on it. Spit it out."

"Well . . . *we* have to be tried, too."

"What?"

"Maybe 'examined' is the word. I don't know. But I know this: we can't go home until we've been judged."

"But what have we *done?*" I burst out."

"I don't know!"

My thoughts were boiling. "Are you sure they'll let us go home then?"

"The Mother Thing refuses to talk about it."

I stopped and took her arm. "What it amounts to," I said bitterly, "is that we are under arrest. Aren't we?"

"Yes—" She added almost in a sob, "But, Kip, I *told* you she was a cop!"

"Great stuff. We pull her chestnuts out of the fire— and now we're arrested—and going to be tried—and we don't even know why! Nice place, Vega Five. 'The natives are friendly.'" They had nursed me—as we nurse a gangster in order to hang him.

"But, Kip—" Peewee was crying openly now. "I'm *sure* it'll be all right. She may be a cop—but she's still the Mother Thing."

"Is she? I wonder." Peewee's manner contradicted her words. She was not one to worry over nothing. Quite the contrary.

My watch was on the washstand. I ungasketed to put it in an inside pocket. When I came out, Peewee was doing the same with Madame Pompadour. "Here," I said, "I'll take her with me. I've got more room."

"No, thank you," Peewee answered bleakly. "I need her with me. Especially now."

"Uh, Peewee, where is this court? This city? Or another one?"

"Didn't I tell you? No, I guess I didn't. It's not on this planet."

"I thought this was the only inhabited—"

"It's not a planet around Vega. Another star. Not even in the Galaxy."

"Say that again?"

"It's somewhere in the Lesser Magellanic Cloud."

Chapter 10

I didn't put up a fight—a hundred and sixty trillion miles from nowhere, I mean. But I didn't speak to the Mother Thing as I got into her ship.

It was shaped like an old-fashioned beehive and it looked barely big enough to jump us to the space port. Peewee and I crowded together on the floor, the Mother Thing curled up in front and twiddled a shiny rack like an abacus; we took off, straight up.

In a few minutes my anger grew from sullenness to a reckless need to settle it. "Mother Thing!"

("One moment, dear. Let me get us out of the atmosphere.") She pushed something, the ship quivered and steadied.

"Mother Thing," I repeated.

("Wait until I lower us, Kip.")

I had to wait. It's as silly to disturb a pilot as it is to snatch the wheel of a car. The little ship took a buffeting; the upper winds must have been dillies. But she could pilot.

Presently there was a gentle bump and I figured we must be at the space port. The Mother Thing turned her head. ("All right, Kip. I sense your fear and resentment. Will it help to say that you two are in no danger? That I would protect you with my body? As you protected mine?")

"Yes, but—"

("Then let be. It is easier to show than it is to explain. Don't clamp your helmet. This planet's air is like your own.")

"Huh? You mean we're *there?*"

"I told you," Peewee said at my elbow. "Just *poof!* and you're there."

I didn't answer. I was trying to guess how far we were from home.

("Come, children.")

It was midday when we left; it was night as we disembarked. The ship rested on a platform that stretched out of sight. Stars in front of me were in unfamiliar constellations; slaunchwise down the sky was a thin curdling which I spotted as the Milky Way. So Peewee had her wires crossed—we were far from home but still in the Galaxy—perhaps we had simply switched to the night side of Vega Five.

I heard Peewee gasp and turned around.

I didn't have strength to gasp.

Dominating that whole side of the sky was a great whirlpool of millions, maybe billions, of stars.

You've seen pictures of the Great Nebula in Andromeda?—a giant spiral of two curving arms, seen at an angle. Of all the lovely things in the sky it is the most beautiful. This was like that.

Only we weren't seeing a photograph nor even by telescope; we were so close (if "close" is the word) that it stretched across the sky twice as long as the Big Dipper as seen from home—so close that I saw the thickening at the center, two great branches coiling around and overtaking each other. We saw it from an angle so that it appeared elliptical, just as M31 in Andromeda does; you could feel its depth, you could see its shape.

Then I *knew* I was a long way from home. *That* was home, up there, lost in billions of crowded stars.

It was some time before I noticed another double spiral on my right, almost as wide-flung but rather lopsided and not nearly as brilliant—a pale ghost of our own gorgeous Galaxy. It slowly penetrated that this second one must be the Greater Magellanic Cloud—if we were in the Lesser and if that fiery whirlpool was our own Galaxy. What I had thought was "The Milky Way" was simply *a* milky way, the Lesser Cloud from inside.

I turned and looked at it again. It had the right shape, a roadway around the sky, but it was pale skim milk compared with our own, about as our Milky Way looks on a murky night. I don't know how it should look, since I'd never seen the Magellanic Clouds; I've never been south of the Rio Grande. But I did know that each cloud is a galaxy in its own right, but smaller than ours and grouped with us.

I looked again at our blazing spiral and was homesick in a way I hadn't been since I was six.

Peewee was huddling to the Mother Thing for comfort. She made herself taller and put an arm around Peewee. ("There, there, dear! I felt the same way when I was very young and saw it for the first time.")

"Mother Thing?" Peewee said timidly. "Where is *home?*"

("See the right half of it, dear, where the outer arm trails into nothingness? We came from a point two-thirds the way out from the center."

"No, no! Not Vega. I want to know where the *Sun* is!"

("Oh, your star. But, dear, at this distance it is the same.")

We learned how far it is from the Sun to the planet Lanador—167,000 light-years. The Mother Thing couldn't tell us directly as she did not know how much time we meant by a "year"—how long it takes Terra to go around the Sun (a figure she might have used once or not at all and as worth remembering as the price of peanuts in Perth). But she did know the distance from Vega to the Sun and told us the distance from Lanador to Vega with that as a yardstick—six thousand one hundred and ninety times as great. 6190 times 27 light-years gives 167,000 light-years. She courteously gave it in powers of ten the way we figure, instead of using factorial five (1 X 2 X 3 X 4 X 5 equals 120) which is how Vegans figure. 167,000 light-years is 9.82×10^{17} miles. Round off 9.82 and call it ten. Then—

$$1,000,000,000,000,000,000 \text{ miles}$$

—is the distance from Vega to Lanador (or from the Sun to Lanador; Vega and the Sun are back-fence neighbors on this scale.)

A thousand million billion miles.

I refuse to have anything to do with such a preposterous figure. It may be "short" as cosmic distances go, but there comes a time when the circuit breakers in your skull trip out from overload.

The platform we were on was the roof of an enormous triangular building, miles on a side. We saw that triangle repeated in many places and always with a two-armed spiral in each corner. It was the design the Mother Thing wore as jewelry.

It is the symbol for "Three Galaxies, One Law."

I'll lump here things I learned in driblets: The Three Galaxies are like our Federated Free Nations, or the United Nations before that, or the League of Nations still earlier; Lanador houses their offices and courts and files—the League's capital, the way the FFN is in New York and the League of Nations used to be in Switzerland. The cause is historical; the people of Lanador are the Old Race; that's where civilization began.

The Three Galaxies are an island group, like Hawaii State, they haven't any other close neighbors. Civilization spread through the Lesser Cloud, then through the Greater Cloud and is seeping slowly through our own Galaxy—that is taking longer; there are fifteen or twenty times as many stars in our Galaxy as in the other two.

When I began to get these things straight I wasn't quite as sore. The Mother Thing was a very important person at home but here she was a minor official—all she could do was bring us in. Still, I wasn't more than coolly polite for a while—she might have looked the other way while we beat it for home.

They housed us in that enormous building in a part you could call a "transients" hotel," although "detention barracks" or "jail" is closer. I can't complain about accommodations but I was getting confoundedly tired of being locked up every time I arrived in a new place. A robot met us and took us down inside—there are robots wherever you turn on Lanador. I don't mean things looking like the Tin Woodman; I mean machines that do things for you, such as this one which led us to our rooms, then hung around like a bellhop expecting a tip. It was a three-wheeled cart with a big basket on top, for luggage if we had any. It met us, whistled to the Mother Thing in Vegan and led us away, down a lift and through a wide and endlessly long corridor.

I was given "my" room again—a fake of a fake, with all errors left in and new ones added. The sight of it was not reassuring; it shrieked that they planned to keep us there as long as—well, as long as *they* chose.

But the room was complete even to a rack for Oscar and a bathroom outside. Just beyond "my" room was a fake of another kind—a copy of that Arabian Nights horror Peewee had occupied on Vega Five. Peewee seemed delighted, so I didn't point out the implications.

The Mother Thing hovered around while we got out of space suits. ("Do you think you will be comfortable?")

"Oh, sure," I agreed unenthusiastically.

("If you want food or anything, just say so. It will come.")

"So? Is there a telephone somewhere?"

("Simply speak your wishes. You will be heard.")

I didn't doubt her—but I was almost as tired of rooms that were bugged as of being locked up; a person ought to have privacy.

"I'm hungry now," Peewee commented. "I had an early breakfast."

We were in her room. A purple drapery drew back, a light glowed in the wall. In about two minutes a section of wall disappeared; a slab at table height stuck out like a tongue. On it were dishes and silverware, cold cuts, fruit, bread, butter, and a mug of steaming cocoa. Peewee clapped and squealed. I looked at it with less enthusiasm.

("You see?") the Mother Thing went on with a smile in her voice. ("Ask for what you need. If you need me, I'll come. But I must go now.")

"Oh, please don't go, Mother Thing."

("I must, Peewee dear. But I will see you soon. By the bye, there are two more of your people here.")

"Huh?" I put in. "Who? Where?"

("Next door.") She was gone with gliding swiftness; the bellhop speeded up to stay ahead of her.

I spun around. "Did you hear that?"

"I certainly did!"

"Well—you eat if you want to; I'm going to look for those other humans."

"Hey! Wait for me!"

"I thought you wanted to eat."

"Well . . ." Peewee looked at the food. "Just a sec." She hastily buttered two slices of bread and handed one to me. I was not in that much of a hurry; I ate it. Peewee gobbled hers, took a gulp from the mug and offered it to me. "Want some?"

It wasn't quite cocoa; there was a meaty flavor, too. But it was good. I handed it back and she finished it. "Now I can fight wildcats. Let's go, Kip."

"Next door" was through the foyer of our three-room suite and fifteen yards down the corridor, where we came to a door arch. I kept Peewee back and glanced in cautiously.

It was a diorama, a fake scene.

This one was better than you see in museums. I was looking through a bush at a small clearing in wild country. It ended in a limestone bank. I could see overcast sky and a cave mouth in the rocks. The ground was wet, as if from rain.

A cave man hunkered down close to the cave. He was gnawing the carcass of a small animal, possibly a squirrel.

Peewee tried to shove past me; I stopped her. The cave mad did not appear to notice us which struck me as a good idea. His legs looked short but I think he weighed twice what I do and he was muscled like a weight lifter, with short, hairy forearms and knotty biceps and calves. His head was huge, bigger than mine and longer, but his forehead and chin weren't much. His teeth were large and yellow and a front one was broken. I heard bones crunching.

In a museum I would have expected a card reading "Neanderthal Man—*circa* Last Ice Age." But wax dummies of extinct breeds don't crack bones.

Peewee protested, "Hey, let me look."

He heard. Peewee stared at him, he stared toward us. Peewee squealed; he whirled and ran into the cave, waddling but making time.

I grabbed Peewee. "Let's get out of here!"

"Wait a minute," she said calmly. "He won't come out in a hurry." She tried to push the bush aside.

"Peewee!"

"Try this," she suggested. Her hand was shoving air. "They've got him penned."

I tried it. Something transparent blocked the arch. I could push it a little but not more than an inch. "Plastic?" I suggested. "Like Lucite but springier?"

"Mmm . . ." said Peewee. "More like the helmet of my suit. Tougher, though—and I'll bet light passes only one way. I don't think he saw us."

"Okay, let's get back to our rooms. Maybe we can lock them."

She went on feeling that barrier. "Peewee!" I said sharply. "You're not listening."

"What were you doing talking," she answered reasonably, "when I wasn't listening?"

"Peewee! This is no time to be difficult."

"You sound like Daddy. He dropped that rat he was eating—he might come back."

"If he does, you won't be here, because I'm about to drag you—and if you bite, I'll bite back. I warn you."

She looked around with a trace of animosity. "I wouldn't bite you, Kip, no matter what you did. But if you're going to be stuffy—oh, well, I doubt if he'll come out for an hour or so. We'll come back."

"Okay." I pulled her away.

But we did not leave. I heard a loud whistle and a shout: "Hey, buster! Over here!"

The words were not English, but I understood—well enough. The yell came from an archway across the corridor and a little farther on. I hesitated, then moved toward it because Peewee did so.

A man about forty-five was loafing in this doorway. He was no Neanderthal; he was civilized—or somewhat so. He wore a long heavy woolen tunic, belted in at the waist, forming a sort of kilt. His legs below that were wrapped in wool and he was shod in heavy short boots, much worn. At the belt and supported by a shoulder sling was a short, heavy sword; there was a dagger on the other side of the belt. His hair was short and he was clean-shaven save for a few days' gray stubble. His expression was neither friendly nor unfriendly; it was sharply watchful.

"Thanks," he said gruffly. "Are you the jailer?"

Peewee gasped. "Why, that's Latin!"

What do you do when you meet a Legionary? Right after a cave man? I answered: "No, I am a prisoner myself." I said it in Spanish and repeated it in pretty fair classical Latin. I used Spanish because Peewee hadn't been quite correct. It was not Latin he spoke, not the Latin of Ovid and Gaius Julius Caesar. Nor was it Spanish. It was in between, with an atrocious accent and other differences. But I could worry out the meaning.

He sucked his lip and answered, "That's bad. I've been trying for three days to attract attention and all I get is another prisoner. But that's how the die rolls. Say, that's a funny accent you have."

"Sorry, amigo, but I have trouble understanding you, too." I repeated it in Latin, then split the difference. I added, in improvised lingua franca, "Speak slowly, will you?"

"I'll speak as I please. And don't call me 'amico'; I'm a Roman citizen—so don't get gay."

That's a free translation. His advice was more vulgar—I think. It was close to a Spanish phrase which certainly is vulgar.

"What's he saying?" demanded Peewee. "It *is* Latin, isn't it? Translate!"

I was glad she hadn't caught it. "Why, Peewee, don't you know 'the language of poetry and science'?"

"Oh, don't be a smartie! Tell me."

"Don't crowd me, hon. I'll tell you later. I'm having trouble following it."

"What is that barbarian grunting?" the Roman said pleasantly. "Talk language, boy. Or will you have ten with the flat of the sword?"

He seemed to be leaning on nothing—so I felt the air. It was solid; I decided not to worry about his threat. "I'm talking as best I can. We spoke to each other in our own language."

"Pig grunts. Talk Latin. If you can." He looked at Peewee as if just noticing her. "Your daughter? Want to sell her? If she had meat on her bones, she might be worth a half denario."

Peewee clouded up. "I understood that!" she said fiercely. "Come out here and fight!"

"Try it in Latin," I advised her. "If he understands you, he'll probably spank you."

She looked uneasy. "You wouldn't let him?"

"You know I wouldn't."

"Let's go back."

"That's what I said earlier." I escorted her past the cave man's lair to our suite. "Peewee, I'm going back and see what our noble Roman has to say. Do you mind?"

"I certainly do!"

"Be reasonable, hon. If we could be hurt by them, the Mother Thing would know it. After all, she told us they were here."

"I'll go with you."

"What for? I'll tell you everything I learn. This may be a chance to find out what this silliness means. What's *he* doing here? Have they kept him in deep-freeze a couple of thousand years? How long has he been awake? What does he know that we don't? We're in a bad spot; all the data I can dig up we need. You can help by keeping out. If you're scared, send for the Mother Thing."

She pouted. "I'm not scared. All right—if that's the way you want it."

"I do. Eat your dinner."

Jo-Jo the dogface boy was not in sight; I gave his door a wide berth. If a ship can go anywhere in *no* time, could it skip a dimension and go anywhere to *any* time? How would the math work out? The soldier was still lounging at his door. He looked up. "Didn't you hear me say to stick around?"

"I heard you," I admitted, "but we're not going to get anywhere if you take that attitude. I'm not one of your privates."

"Lucky for you!"

"Do we talk peacefully? Or do I leave?"

He looked me over. "Peace. But don't get smart with me, barbarian."

He called himself "Iunio." He had served in Spain and Gaul, then transferred to the VIth Legion, the "Victrix" —which he felt that even a barbarian should know of. His legion's garrison was Eboracum, north of Londinium in Britain, but he had been on advance duty as a brevet centurion (he pronounced it "centurio")—his permanent rank was about like top sergeant. He was smaller than I am but I would not want to meet him in an alley. Nor at the palisades of a castra.

He had a low opinion of Britons and all barbarians including me ("nothing personal—some of my best friends are barbarians"), women, the British climate, high brass, and priests; he thought well of Caesar, Rome, the gods, and his own professional ability. The army wasn't what it used to be and the slump came from treating auxiliaries like Roman citizens.

He had been guarding the building of a wall to hold back barbarians—a nasty lot who would sneak up and slit your throat and eat you—which no doubt had happened to him, since he was now in the nether regions.

I thought he was talking about Hadrian's Wall, but it was three days' march north of there, where the seas were closest together. The climate there was terrible and the natives were bloodthirsty beasts who dyed their bodies and didn't appreciate civilization—you'd think the Eagles were trying to steal their dinky island. Provincial . . . like me. No offense meant.

Nevertheless he had bought a little barbarian to wife and had been looking forward to garrison duty at Eboracum—when this happened. Iunio shrugged. "Perhaps if I had been careful with lustrations and sacrifices, my luck wouldn't have run out. But I figure that if a man does his duty and keeps himself and his weapons clean, the rest is the C.O.'s worry. Careful of that doorway; it's witched."

The longer he talked the easier it was to understand him. The "-us" endings turned to "-o" and his vocabulary was not that of *De Bello Gallico* —"horse" wasn't "equus"; it was "caballo." His idioms bothered me, plus the fact that his Latin was diluted by a dozen barbarian tongues. But you can blank out every third word in a newspaper and still catch the gist.

I learned a lot about the daily life and petty politics of the Victrix and nothing that I wanted to know. Iunio did not know how he had gotten where he was nor why—except that he was dead and awaiting disposition in a receiving barracks somewhere in the nether world—a theory which I was not yet prepared to accept.

He knew the year of his "death"—Year Eight of the Emperor and Eight Hundred and Ninety-Nine of Rome. I wrote out the dates in Roman numerals to make sure. But I did not remember when Rome was founded nor could I identify the "Caesar" even by his full name —there have been so many Caesars. But Hadrian's Wall had been built and Britain was still occupied; that placed Iunio close to the third century.

He wasn't interested in the cave man across the way—it embodied to him the worst vice of a barbarian: cowardice. I didn't argue but I would be timid, too, if I had saber-toothed tigers yowling at my door. (Did they have saber-tooths then? Make it "cave bears.")

Iunio went back and returned with hard dark bread, cheese, and a cup. He did not offer me any and I don't think it was the barrier. He poured a little of his drink on the floor and started to chomp. It was a mud floor; the walls were rough stone and the ceiling was supported by wooden beams. It may have been a copy of dwellings during the occupation of Britain, but I'm no expert.

I didn't stay much longer. Not only did bread and cheese remind me that I was hungry, but I offended Iunio. I don't know what set him off, but he discussed me with cold thoroughness, my eating habits, ancestry, appearance, conduct, and method of earning a living. Iunio was pleasant—as long as you agreed with him, ignored insults, and deferred to him. Many older people demand this, even in buying a thirty-nine-cent can of talcum; you learn to give it without thinking—otherwise you get a reputation as a fresh kid and potential juvenile delinquent. The less respect an older person deserves the more certain he is to demand it from anyone younger. So I left, as Iunio didn't know anything helpful anyhow. As I went back I saw the cave man peering out his cave. I said, "Take it easy, Jo-Jo," and went on.

I bumped into another invisible barrier blocking our archway. I felt it, then said quietly, "I want to go in." The barrier melted away and I walked in—then found that it was back in place.

My rubber soles made no noise and I didn't call out because Peewee might be asleep. Her door was open and I peeped in. She was sitting tailor-fashion on that incredible Oriental divan, rocking Madame Pompadour and crying.

I backed away, then returned whistling, making a racket, and calling to her. She popped out of her door, with smiling face and no trace of tears. "Hi, Kip! It took you long enough."

"That guy talks too much. What's new?"

"Nothing. I ate and you didn't come back, so I took a nap. You woke me. What did you find out?"

"Let me order dinner and I'll tell you while I eat."

I was chasing the last bit of gravy when a bellhop robot came for us. It was like the other one except that it had in glowing gold on its front that triangle with three spirals. "Follow me," it said in English.

I looked at Peewee. "Didn't the Mother Thing say she was coming back?"

"Why, I thought so."

The machine repeated, "Follow me. Your presence is required."

I laid my ears back. I have taken lots of orders, some of which I shouldn't have, but I had never yet taken orders from a piece of machinery. "Go climb a rope!" I said. "You'll have to drag me."

This is not what to say to a robot. It did.

Peewee yelled, "*Mother Thing! Where are you? Help us!*"

Her birdsong came out of the machine. ("It's all right, dears. The servant will lead you to me.")

I quit struggling and started to walk. That refugee from an appliance dealer took us into another lift, then into a corridor whose walls whizzed past as soon as we entered. It nudged us through an enormous archway topped by the triangle and spirals and herded us into a pen near one wall. The pen was not apparent until we moved—more of that annoying solid air.

It was the biggest room I have ever been in, triangular, unbroken by post or pillar, with ceiling so high and walls so distant that I half expected local thunderstorms. An enormous room makes me feel like an ant; I was glad to be near a wall. The room was not empty —hundreds in it—but it looked empty because they were all near the walls; the giant floor was bare.

But there were three wormfaces out in the center— Wormface's trial was in progress.

I don't know if our own Wormface was there. I would not have known even if they had not been a long way off as the difference between two wormfaces is the difference between having your throat cut and being beheaded. But, as we learned, the presence or absence of the individual offender was the least important part of a trial. Wormface was being tried, present or not—alive or dead.

The Mother Thing was speaking. I could see her tiny figure, also far out on the floor but apart from the wormfaces. Her birdsong voice reached me faintly but I heard her words clearly—in English; from somewhere near us her translated words were piped to us. The feel of her was in the English translation just as it was in her bird tones.

She was telling what she knew of wormface conduct, as dispassionately as if describing something under a microscope, like a traffic officer testifying: "At 9:17 on the fifth, while on duty at—" etc. The facts. The Mother Thing was finishing her account of events on Pluto. She chopped it off at the point of explosion.

Another voice spoke, in English. It was flat with a nasal twang and reminded me of a Vermont grocer we had dealt with one summer when I was a kid. He was a man who never smiled nor frowned and what little he said was all in the same tone, whether it was, "She is a good woman," or, "That man would cheat his own son," or, "Eggs are fifty-nine cents," cold as a cash register. This voice was that sort.

It said to the Mother Thing: "Have you finished?"

"I have finished."

"The other witnesses will be heard. Clifford Russell—"

I jumped, as if that grocer had caught me in the candy jar.

The voice went on: "—listen carefully." Another voice started.

My *own*—it was the account I had dictated, flat on my back on Vega Five.

But it wasn't all of it; it was just that which concerned wormfaces. Adjectives and whole sentences had been cut—as if someone had taken scissors to a tape recording. The facts were there; what I thought about them was missing.

It started with ships landing in the pasture back of our house; it ended with that last wormface stumbling blindly down a hole. It wasn't long, as so much had been left out—our hike across the Moon, for example. My description of Wormface was left in but had been trimmed so much that I could have been talking about Venus de Milo instead of the ugliest thing in creation.

My recorded voice ended and the Yankee-grocer voice said, "Were those your words?"

"Huh? Yes."

"Is the account correct?"

"Yes, but—"

"Is it correct?"

"Yes."

"Is it complete?"

I wanted to say that it certainly was *not*—but I was beginning to understand the system. "Yes."

"Patricia Wynant Reisfeld—"

Peewee's story started earlier and covered all those days when she had been in contact with wormfaces while I was not. But it was not much longer, for, while Peewee has a sharp eye and a sharper memory, she is loaded with opinions. Opinions were left out.

When Peewee had agreed that her evidence was correct and complete the Yankee voice stated, "All witnesses have been heard, all known facts have been integrated. The three individuals may speak for themselves."

I think the wormfaces picked a spokesman, perhaps *the* Wormface, if he was alive and there. Their answer, as translated into English, did not have the guttural accent with which Wormface spoke English; nevertheless it was a wormface speaking. That bone-chilling

217

yet highly intelligent viciousness, as unmistakable as a punch in the teeth, was in every syllable.

Their spokesman was so far away that I was not upset by his looks and after the first stomach-twisting shock of that voice I was able to listen more or less judicially. He started by denying that this court had jurisdiction over his sort. He was responsible only to his mother-queen and she only to their queen-groups—that's how the English came out.

That defense, he claimed, was sufficient. However, if the "Three Galaxies" confederation existed—which he had no reason to believe other than that he was now being detained unlawfully before this hiveful of creatures met as a kangaroo court—if it existed, it still had no jurisdiction over the Only People, first, because the organization did not extend to his part of space; second, because even if it were there, the Only People had never joined and therefore its rules (if it had rules) could not apply; and third, it was inconceivable that their queen-group would associate itself with this improbable "Three Galaxies" because people do not contract with animals.

This defense was also sufficient.

But disregarding for the sake of argument these complete and sufficient defenses, this trial was a mockery because no offense existed even under the so-called rules of the alleged "Three Galaxies." They (the wormfaces) had been operating in their own part of space engaged in occupying a useful but empty planet, Earth. No possible crime could lie in colonizing land inhabited merely by animals. As for the agent of Three Galaxies, she had butted in; she had not been harmed; she had merely been kept from interfering and had been detained only for the purpose of returning her where she belonged.

He should have stopped. Any of these defenses might have stood up, especially the last one. I used to think of the human race as "lords of creation"—but things had happened to me since. I was not sure that this assemblage would think that humans had rights compared with wormfaces. Certainly the wormfaces were ahead of us in many ways. When we clear jungle to make farms, do we worry if baboons are there first?

But he discarded these defenses, explained that they were intellectual exercises to show how foolish the whole thing was under *any* rules, from *any* point of view. He would now make his defense.

It was an attack.

The viciousness in his voice rose to a crescendo of hatred that made every word slam like a blow. How *dared* they do this? They were mice voting to bell the cat! (I know—but that's how it came out in translation.) They were animals to be eaten, or merely vermin to be exterminated. Their mercy would be rejected if offered, no negotiation was possible, their crimes would never be forgotten, the Only People would destroy them!

I looked around to see how the jury was taking it. This almost-empty hall had hundreds of creatures around the three sides and many were close to us. I had been too busy with the trial to do more than glance at them. Now I looked, for the wormface's blast was so disturbing that I welcomed a distraction.

They were all sorts and I'm not sure that any two were alike. There was one twenty feet from me who was as horrible as Wormface and amazingly like him— except that this creature's grisly appearance did not inspire disgust. There were others almost human in appearance, although they were greatly in the minority. There was one really likely-looking chick as human as I am—except for iridescent skin and odd and skimpy notions of dress. She was so pretty that I would have sworn that the iridescence was just make-up—but I probably would have been wrong. I wondered in what language the diatribe was reaching her? Certainly not English.

Perhaps she felt my stare, for she looked around and unsmilingly examined me, as I might a chimpanzee in a cage. I guess the attraction wasn't mutual.

There was every gradation from pseudo-wormface to the iridescent girl—not only the range between, but also way out in left field; some had their own private aquaria.

I could not tell how the invective affected them. The girl creature was taking it quietly, but what can you say about a walrus thing with octopus arms? If he twitches, is he angry? Or laughing? Or itches where the twitch is?

The Yankee-voiced spokesman let the wormface rave on.

Peewee was holding my hand. Now she grabbed my ear, tilted her face and whispered, "He talks nasty." She sounded awed.

The wormface ended with a blast of hate that must have overtaxed the translator for instead of English we heard a wordless scream.

The Yankee voice said flatly, "But do you have anything to say in your defense?"

The scream was repeated, then the wormface became coherent. "I have made my defense—that no defense is necessary."

The emotionless voice went on, to the Mother Thing. "Do you speak for them?"

She answered reluctantly, "My lord peers . . . I am forced to say . . . that I found them to be quite naughty." She sounded grieved.

"You find against them?"

"I do."

"Then you may not be heard. Such is the Law."

" 'Three Galaxies, One Law.' I may not speak."

The flat voice went on, "Will any witness speak favorably?"

There was silence.

That was my chance to be noble. We humans were their victims; we were in a position to speak up, point out that from their standpoint they hadn't done anything wrong, and ask mercy—if they would promise to behave in the future.

Well, I didn't. I've heard all the usual Sweetness and Light that kids get pushed at them—how they should always forgive, how there's some good in the worst of us, etc. But when I see a black widow, I step on it; I don't plead with it to be a good little spider and please stop poisoning people. A black widow spider can't help it—but that's the point.

The voice said to the wormfaces: "Is there any race anywhere which might speak for you? If so, it will be summoned."

The spokesman wormface spat at the idea. That another race might be character witnesses for them disgusted him.

"So be it," answered the Yankee voice. "Are the facts sufficient to permit a decision?"

Almost immediately the voice answered itself: "Yes."

"What is the decision?"

Again it answered itself: "Their planet shall be rotated."

It didn't sound like much—shucks, all planets rotate—and the flat voice held no expression. But the verdict scared me. The whole room seemed to shudder.

The Mother Thing turned and came toward us. It was a long way but she reached us quickly. Peewee flung herself on her; the solid air that penned us solidified still more until we three were in a private room, a silvery hemisphere.

Peewee was trembling and gasping and the Mother Thing comforted her. When Peewee had control of herself, I said nervously, "Mother Thing? What did he mean? 'Their planet shall be rotated.'"

She looked at me without letting go of Peewee and her great soft eyes were sternly sad. ("It means that their planet is tilted ninety degrees out of the space-time of your senses and mine.")

Her voice sounded like a funeral dirge played softly on a flute. Yet the verdict did not seem tragic to me. I knew what she meant; her meaning was even clearer in Vegan than in English. If you rotate a plane figure about an axis in its plane—it disappears. It is no longer in a plane and Mr. A. Square of Flatland is permanently out of touch with it.

But it doesn't cease to exist; it just is no longer where it was. It struck me that the wormfaces were getting off easy. I had halfway expected their planet to be blown up (and I didn't doubt that Three Galaxies could do so), or something equally drastic. As it was, the wormfaces were to be run out of town and would never find their way back—there are so many, many dimensions—but they wouldn't be hurt; they were just being placed in Coventry.

But the Mother Thing sounded as if she had taken unwilling part in a hanging.

So I asked her.

("You do not understand, dear gentle Kip—*they do not take their star with them.*")

"Oh—" was all I could say.

Peewee turned white.

Stars are the source of life—planets are merely life's containers. Chop off the star . . . and the planet gets colder . . . and colder . . . and *colder*—then still colder.

How long until the very air freezes? How many hours or days to absolute zero? I shivered and got goose pimples. Worse than Pluto—

"Mother Thing? How long before they do this?" I had a queasy misgiving that I should have spoken, that even wormfaces did not deserve *this*. Blow them up, shoot them down—but don't freeze them.

("It is done,") she sang in that same dirgelike way.

"What?"

("The agent charged with executing the decision waits for the word . . . the message goes out the instant we hear it. They were rotated out of our world even before I turned to join you. It is better so.")

I gulped and heard an echo in my mind: *"—'twere well it were done quickly."*

But the Mother Thing was saying rapidly, ("Think no more on 't, for now you must be brave!")

"Huh? What, Mother Thing? What happens now?"

("You'll be summoned any moment—for your own trial.")

I simply stared, I could not speak—I had thought it was all over. Peewee looked still thinner and whiter but did not cry. She wet her lips and said quietly, "You'll come with us, Mother Thing?"

("Oh, my children! I cannot. You must face this alone.")

I found my voice. "But what are *we* being tried for? We haven't hurt anybody. We haven't done a thing."

("Not you personally. Your race is on trial. Through you.")

Peewee turned away from her and looked at me—and I felt a thrill of tragic pride that in our moment of extremity she had turned, not to the Mother Thing, but to *me*, another human being.

I knew that she was thinking of the same thing I was: a ship, a ship hanging close to Earth, only an instant away and yet perhaps uncounted trillion miles in some pocket of folded space, where no DEW line gives warning, where no radar can reach.

The Earth, green and gold and lovely, turning lazily in the warm light of the Sun—

A flat voice— No more Sun.

No stars.

The orphaned Moon would bobble once, then continue around the Sun, a gravestone to the hopes of men. The few at Lunar Base and Luna City and Tombaugh Station would last weeks or even months, the only human beings left alive. Then they would go—if not of suffocation, then of grief and loneliness.

Peewee said shrilly, "Kip, she's not serious! Tell me she's not!"

I said hoarsely, "Mother Thing—are the executioners already waiting?"

She did not answer. She said to Peewee, ("It is very serious, my daughter. But do not be afraid. I exacted a promise before I surrendered you. If things go against your race, you two will return with me and be suffered to live out your little lives in my home. So stand up and tell the truth . . . and do not be afraid.")

The flat voice entered the closed space: "The human beings are summoned."

Chapter 11

We walked out onto that vast floor. The farther we went the more I felt like a fly on a plate. Having Peewee with me was a help; nevertheless it was that nightmare where you find yourself not decently dressed in a public place. Peewee clutched my hand and held Madame Pompadour pressed tightly to her. I wished that I had suited-up in Oscar—I wouldn't have felt quite so under a microscope with Oscar around me.

Just before we left, the Mother Thing placed her hand against my forehead and started to hold me with her eyes. I pushed her hand aside and looked away. "No," I told her. "No treatments! I'm not going to—oh, I know you mean well but I won't take an anesthetic. Thanks."

She did not insist; she simply turned to Peewee. Peewee looked uncertain, then shook her head. "We're ready," she piped.

The farther out we got on that great bare floor the more I regretted that I had not let the Mother Thing do whatever it was that kept one from worrying. At least I should have insisted that Peewee take it.

Coming at us from the other walls were two other flies; as they got closer I recognized them: the Neanderthal and the Legionary. The cave man was being dragged invisibly; the Roman covered ground in a long, slow, easy lope. We all arrived at the center at the same time and were stopped about twenty feet apart, Peewee and I at one point of a triangle, the Roman and the cave man each at another.

I called out, "Hail, Iunio!"

"Silence, barbarian." He looked around him, his eyes estimating the crowd at the walls.

He was no longer in casual dress. The untidy leggings

were gone; strapped to his right shin was armor. Over the tunic he wore full cuirass and his head was brave with plumed helmet. All metal was burnished, all leather was clean.

He had approached with his shield on his back, route-march style. But even as we were stopped he unslung it and raised it on his left arm. He did not draw his sword as his right hand held his javelin at the ready—carried easily while his wary eyes assessed the foe.

To his left the cave man hunkered himself small, as an animal crouches who has no place to hide.

"Iunio!" I called out. "Listen!" The sight of those two had me still more worried. The cave man I could not talk to but perhaps I could reason with the Roman. "Do you know why we are here?"

"I know," he tossed over his shoulder. "Today the Gods try us in their arena. This is work for a soldier and a Roman citizen. You're no help so keep out. No—watch behind me and shout. Caesar will reward you."

I started to try to talk sense but was cut off by a giant voice from everywhere:

"YOU ARE NOW BEING JUDGED!"

Peewee shivered and got closer. I twisted my left hand out of her clutch, substituted my right, and put my left arm around her shoulders. "Head up, partner," I said softly. "Don't let them scare you."

"I'm not scared," she whispered as she trembled. "Kip? You do the talking."

"Is that the way you want it?"

"Yes. You don't get mad as fast as I do—and if I lost my temper . . . well, that'd be *awful.*"

"Okay."

We were interrupted by that flat, nasal twang. As before, it seemed close by. "This case derives from the one preceding it. The three temporal samples are from a small Lanador-type planet around a star in an out-center part of the Third Galaxy. It is a very primitive area having no civilized races. This race, as you see from the samples, is barbaric. It has been examined twice before and would not yet be up for routine examination had not new facts about it come out in the case which preceded it."

The voice asked itself: "When was the last examination made?"

It answered itself: "Approximately one half-death of Thorium-230 ago." It added, apparently to us only: "About eighty thousand of your years."

Iunio jerked his head and looked around, as if trying to locate the voice. I concluded that he had heard the same figure in his corrupt Latin. Well, I was startled too—but I was numb to that sort of shock.

"Is it necessary again so soon?"

"It is. There has been a discontinuity. They are developing with unexpected speed." The flat voice went on, speaking to us: "I am your judge. Many of the civilized beings you see around you are part of me. Others are spectators, some are students, and a few are here because they hope to catch me in a mistake." The voice added, "This they have not managed to do in more than a million of your years."

I blurted out, "You are more than a million years old?" I did not add that I didn't believe it.

The voice answered, "I am older than that, but no part of me is that old. I am partly machine, which part can be repaired, replaced, recopied; I am partly alive, these parts die and are replaced. My living parts are more than a dozen dozens of dozens of civilized beings from throughout Three Galaxies, any dozen dozens of which may join with my non-living part to act. Today I am two hundred and nine qualified beings, who have at their instant disposal all knowledge accumulated in my non-living part and all its ability to analyze and integrate."

I said sharply, "Are your decisions made unanimously?" I thought I saw a loophole—I never had much luck mixing up Dad and Mother but there had been times as a kid when I had managed to confuse issues by getting one to answer one way and the other to answer another.

The voice added evenly, "Decisions are always unanimous. It may help you to think of me as one person." It addressed everyone: "Standard sampling has been followed. The contemporary sample is the double one; the intermediate sample for curve check is the clothed single sample and was taken by standard random at a spacing of approximately one half-death of Radium-226—" The voice supplemented: "—call it sixteen hundred of your years. The remote curve-check sample, by standard procedure, was taken at two dozen times that distance."

The voice asked itself: "Why is curve-check spacing so short? Why not at least a dozen times that?"

"Because this organism's generations are very short. It mutates rapidly."

The explanation appeared to satisfy for it went on, "The youngest sample will witness first."

I thought he meant Peewee and so did she; she cringed. But the voice barked and the cave man jerked. He did not answer; he simply crouched more deeply into himself.

The voice barked again.

It then said to itself, "I observe something."

"Speak."

"This creature is not ancestor to those others."

The voice of the machine almost seemed to betray emotion, as if my dour grocer had found salt in his sugar bin. "The sample was properly taken."

"Nevertheless," it answered, "it is not a correct sample. You must review all pertinent data."

For a long five seconds was silence. Then the voice spoke: "This poor creature is not ancestor to these others; he is cousin only. He has no future of his own. Let him be returned at once to the space-time whence he came."

The Neanderthal was dragged rapidly away. I watched him out of sight with a feeling of loss. I had been afraid of him at first. Then I had despised him and was ashamed of him. He was a coward, he was filthy, he stank. A dog was more civilized. But in the past five minutes I had decided that I had better love him, see his good points—for, unsavory as he was, he was *human*. Maybe he wasn't my remote grandfather, but I was in no mood to disown even my sorriest relation.

The voice argued with itself, deciding whether the trial could proceed. Finally it stated: "Examination will continue. If enough facts are not developed, another remote sample of correct lineage will be summoned. Iunio."

The Roman raised his javelin higher. "Who calls Iunio?"

"Stand forth and bear witness."

Just as I feared, Iunio told the voice where to go and what to do. There was no protecting Peewee from his language; it echoed back in English—not that it mattered now whether Peewee was protected from "unladylike" influences.

The flat voice went on imperturbably: "Is this your voice? Is this your witnessing?" Immediately another voice started up which I recognized as that of the Roman, answering questions, giving accounts of battle, speaking of treatment of prisoners. This we got only in English but the translation held the arrogant timbre of Iunio's voice.

Iunio shouted "Witchcraft!" and made horns at them.

The recording cut off. "The voice matches," the machine said dryly. "The recording will be integrated."

But it continued to peck at Iunio, asking him details about who he was, why he was in Britain, what he had done there, and why it was necessary to serve Caesar. Iunio gave short answers, then blew his top and gave none. He let out a rebel yell that bounced around that mammoth room, drew back and let fly his javelin.

It fell short. But I think he broke the Olympic record. I found myself cheering.

Iunio drew his sword while the javelin was still rising. He flung it up in a gladiatorial challenge, shouting, "Hail, Caesar!" and dropped into guard.

He reviled them. He told them what he thought of vermin who were not citizens, not even *barbarians!*

I said to myself, "Oh, oh! There goes the game. Human race, you've had it."

Iunio went on and on, calling on his gods to help him, each way worse than the last, threatening them with Caesar's vengeance in gruesome detail. I hoped that, even though it was translated, Peewee would not understand much of it. But she probably did; she understood entirely too much.

I began to grow proud of him. That wormface, in diatribe, was evil; Iunio was not. Under bad grammar, worse language, and rough manner, that tough old sergeant had courage, human dignity, and a basic gallantry. He might be an old scoundrel—but he was *my* kind of scoundrel.

He finished by demanding that they come at him, one at a time—or let them form a turtle and he would take them all on at once. "I'll make a funeral pyre of you! I'll temper my blade in your guts! I, who am about to die, will show you a Roman's grave—piled high with Caesar's enemies!"

He had to catch his breath. I cheered again and Peewee joined in. He looked over his shoulder and grinned.

"Slit their throats as I bring them down, boy! There's work to do!"

The cold voice said: "Let him now be returned to the space-time whence he came."

Iunio looked startled as invisible hands pulled him along. He called on Mars and Jove and laid about him. The sword clattered to the floor—picked itself up and returned itself to his scabbard. Iunio was moving rapidly away; I cupped my hands and yelled, "Good-bye, Iunio!"

"Farewell, boy! They're *cowards!*" He shook himself. "Nothing but filthy witchcraft!" Then he was gone.

"Clifford Russell—"

"Huh? I'm here." Peewee squeezed my hand.

"Is this your voice?"

I said, "Wait a minute—"

"Yes? Speak."

I took a breath. Peewee pushed closer and whispered, "Make it good, Kip. They mean it."

"I'll try, kid," I whispered, then went on, "What is this? I was told you intend to judge the human race."

"That is correct."

"But you *can't.* You haven't enough to go on. No better than witchcraft, just as Iunio said. You brought in a cave man—then decided he was a mistake. That isn't your only mistake. You had Iunio here. Whatever he was—and I'm not ashamed of him; I'm proud of him—he's got nothing to do with *now.* He's been dead two thousand years, pretty near—if you've sent him back, I mean—and all that he was is dead with him. Good or bad, he's not what the human race is *now.*"

"I know that. You two are the test sample of your race now."

"Yes—but you can't judge from *us.* Peewee and I are about as far from average as any specimens can be. We don't claim to be angels, either one of us. If you condemn our race on what *we* have done, you do a great injustice. Judge *us*—or judge *me*, at least—"

"Me, too!"

"—on whatever I've done. But don't hold my people responsible. That's not scientific. That's not valid mathematics."

"It is valid."

"It is *not*. Human beings aren't molecules; they're all different." I decided not to argue about jurisdiction; the wormfaces had ruined that approach.

"Agreed, human beings are not molecules. But they are not individuals, either."

"Yes, they are!"

"They are not independent individuals; they are parts of a single organism. Each cell in your body contains your whole pattern. From three samples of the organism you call the human race I can predict the future potentialities and limits of that race."

"We have no limits! There's no telling what our future will be."

"It may be that you have no limits," the voice agreed. "That is to be determined. But, if true, it is not a point in your favor. For *we* have limits."

"Huh?"

"You have misunderstood the purpose of this examination. You speak of 'justice.' I know what you think you mean. But no two races have ever agreed on the meaning of that term, no matter how they say it. It is not a concept I deal with here. This is not a court of justice."

"Then what is it?"

"You would call it a 'Security Council.' Or you might call it a committee of vigilantes. It does not matter what you call it; my sole purpose is to examine your race and see if you threaten our survival. If you do, I will now dispose of you. The only certain way to avert a grave danger is to remove it while it is small. Things that I have learned about you suggest a possibility that you may someday threaten the security of Three Galaxies. I will now determine the facts."

"But you said that you have to have at least three samples. The cave man was no good."

"We have three samples, you two and the Roman. But the facts could be determined from one sample. The use of three is a custom from earlier times, a cautious habit of checking and rechecking. I cannot dispense 'justice'; I can make sure not to produce error."

I was about to say that he was wrong, even if he was a million years old. But the voice went on, "I continue the examination. Clifford Russell, is this your voice?"

My voice sounded then—and again it was my own dictated account, but this time everything was left in—purple adjectives, personal opinions, comments about other matters, every word and stutter.

I listened to enough of it, held up my hand. "All right, all right, I said it."

The recording stopped. "Do you now confirm it?"

"Eh? Yes."

"Do you wish to add, subtract, or change?"

I thought hard. Aside from a few wisecracks that I had tucked in later it was a straight-forward account. "No. I stand on it."

"And is this also your voice?"

This one fooled me. It was that endless recording I had made for Prof Joe about—well, everything on Earth . . . history, customs, peoples, the works. Suddenly I knew why Prof Joe had worn the same badge the Mother Thing wore. What did they call that?—"Planting a stool pigeon." Good Old Prof Joe, the no-good, had been a stoolie.

I felt sick.

"Let me hear more of it."

They accommodated me. I didn't really listen; I was trying to remember, not what I was hearing, but what else I might have said—what I had admitted that could be used against the human race. The Crusades? Slavery? The gas chambers at Dachau? *How much had I said?*

The recording droned on. Why, that thing had taken *weeks* to record; we could stand here until our feet went flat.

"It's my voice."

"Do you stand on this, too? Or do you wish to correct, revise, or extend?"

I said cautiously, "Can I do the whole thing over?"

"If you so choose."

I started to say that I would, that they should wipe the tape and start over. But would they? Or would they keep both and compare them? I had no compunction about lying—"tell the truth and shame the devil" is no virtue when your family and friends and your whole race are at stake.

But could they tell if I lied?

"The Mother Thing said to tell the truth and not to be afraid."

"But she's not on our side!"

"Oh, yes, she is."

I had to answer. I was so confused that I couldn't think. I had tried to tell the truth to Prof Joe . . . oh, maybe I had shaded things, not included every horrid thing that makes a headline. But it was essentially true.

Could I do better under pressure? Would they let me start fresh and accept any propaganda I cooked up? Or would the fact that I changed stories be used to condemn our race?

"I stand on it!"

"Let it be integrated. Patricia Wynant Reisfeld—"

Peewee took only moments to identify and allow to be integrated her recordings; she simply followed my example.

The machine voice said: "The facts have been integrated. By their own testimony, these are a savage and brutal people, given to all manner of atrocities. They eat each other, they starve each other, they kill each other. They have no art and only the most primitive of science, yet such is their violent nature that even with so little knowledge they are now energetically using it to exterminate each other, tribe against tribe. Their driving will is such that they may succeed. But if by some unlucky chance they fail, they will inevitably, in time, reach other stars. It is this possibility which must be calculated: how soon they will reach us, if they live, and what their potentialities will be then."

The voice continued to us: "This is the indictment against you—your own savagery, combined with superior intelligence. What have you to say in your defense?"

I took a breath and tried to steady down. I knew that we had lost—yet I had to try.

I remembered how the Mother Thing had spoken. "My lord peers—"

"Correction. We are not your 'lords,' nor has it been established that you are our equals. If you wish to address someone, you may call me the 'Moderator.' "

"Yes, Mr. Moderator—" I tried to remember what Socrates had said to his judges. He knew ahead of time that he was condemned just as we knew—but somehow, though he had been forced to drink hemlock, he had won and they had lost.

No! I couldn't use his *Apologia*—all he had lost was his *own* life. This was *everybody*.

"—you say we have no art. Have you see the Parthenon?"

"Blown up in one of your wars."

"Better see it before you rotate us—or you'll be missing something. Have you read our poetry? 'Our revels now are ended: these our actors, as I foretold you, were all spirits, and are melted into air, into thin air: And, like the baseless fabric of this vision, the cloud-capped towers, the gorgeous palaces, the solemn temples, the great globe itself . . . itself—yea—all which it . . . inherit—shall dissolve—"

I broke down. I heard Peewee sobbing beside me. I don't know why I picked that one—but they say the subconscious mind never does things "accidentally." I guess it had to be that one.

"As it well may," commented the merciless voice.

"I don't think it's any of your *business* what we do—as long as we leave you alone—" My stammer was back and I was almost sobbing.

"We have made it our business."

"We aren't under your government and—"

"Correction. Three Galaxies is not a government; conditions for government cannot obtain in so vast a space, such varied cultures. We have simply formed police districts for mutual protection."

"But—even so, we haven't troubled your cops. We were in our own backyards—I *was* in my own backyard!—when these wormface things came along and started troubling *us*. We haven't hurt *you*."

I stopped, wondering where to turn. I couldn't guarantee good behavior, not for the whole human race—the machine knew it and I knew it.

"Inquiry." It was talking to itself again. "These creatures appear to be identical with the Old Race, allowing for mutation. What part of the Third Galaxy are they from?"

It answered itself, naming co-ordinates that meant nothing to me. "But they are not of the Old Race; they are ephemerals. That is the danger; they change too fast."

"Didn't the Old Race lose a ship out that way a few half-deaths of Thorium-230 ago? Could that account for the fact that the youngest sample failed to match?"

It answered firmly, "It is immaterial whether or not

they may be descended from the Old Race. An examination is in progress; a decision must be made."

"The decision must be sure."

"It will be." The bodyless voice went on, to us: "Have either of you anything to add in your defense?"

I had been thinking of what had been said about the miserable state of our science. I wanted to point out that we had gone from muscle power to atomic power in only two centuries—but I was afraid that fact would be used against us. "Peewee, can you think of *anything?*"

She suddenly stepped forward and shrilled to the air, "Doesn't it count that Kip saved the Mother Thing?"

"No," the cold voice answered. "It is irrelevant."

"Well, it ought to count!" She was crying again. "You ought to be *ashamed* of yourselves! Bullies! *Cowards!* Oh, you're worse than wormfaces!"

I pulled her back. She hid her head against my shoulder and shook. Then she whispered, "I'm sorry, Kip. I didn't mean to. I guess I've ruined it."

"It was ruined anyhow, honey."

"Have you anything more to say?" old no-face went on relentlessly.

I looked around at the hall. —*the cloud-capped towers . . . the great globe itself*— "Just this!" I said savagely. "It's not a defense, you don't *want* a defense. All right, take away our star— You will if you can and I guess you can. Go ahead! We'll *make* a star! Then, someday, we'll come back and hunt you down—*all of you!*"

"That's telling 'em, Kip! That's telling them!"

Nobody bawled me out. I suddenly felt like a kid who has made a horrible mistake at a party and doesn't know how to cover it up.

But I meant it. Oh, I didn't think we could *do* it. Not yet. But we'd *try.* "Die trying" is the proudest human thing.

"It is possible that you will," that infuriating voice went on. "Are you through?"

"I'm through." We all were through . . . every one of us.

"Does anyone speak for them? Humans, will any race speak for you?"

We didn't *know* any other races. Dogs— Maybe dogs would.

"I speak for them!"

Peewee raised her head with a jerk. "Mother Thing!"

Suddenly she was in front of us. Peewee tried to run to her, bounced off that invisible barrier. I grabbed her. "Easy, hon. She isn't there—it's some sort of television."

"My lord peers . . . you have the advantage of many minds and much knowledge—" It was odd to see her singing, hear her in English; the translation still held that singing quality.

"—but *I* know them. It is true that they are violent— especially the smaller one—but they are not more violent than is appropriate to their ages. Can we expect mature restraint in a race whose members all must die in early childhood? And are not we ourselves violent? Have we not this day killed our billions? Can any race survive without a willingness to fight? It is true that these creatures are often more violent than is necessary or wise. But, my peers, they all are so very young. Give them time to learn."

"That is exactly what there is to fear, that they may learn. Your race is overly sentimental; it distorts your judgment."

"Not true! We are compassionate, we are *not* foolish. I myself have been the proximate cause of how many, many adverse decisions? You know; it is in your records—I prefer not to remember. And I shall be again. When a branch is diseased beyond healing, it must be pruned. We are not sentimental; we are the best watchers you have ever found, for we do it without anger. Toward evil we have no mercy. But the mistakes of a child we treat with loving forbearance."

"Have you finished?"

"I say that this branch need not be pruned! I have finished."

The Mother Thing's image vanished. The voice went on, "Does any other race speak for them?"

"I do." Where she had been now stood a large green monkey. He stared at us and shook his head, then suddenly did a somersault and finished looking at us between his legs. "I'm no friend of theirs but I am a lover of 'justice'—in which I differ from my colleagues in this Council." He twirled rapidly several times. "As our sister has said, this race is young. The infants of my own noble race bite and scratch each other—some even die from it. Even *I* behaved so, at one time." He jumped into the air, landed on his hands, did a flip from that position. "Yet does anyone here deny that *I* am civilized?" He stopped, looked at us thoughtfully while scratching. "These are brutal savages and I don't see how anyone could ever *like* them—but *I* say: give them their chance!"

His image disappeared.

The voice said, "Have you anything to add before a decision is reached?"

I started to say: No, get it over with—when Peewee grabbed my ear and whispered. I listened, nodded, and spoke. "Mr. Moderator—if the verdict is against us—can you hold off your hangmen long enough to let us *go home?* We know that you can send us home in only a few minutes."

The voice did not answer quickly. "Why do you wish this? As I have explained, you are not personally on trial. It has been arranged to let you live."

"We know. We'd rather be home, that's all—with our people."

Again a tiny hesitation. "It shall be done."

"Are the facts sufficient to permit a decision?"

"Yes."

"What is the decision?"

"This race will be re-examined in a dozen half-deaths of radium. Meanwhile there is danger to it from itself. Against this mischance it will be given assistance. During the probationary period it will be watched closely by Guardian Mother—" the machine trilled the true Vegan name of the Mother Thing "—the cop on that beat, who will report at once any ominous change. In the meantime we wish this race good progress in its long journey upward.

"Let them now be returned forthwith to the space-time whence they came."

Chapter 12

I didn't think it was safe to make our atmosphere descent in New Jersey without filing a flight plan. Princeton is near important targets; we might be homed-on by everything up to A-missiles. The Mother Thing got that indulgent chuckle in her song: ("I fancy we can avoid that.")

She did. She put us down in a side street, sang goodbye and was gone. It's not illegal to be out at night in space suits, even carrying a rag dolly. But it's unusual—cops hauled us in. They phoned Peewee's father and in twenty minutes we were in his study, drinking cocoa and talking and eating shredded wheat.

Peewee's mother almost had a fit. While we told our story she kept gasping, "I can't believe it!" until Professor Reisfeld said, "Stop it, Janice. Or go to bed." I don't blame her. Her daughter disappears on the Moon and is given up for dead—then miraculously reappears on Earth. But Professor Reisfeld believed us. The way the Mother Thing had "understanding" he had "acceptance." When a fact came along, he junked theories that failed to match.

He examined Peewee's suit, had her switch on the helmet, shined a light to turn it opaque, all with a little smile. Then he reached for the phone. "Dario must see this."

"At midnight, Curt?"

"Please, Janice. Armageddon won't wait for office hours."

"Professor Reisfeld?"

"Yes, Kip?"

"Uh, you may want to see other things first."

"That's possible."

I took things from Oscar's pockets—two beacons, one for each of us, some metal "paper" covered with equations, two "happy things," and two silvery spheres. We had stopped on Vega Five, spending most of the time under what I suppose was hypnosis while Prof Joe and another professor thing pumped us for what we knew of human mathematics. They hadn't been learning math from us—oh, no! They wanted the language we use in mathematics, from radicals and vectors to those weird symbols in higher physics, so that *they* could teach *us;* the results were on the metal paper.

First I showed Professor Reisfeld the beacons. "The Mother Thing's beat now includes us. She says to use these if we need her. She'll usually be close by—a thousand light-years at most. But even if she is far away, she'll come."

"Oh." He looked at mine. It was neater and smaller than the one she haywired on Pluto. "Do we dare take it apart?"

"Well, it's got a lot of power tucked in it. It might explode."

"Yes, it might." He handed it back, looking wistful.

A "happy thing" can't be explained. They look like those little abstract sculptures you feel as well as look at. Mine was like obsidian but warm and not hard; Peewee's was more like jade. The surprise comes when you touch one to your head. I had Professor Reisfeld do so and he looked awed—the Mother Thing is all around you and you feel warm and safe and *understood.*

He said, "She loves you. The message wasn't for me. Excuse me."

"Oh, she loves *you*, too."

"Eh?"

"She loves everything small and young and fuzzy and helpless. That's why she's a 'mother thing.' "

I didn't realize how it sounded. But he didn't mind. "You say she is a police officer?"

"Well, she's more of a juvenile welfare officer—this is a slum neighborhood we're in, backward and pretty tough. Sometimes she has to do things she doesn't like. But she's a good cop and somebody has to do nasty jobs. She doesn't shirk them."

"I'm sure she wouldn't."

"Would you like to try it again?"

"Do you mind?"

"Oh, no, it doesn't wear out."

He did and got that warm happy look. He glanced at Peewee, asleep with her face in her cereal. "I need not have worried about my daughter, between the Mother Thing—and you."

"It was a team," I explained. "We couldn't have made it without Peewee. The kid's got guts."

"Too much, sometimes."

"Other times you need that extra. These spheres are recorders. Do you have a tape recorder, Professor?"

"Certainly, sir." We set it up and let a sphere talk to it. I wanted a tape because the spheres are one-shot—the molecules go random again. Then I showed him the metal paper. I had tried to read it, got maybe two inches into it, then just recognized a sign here and there. Professor Reisfeld got halfway down the first page, stopped. "I had better make those phone calls."

At dawn a sliver of old Moon came up and I tried to judge where Tombaugh Station was. Peewee was asleep on her Daddy's couch, wrapped in his bathrobe and clutching Madame Pompadour. He had tried to carry her to bed but she had wakened and become very, very difficult, so he put her down. Professor Reisfeld chewed an empty pipe and listened to my sphere whispering softly to his recorder. Occasionally he darted a question at me and I'd snap out of it.

Professor Giomi and Dr. Bruck were at the other end of the study, filling a blackboard, erasing and filling it again, while they argued over that metal paper. Geniuses are common at the Institute for Advanced Study but these two wouldn't be noticed anywhere; Bruck looked like a truckdriver and Giomi like an excited Iunio. They both had that Okay-I-get-you that Professor Reisfeld had. They were excited but Dr. Bruck showed it only by a tic in his face—which Peewee's Daddy told me was a guarantee of nervous breakdowns—not for Bruck, for other physicists.

Two mornings later we were still there. Professor Reisfeld had shaved; the others hadn't. I napped and once I took a shower. Peewee's Daddy listened to recordings —he was now replaying Peewee's tape. Now and then Bruck and Giomi called him over, Giomi almost hysterical and Bruck stolid. Professor Reisfeld always asked a question or two, nodded and came back to his chair. I don't think he could work that math—but he could soak up results and fit them with other pieces.

I wanted to go home once they were through with me but Professor Reisfeld said please stay; the Secretary General of the Federated Free Nations was coming.

I stayed. I didn't call home because what was the use in upsetting them? I would rather have gone to New York City to meet the Secretary General, but Professor Reisfeld had invited him here—I began to realize that anybody really important would come if Professor Reisfeld asked him.

Mr. van Duivendijk was slender and tall. He shook hands and said, "I understand that you are Dr. Samuel C. Russell's son."

"You know my father, sir?"

"I met him years ago, at the Hague."

Dr. Bruck turned—he had barely nodded at the Secretary General. "You're Sam Russell's boy?"

"Uh, you know him, too?"

"Of course. *On the Statistical Interpretation of Imperfect Data.* Brilliant." He turned back and got more chalk on his sleeve. I hadn't known that Dad had written such a thing, nor suspected that he knew the top man in the Federation. Sometimes I think Dad is eccentric.

Mr. van D. waited until the double domes came up for air, then said, "You have something, gentlemen?"

"Yeah," said Bruck.

"Superb!" agreed Giomi.

"Such as?"

"Well—" Dr. Bruck pointed at a line of chalk. "That says you can damp out a nuclear reaction at a distance."

"What distance?"

"How about ten thousand miles? Or must you do it from the Moon?"

"Oh, ten thousand miles is sufficient, I imagine."

"You could do it from the Moon," Giomi interrupted, "if you had enough power. Magnificent!"

"It is," agreed van Duivendijk. "Anything else?"

"What do you want?" demanded Bruck. "Egg in your suds?"

"Well?"

"See that seventeenth line? It may mean anti-gravity, I ain't promising. Or, if you rotate ninety degrees, this unstable Latin thinks it's time travel."

"It is!"

"If he's right, the power needed is a fair-sized star— so forget it." Bruck stared at hen's tracks. "A new approach to matter conversion—possibly. How about a power pack for your vest pocket that turns out more ergs than the Brisbane reactor?"

"This can be done?"

"Ask your grandson. It won't be soon." Bruck scowled. "Dr. Bruck, why are you unhappy?" asked Mr. van D.

Bruck scowled harder. "Are you goin' to make this 'Top Secret'? I don't like classifying mathematics. It's shameful."

I batted my ears. I had explained to the Mother

Thing about "classified" and I think I shocked her. I said that the FFN *had* to have secrets for survival, just like Three Galaxies. She couldn't see it. Finally she had said that it wouldn't make any difference in the long run. But I had worried because while I don't like science being "secret," I don't want to be reckless, either.

Mr. van D. answered, "I don't like secrecy. But I have to put up with it."

"I knew you would say that!"

"Please. Is this a U.S. government project?"

"Eh? Of course not."

"Nor a Federation one. Very well, you've shown me some equations. I can't tell you not to publish them. They're yours."

Bruck shook his head. "Not ours." He pointed at me. "His."

"I see." The Secretary General looked at me. "I am a lawyer, young man. If you wish to publish, I see no way to stop you."

"Me? It's not mine—I was just—well, a messenger."

"You seem to have the only claim. Do you wish this published? Perhaps with all your names?" I got the impression that he wanted it published.

"Well, sure. But the third name shouldn't be mine; it should be—" I hesitated. You can't put a birdsong down as author. "—uh, make it 'Dr. M. Thing.'"

"Who is he?"

"She's a Vegan. But we could pretend it's a Chinese name."

The Secretary General stayed on, asking questions, listening to tapes. Then he made a phone call—to the Moon. I knew it could be done, I never expected to see it. "Van Duivendijk here . . . yes, the Secretary General. Get the Commanding General . . . Jim? . . . This connection is terrible . . . Jim, you sometimes order practice maneuvers . . . My call is unofficial but you might check a valley—" He turned to me; I answered quickly.

"—a valley just past the mountains east of Tombaugh Station. I haven't consulted the Security Council; this is between friends. But if you go into that valley I very strongly suggest that it be done in force, with all weapons. It may have snakes in it. The snakes will be camouflaged. Call it a hunch. Yes, the kids are fine and so is Beatrix. I'll phone Mary and tell her I talked with you."

The Secretary General wanted my address. I couldn't say when I would be home because I didn't know how I would get there—I meant to hitchhike but didn't say so. Mr. van D.'s eyebrows went up. "I think we owe you a ride home. Eh, Professor?"

"That would not be overdoing it."

"Russell, I heard on your tape that you plan to study engineering—with a view to space."

"Yes, sir. I mean, 'Yes, Mr. Secretary.' "

"Have you considered studying law? Many young engineers want to space—not many lawyers. But the Law goes everywhere. A man skilled in space law and meta-law would be in a strong position."

"Why not both?" suggested Peewee's Daddy. "I deplore this modern overspecialization."

"That's an idea," agreed Mr. van Duivendijk. "He could then write his own terms."

I was about to say I should stick to electronics—when suddenly I knew what I wanted to do. "Uh, I don't think I could handle both."

"Nonsense!" Professor Reisfeld said severely.

"Yes, sir. But I want to make space suits that work better. I've got some ideas."

"Mmm, that's mechanical engineering. And many other things, I imagine. But you'll need an M.E. degree." Professor Reisfeld frowned. "As I recall your tape, you passed College Boards but hadn't been accepted by a good school." He drummed his desk. "Isn't that silly, Mr.

Secretary? The lad goes to the Magellanic Clouds but can't go to the school he wants."

"Well, Professor? You pull while I push?"

"Yes. But wait." Professor Reisfeld picked up his phone. "Susie, get me the President of M.I.T. I know it's a holiday; I don't care if he's in Bombay or in bed; get him. Good girl." He put down the phone. "She's been with the Institute five years and on the University switchboard before that. She'll get him."

I felt embarrassed and excited. M.I.T.—anybody would jump at the chance. But tuition alone would stun you. I tried to explain that I didn't have the money. "I'll work the rest of this school year and next summer —I'll save it."

The phone rang. "Reisfeld here. Hi, Oppie. At the class reunion you made me promise to tell you if Bruck's tic started bothering him. Hold onto your chair; I timed it at twenty-one to the minute. That's a record. . . . Slow down; you won't send *anybody*, unless I get my pound of flesh. If you start your lecture on academic freedom and 'the right to know,' I'll hang up and call Berkeley. I can do business there—and I know I can here, over on the campus. . . . Not much, just a four-year scholarship, tuition and fees. . . . Don't scream at me; use your discretionary fund—or make it a wash deal in bookkeeping. You're over twenty-one; you can do arithmetic. . . . Nope, no hints. Buy a pig in a poke or your radiation lab won't be in on it. Did I say 'radiation lab'? I meant the entire physical science department. You can flee to South America, don't let me sway you. . . . What? I'm an embezzler, too. Hold it." Professor Reisfeld said to me, "You applied for M.I.T.?"

"Yes, sir, but—"

"He's in your application files, 'Clifford C. Russell.' Send the letter to his home and have the head of your team fetch my copy. . . . Oh, a broad team, headed by a mathematical physicist—Farley, probably; he's got imagination. This is the biggest thing since the apple konked Sir Isaac. . . . Sure, I'm a blackmailer, and you are a chair warmer and a luncheon speaker. When are you returning to the academic life? . . . Best to Beulah. 'Bye."

He hung up. "That's settled. Kip, the one thing that confuses me is why those worm-faced monsters wanted *me*."

I didn't know how to say it. He had told me only the day before that he had been correlating odd data—unidentified sightings, unexpected opposition to space travel, many things that did not fit. Such a man is likely to get answers—and be listened to. If he had a weakness, it was modesty—which he hadn't passed on to Peewee. If I told him that invaders from outer space had grown nervous over his intellectual curiosity, he would have pooh-poohed it. So I said, "They never told us, sir. But they thought you were important enough to grab."

Mr. van Duivendijk stood up. "Curt, I won't waste time listening to nonsense. Russell, I'm glad your schooling is arranged. If you need me, call me."

When he was gone, I tried to thank Professor Reisfeld. "I meant to pay my way, sir. I would have earned the money before school opens again."

"In less than three weeks? Come now, Kip."

"I mean the rest of this year and—"

"Waste a year? No."

"But I already—" I looked past his head at green leaves in their garden. "Professor . . . what date is it?"

"Why, Labor Day, of course."

(*"—forthwith to the space-time whence they came."*) Professor Reisfeld flipped water in my face. "Feeling better?"

"I—I guess so. We were gone for *weeks*."

"Kip, you've been through too much to let this shake you. You can talk it over with the stratosphere twins—"

He gestured at Giomi and Bruck. "—but you won't understand it. At least I didn't. Why not assume that a hundred and sixty-seven thousand light-years leaves room for Tennessee windage amounting to only a hair's breadth of a fraction of one per cent? Especially when the method doesn't properly use space-time at all?"

When I left, Mrs. Reisfeld kissed me and Peewee blubbered and had Madame Pompadour say good-bye to Oscar, who was in the back seat because the Professor was driving me to the airport.

On the way he remarked, "Peewee is fond of you."

"Uh, I hope so."

"And you? Or am I impertinent?"

"Am I fond of Peewee? I certainly am! She saved my life four or five times." Peewee could drive you nuts. But she was gallant and loyal and smart—and had guts.

"You won a life-saving medal or two yourself."

I thought about it. "Seems to me I fumbled everything I tried. But I had help and an awful lot of luck." I shivered at how luck alone had kept me out of the soup—real soup.

" 'Luck' is a question-begging word," he answered. "You spoke of the 'amazing luck' that you were listening when my daughter called for help. That wasn't luck."

"Huh? I mean, 'Sir'?"

"Why were you on that frequency? Because you were wearing a space suit. Why were you wearing it? Because you were determined to space. When a space ship called, you answered, If that is luck, then it is luck every time a batter hits a ball. Kip, 'good luck' follows careful preparation; 'bad luck' comes from sloppiness. You convinced a court older than Man himself that you and your kind were worth saving. Was that mere chance?"

"Uh . . . fact is, I got mad and almost ruined things. I was tired of being shoved around."

"The best things in history are accomplished by people who get 'tired of being shoved around.' " He frowned. "I'm glad you like Peewee. She is about twenty years old intellectually and six emotionally; she usually antagonizes people. So I'm glad she has gained a friend who is smarter than she is."

My jaw dropped. "But, Professor, Peewee is much smarter than I am. She runs me ragged."

He glanced at me. "She's run me ragged for years—and I'm not stupid. Don't downgrade yourself, Kip."

"It's the truth."

"So? The greatest mathematical psychologist of our time, a man who always wrote his own ticket even to retiring when it suited him—very difficult, when a man is in demand—this man married his star pupil. I doubt if their offspring is less bright than my own child."

I had to untangle this to realize that he meant *me*. Then I didn't know what to say. How many kids really know their parents? Apparently I didn't.

He went on, "Peewee is a handful, even for me. Here's the airport. When you return for school, please plan on visiting us. Thanksgiving, too, if you will—no doubt you'll go home Christmas."

"Uh, thank you, sir. I'll be back."

"Good."

"Uh, about Peewee—if she gets too difficult, well, you've got the beacon. The Mother Thing can handle her."

"Mmm, that's a thought."

"Peewee tries to get around her but she never does. Oh—I almost forgot. Whom may I tell? Not about Peewee. About the whole thing."

"Isn't that obvious?"

"Sir?"

"Tell anybody anything. You won't very often. Almost no one will believe you."

I rode home in a courier jet—those things go *fast*. Professor Reisfeld had insisted on lending me ten dollars when he found out that I had only a dollar sixty-seven, so I got a haircut at the bus station and bought two tickets to Centerville to keep Oscar out of the luggage compartment; he might have been damaged. The best thing about that scholarship was that now I needn't ever sell him—not that I would.

Centerville looked mighty good, from elms overhead to the chuckholes under foot. The driver stopped near our house because of Oscar; he's clumsy to carry. I went to the barn and racked Oscar, told him I'd see him later, and went in the back door.

Mother wasn't around, Dad was in his study. He looked up from reading. "Hi, Kip."

"Hi, Dad."

"Nice trip?"

"Uh, I didn't go to the lake."

"I know. Dr. Reisfeld phoned—he briefed me thoroughly."

"Oh. It was a nice trip—on the whole." I saw that he was holding a volume of the Britannica, open to "Magellanic Clouds."

He followed my glance. "I've never seen them," he said regretfully. "I had a chance once, but I was busy except one cloudy night."

"When was that, Dad?"

"In South America, before you were born."

"I didn't know you had been there."

"It was a cloak-and-daggerish government job—not one to talk about. Are they beautiful?"

"Uh, not exactly." I got another volume, turned to "Nebulae" and found the Great Nebula of Andromeda. "*Here* is beauty. That's the way *we* look."

Dad sighed. "It must be lovely."

"It is. I'll tell you all about it. I've got a tape, too."

252

"No hurry. You've had quite a trip. Three hundred and thirty-three thousand light-years—is that right?"

"Oh, no, just half that."

"I meant the round trip."

"Oh. But we didn't come back the same way."

"Eh?"

"I don't know how to put it, but in these ships, if you make a jump, *any* jump, the short way back is the long way 'round. You go straight ahead until you're back where you started. Well, not 'straight' since space is curved—but straight as can be. That returns everything to zero."

"A cosmic great-circle?"

"That's the idea. All the way around in a straight line."

"Mmm—" He frowned thoughtfully. "Kip, how far is it, around the Universe? The red-shift limit?"

I hesitated. "Dad, I asked—but the answer didn't mean anything." (The Mother Thing had said, "How can there be 'distance' where there is *nothing?*") "It's not a distance; it's more of a condition. I didn't *travel* it; I just *went*. You don't go *through*, you slide past."

Dad looked pensive. "I should know not to ask a mathematical question in words."

I was about to suggest that Dr. Bruck could help when Mother sang out: "Hello, my darlings!"

For a split second I thought I was hearing the Mother Thing.

She kissed Dad, she kissed me. "I'm glad you're home, dear."

"Uh—" I turned to Dad.

"She knows."

"Yes," Mother agreed in a warm indulgent tone, "and I don't mind where my big boy goes as long as he comes home safely. I know you'll go as far as you want to." She patted my cheek. "And I'll always be proud of you. Myself, I've just been down to the corner for another chop."

Next morning was Tuesday, I went to work early. As I expected, the fountain was a mess. I put on my white jacket and got cracking. Mr. Charton was on the phone; he hung up and came over. "Nice trip, Kip?"

"Very nice, Mr. Charton."

"Kip, there's something I've been meaning to say. Are you still anxious to go to the Moon?"

I was startled. Then I decided that he couldn't know.

Well, I hadn't seen the Moon, hardly, I was still eager —though not as much in a hurry. "Yes, sir. But I'm going to college first."

"That's what I mean. I— Well, I have no children. If you need money, say so."

He had hinted at pharmacy school—but never this. And only last night Dad had told me that he had bought an education policy for me the day I was born—he had been waiting to see what I would do on my own. "Gee, Mr. Charton, that's mighty nice of you!"

"I approve of your wanting an education."

"Uh, I've got things lined up, sir. But I might need a loan someday."

"Or not a loan. Let me know." He bustled away, plainly fussed.

I worked in a warm glow, sometimes touching the happy thing, tucked away in a pocket. Last night I had let Mother and Dad put it to their foreheads. Mother had cried; Dad said solemnly, "I begin to understand, Kip." I decided to let Mr. Charton try it when I could work around to it. I got the fountain shining and checked the air conditioner. It was okay.

About midafternoon Ace Quiggle came in, plunked himself down. "Hi, Space Pirate! What do you hear from the Galactic Overlords? Yuk yuk yukkity yuk!"

What would he have said to a straight answer? I touched the happy thing and said, "What'll it be, Ace?"

"My usual, of course, and snap it up!"

"A choc malt?"

"You know that. Look alive, Junior! Wake up and get hep to the world around you."

"Sure thing, Ace." There was no use fretting about Ace; his world was as narrow as the hole between his ears, no deeper than his own hog wallow. Two girls came in; I served them cokes while Ace's malt was in the mixer. He leered at them. "Ladies, do you know Commander Comet here?" One of them tittered; Ace smirked and went on: "I'm his manager. You want hero-ing done, see me. Commander, I've been thinking about that ad you're goin' to run."

"Huh?"

"Keep your ears open. 'Have Space Suit—Will Travel,' that doesn't say enough. To make money out of that silly clown suit, we got to have oomph. So we add: 'Bug-Eyed Monsters Exterminated—World Saving a Specialty—Rates on Request.' Right?"

I shook my head. "No, Ace."

"S'matter with you? No head for business?"

"Let's stick to the facts. I don't charge for world saving and don't do it to order; it just happens. I'm not sure I'd do it on purpose—with *you* in it."

Both girls tittered, Ace scowled. "Smart guy, eh? Don't you know that the customer is always right?"

"Always?"

"He certainly is. See that you remember it. Hurry up that malt!"

"Yes, Ace." I reached for it; he shoved thirty-five cents at me; I pushed it back. "This is on the house."

I threw it in his face.